THE FLIGHT OF THE DARKSTAR DRAGON

A DARKSTAR NOVEL

BENEDICT PATRICK

The Flight of the Darkstar Dragon
Copyright 2019 Benedict Patrick
All rights reserved.

www.benedictpatrick.com

Cover design by Jenny Zemanek
www.seedlingsonline.com

Published by One More Page Publishing

ISBN: 9781693299919

CONTENTS

Chapter One	Pg 1
Chapter Two	Pg 19
Chapter Three	Pg 30
Chapter Four	Pg 47
Chapter Five	Pg 59
Chapter Six	Pg 71
Chapter Seven	Pg 85
Chapter Eight	Pg 103
Chapter Nine	Pg 115
Chapter Ten	Pg 138
Chapter Eleven	Pg 157
Chapter Twelve	Pg 169
Chapter Thirteen	Pg 179
Chapter Fourteen	Pg 190
Chapter Fifteen	Pg 207
A Word from the Author	Pg 228

ACKNOWLEDGEMENTS

As always, the support and love it has taken to help this story set sail has come from so many people. This is not an exhaustive list, but I would like to thank the following for helping make *The Flight of the Darkstar Dragon* happen:

Jenny, for the gorgeous artwork that graces this book's cover. So much has been said about your work already, and I have no doubt your talents elevate my stories through association.

Alida and Laura, for sorting through the mess of ideas and words.

Richard, Craig, Alex, Timy, Phil, Adele and Kathryn, for taking early looks at the story, and helping me sort out my 'blimeys' from my 'bloody hells'.

Ágnes, Jacinta, and Dad, for being my safety nets, and catching those final tweaks before the big reveal.

And Mark, for having a few tries, even if you never reached the finish line on time!

And I also need to mention so many people who did not affect the book directly, but helped me to shamble through life during the months it took me to get these words out of my head:

My Crit Faced buddies, for consistently being one of the highlights of the month.

All of the Terrible Ten, for the inspiration, education, and lack of pants.

The wonderful Reading Knacks – I might not always make our Monday catch-ups, but you guys are ready when I do finally get online. And you are unparallelled at keeping secrets!

Geoff and Julien, for showing interest, and providing some of the biggest thrills in this writing gig so far.

All the readers out there who have gotten in touch over the years – chatting with you has been the fuel that has kept my fingers typing.

Everyone over at r/fantasy, which remains my favourite place to hang out online.

Helen and Craig, for always being there when we need you.

Everyone back in Ireland (and Manchester, and Australia) – Mum, Dad, Jacinta, and the ever-increasing family tree.

Finally, to my wonderful family here in Scotland – Adele, Darcy and Finn. I feel constantly blessed to share my life with the three of you.

ONE

Min screamed.

It was an excruciating sensation, being pulled back together. She could not fully remember being taken apart in the first place, but had the distinct impression that reforming was more painful, not unlike trying to shove your fist into a bottle of rum with the top smashed off.

She grew dimly aware the process was coming to an end when she heard herself screaming out loud, instead of only in her head. Then her face hit the deck.

The *Narwhal*, she realised, sending a fragment of a prayer to her family's patron spirits, comforted by the familiar feel of the heel-polished deck currently supporting her cheek. She was still on board her ship, the *Melodious Narwhal*.

Gasping for air, still reeling from the pain spasming through her body like a stomach's aftershocks after a particularly painful vomiting session, Min looked around. The familiar sight was a balm to her current agony.

From her position flat on the deck, the *Melodious Narwhal* appeared to be intact. Perhaps it too had been torn apart and reassembled, but if so, her beautiful skyship had been reformed just as thoroughly as Min had been. The *Narwhal*'s trio of masts still rose above her, the sails attached to each still unfurled, unblemished. At the stern, the wheel called to her, asking her to grab it again and take control.

However, between Min and control of the *Narwhal* lay chaos. Chaos in the form of her crew.

It was immediately obvious to Min that her crew had gone through the same experience she had. Those she could see were rolling about on the deck, screaming shamelessly, having similarly lost control of their senses.

By the many hells, it'll be hard to get them back in line after something like this.

Min paused, the pain ebbing, her eyes focussed on one of the seamen whose incoherent screams were becoming more intelligible by the moment as he called for his mother in his hour of need. Min, however, was casting her mind to the seconds before she and her crew were pulled apart.

Her mind would not travel back that far.

What had happened? How in Gorya's frigid hell had they gotten into this state?

With a grunt of effort, Min grabbed the *Narwhal's* railing and did her best to pull herself to her feet. Like a puppet with most of its strings cut, she only managed to get to her knees, but it was enough to peer over the side and get a look at where they were.

They were no longer sailing in New Windward waters.

Whatever had happened to the *Melodious Narwhal*, it had resulted in them being taken somewhere… else.

It appeared to be nighttime; the sky was almost, but not quite, black, and a plethora of stars glinted above. However, the world about Min – the deck of the *Narwhal*, the other crew members, even her own hands when she held them up to inspect – was suffused by a dull purple glow.

Where was it coming from?

Steadying herself, still recovering from her displacement, Min struggled to locate the light source. Try as she might, she could not glimpse any land beneath them, only an empty near-blackness.

"Where are we, Captain?" groaned Kanika, one of the apprentice seamen who was struggling to regain control of herself nearby. "Master Aarav's nuts, I can't even remember what happened."

Min pursed her lips. "Seems to be going around."

So, she was not the only one to have lost memories. Interesting. This felt less like a natural phenomenon and more like an attack of some kind. Still, Min had never heard of any pirate crew with enough magical strength to pull something like this off.

"She ain't no captain."

The grumble came from Sung, the *Narwhal's* first mate and Kanika's immediate superior. Unlike with Kanika, Min had yet to win Sung's approval. Despite the fact that both their families hailed from Goryeoa – the only eastern island state to join the New Windward union – Sung clearly felt no affinity towards Min, bad-mouthing her at every turn to the rest of the crew, especially those on the port watch, which Sung was in charge of. The rest of the differences between Min and Sung were clear enough as well. Sung was almost twice Min's age, and her leathery face told the tales that often accompanied a life on the waves. The first mate kept her head clean-shaven, a popular choice for Goryeoan sailors who did not want to bother with managing their hair. Min had long ago cropped hers into a short, chin-length bob, which was persistently in disarray, never properly tended to, but she could not find it in her to remove her hair entirely.

"True," Min admitted, forcing herself to stand up straight, to be the first among them to do so. She inhaled – *bloody hell, that hurt* – then raised her voice. "Listen up, men. Anyone here have any memory of what happened to us?"

Silence.

Not good.

She saw the seeds of fear start to properly germinate on many of their faces. Min might not be captain, but the *Narwhal* was hers. Best not to lose the crew now.

"Fine," she said. There was no rocking motion, no gentle up and down of waves caressing the *Narwhal*. That meant they were in the air.

That was good.

"We're aloft, where we're safe. Let's keep it that way." She dusted an imagined speck of dust from her navy-blue admiral's jacket, drawing attention to it and the ceremonial sabre she wore at her waist. These were the only visible trappings of her rank – Min wore regular tan shirt and trousers under the jacket – but they seemed enough to remind her crew of who was in charge. "Kanika, check the rigging, make sure it's secure."

The apprentice nodded, running off to her task, seeming thankful to have direction.

"Sung, get the rest of the men to work, get them to inspect their stations. Double – no, triple check everything. If we can't remember what happened, we need to be sure nobody's tampered with the *Narwhal*. And do a head count of your people. I want to know if anyone's missing."

Sung nodded, assessing and then agreeing with Min's commands. "If you say so, First Officer," the first mate drawled, wincing in pain as she moved away.

Arse. Even in such a situation, Sung took the time to remind Min of her contempt? *You'd think she'd have better things to do.* Such as surviving.

"You there," Min shouted, spotting another seaman raising from behind some nearby crates, his hands clutched to his head. "Go check on Jedda. If we're in the air, that means we need her to keep things running. I want to make sure she's okay."

The seaman – sweat glistening on his dark skin – nodded, his mouth open like a goldfish's.

Then the *Narwhal* lurched.

Min froze, as did the rest of her crew.

What the bloody hell was that?

There was another lurch, and the *Narwhal*'s prow pitched forward. It was just a small movement, not a full nosedive, but it was enough to send anything not secured to the deck – including the crew – tumbling forward.

By the many hells, Jedda, what are you up to?

"I'm on it!" Min shouted, struggling to stay upright, scrambling to get below deck. "I'm heading to the belly. The rest of you, tie down anything that isn't already. And try not to die!"

As she entered the main hatch, she heard the mumbled mantra of, "Yes, First Officer," from a score of the older crew, as well as the younger ones who had learned to ape their superiors. She gritted her teeth against the insult.

First, she would save their lives. Then, she would show those ungrateful smart-arses why the powers that be had put her in charge in the first place.

"Jedda!" Min shouted as she burst into the *Narwhal*'s belly, the room that housed the ship's core.

The crystal core should have been brimming with magical energy. Min never tired of coming down here to look at the hypnotic blue light playing under the core's surface; the magical power that New Windward's artificers had captured within, enough to power a skyship for over a decade, if needed.

That light, however, was now absent.

The *Narwhal*'s core was a shadow of its former self. Usually, Min struggled to look directly at it, so bright were the powers that played within. Now, the core pulsed only a dull blue, and Min could swear its colour was draining before her.

The core was losing its magic.

As if to confirm her realisation, the *Narwhal* gave another lurch, more violent this time, sending Min sprawling to the now terribly tilted floor.

"Jedda!" she shouted, the ship's artificer nowhere to be seen. "Where in Frathuda's windowless hell are you? I need to know what's going on."

A head of black hair bobbed up from the other side of the core, the young woman's bronze eyes magnified by the pair of goggles Jedda had strapped over her face, sweat running down her dark brown skin. The look would almost be comical, if not for how terrified and lost Jedda seemed at that moment.

"Min?"

"What's going on?"

Jedda, eyes wide, looked from Min to the core to her various artificer's tools, now tipped to the aft end of the room; the floor of the *Narwhal* canted at an angle that made Min think of childhood adventures, scrambling across the pitched roofs of the Goryeoan quarter back home.

"Ship's tipping," Jedda said, sounding surprised Min even had to ask.

The *Narwhal* gave another lurch. Min, heart thumping, glared at Jedda, and took a deep breath. Jedda was brilliant, the best artificer Min had ever worked with, but the woman could be a little… odd. Especially in stressful situations, which was why she had been posted to a research vessel instead of a military ship.

Min nodded sharply, not able to hide her urgency from her movements. "And why's that, Jedda? What's wrong with the core?"

Jedda, her wide eyes reminding Min of a rodent caught in a campfire light, looked to the core again, then back to her commanding officer.

"It's leaking magic, Min. Losing it quick. Never seen anything like it before."

"Any idea why?"

Jedda looked around, as if the answer should be standing in the room somewhere.

"Never seen anything like it before. It just… it just shouldn't be possible, Min. Even with all the crystals running full pelt, I've never seen a drain like it. Ancestors, I don't think ten crystal arrays could do this."

"How long do we have left?"

Answering Min's question for her, the *Narwhal* lurched again, but this time it did not stop.

Min felt light-footed, as if deck was slowing dropping from beneath her. All around, a dull roaring began. Her throat tightened when she realised it was the sound of the air rushing past as the *Narwhal* fell through the sky.

Min and Jedda locked eyes, and for a heartbeat the first officer just froze. None of her experience, none of the countless expeditions she had gone on during her apprenticeship, had prepared her for this. Skyships just did not fall from the sky.

"Jedda, I need options," Min barked, dodging past some artificer tool that had been thrown to the floor, but was now bouncing back up the deck as gravity lost its grip on everything inside the plummeting ship. "And I'm talking about the falling skyship, damn it – don't dare ask me what I'm talking about."

Jedda gulped, then looked to the dead core. "We're not full velocity, not yet," the artificer said. "Core's dead, but the crystals'll still have some juice left in them, should still be pushing back a bit. Probably the only reason we're not glued to the ceiling." Min felt the distant hum of the *Narwhal's* crystal array through the deck her hand was resting on, and could tell Jedda was right, even though the hum was inconsistent.

"Right," Min acknowledged, preparing to guide her artificer's thoughts, "how do we fix this?"

"There's no way to power the core, Min. It takes a team of artificers weeks to fully charge one, and that's a healthy core without leaks."

"Forget the core, then. What about the rest of the ship? We've got to have something else on board to—"

"To make us fly?" Jedda scoffed. "Why would we have something like that? We've got a core."

"That isn't working."

"But that should never happen! We don't make fail-safes for impossibilities. Without the core, the ship can't fly. That's it."

Min thumped the wall in frustration. "What about the sails? Can we do anything with the sails?"

Jedda shook her head. "Nope. They're good for getting places, not for going up or down. The speed we're falling at, they've already been ripped to shreds by the pressure. The only material we have on board that could cope with this sort of strain is—"

Jedda ripped off her goggles, staring at Min.

"What is it, Jedda?"

"The guidance wings. Maybe the guidance wings…"

For a heartbeat, Min stared back at the artificer, then she bolted out the door behind her, ignoring Jedda's continued shouts.

The *Narwhal's* guidance wings were a terrible idea. They were used for gliding, not to pull the *Narwhal* out of a plummet, but since Min expected them to impact the land below with a crunch at any moment, the small wings were a dice roll she was willing to take a bet on.

It was easy getting back above deck. With the *Narwhal* almost vertical, its nose pointed toward whatever lay below, every step Min took felt like flight, the floor falling away at the same speed as the vessel plunging through the air.

Outside, the *Narwhal* was in chaos. The purple vastness of wherever they now found themselves spread out above Min, with the unbolted belongings of the *Narwhal's* deck streaming through the emptiness above her like the tail on a kite. The sky around them remained saturated with stars, but with other objects as well; strange, swirling blobs of colour that reminded Min of the confusing maps of planets that astronomers promised they could see through their telescopes.

Min should have been focussed on the imminent destruction of her ship, but instead she was captivated by the large object that appeared in the sky to her port side.

A sphere. A massive, glowing, purple sphere. Clearly vast, clearly far from her, clearly the source of the purple hue that saturated the *Narwhal* and her crew.

What in Gorya's frigid hell?

"First Officer!" came a shout that drew Min's attention back to the almost-vertical deck.

It was Sung, gripping hard at the railing. Min spotted a length of rope binding the mate's arm to the relative safety of the *Narwhal*. Despite her rising terror, Min was relieved to see the rest of Sung's watch safe as well, having copied their commanding officer's actions, clinging on to hope with tight knots and white knuckles.

Grunting, straining to keep a grip on the wood, despite the fact that the ship was doing its very best to fall away from her, Min inched her way from the main hatch, toward the mechanism for the guidance wings.

Her first command, she thought, gritting her teeth as she pulled herself across to the edge of the deck. Not even a captain yet, but she had command of a ship. She had a crew. The first out of all her cohort from the academy.

And on their first mission – just a simple, stupid research task – she was going to lose them all.

Swearing at the top of her voice over the roaring wind, Min kicked the lever that held the guidance wings in check, shouting with triumph as she booted the lever free, moving the mechanism that would allow the wings to spring into position.

Nothing happened.

Incredulous, Min looked over the side to see what had gone wrong.

She should have focussed on the wings, to see where the release mechanism had failed.

Instead, Min looked below, and her head swam.

They were falling, she knew. She was looking straight down, but the view below did not seem to be any different from that above her. More purple-soaked emptiness, more distant stars.

How could they be falling toward the stars?

She shook her head, forcing herself to look at the wings again. If they were falling, they were falling toward something. Even if she could not see it properly at the moment, Min was damned if she was going to let her ship hit whatever was waiting for them below.

The chain that held the guidance wings in place was flopping in the air, buffeted by the velocity of the *Narwhal's* fall. The lever had worked fine.

Instead, the wings remained pinned against the *Narwhal's* hull.

"It's the force of the air," Jedda shouted from just behind, causing Min to jump. She turned, shocked to see the artificer had followed from below. Jedda had ropes clipped to her belt, and was using them to tether herself to different points on the *Narwhal's* deck. Hastily, working as she continued to speak, Jedda began fastening a similar contraption to her commanding officer.

"We're falling too fast," the artificer explained. "The wings weren't designed to open under such strain. There's nothing on board that has the strength to get them open, now."

Min felt her heart sink, but not because she agreed with Jedda. The artificer was wrong - they did have something on board strong enough to get the job done.

"I think it's time we visited the arsehole," Min said.

Using Jedda's contraption, but clipping considerably less secure lines than the careful artificer, Min struggled across the deck and made her way back below. The *Narwhal* was vibrating so hard now, Min could not tell if they had reached full velocity, or if the crystals that permitted the *Narwhal* to fly were still powered by the last of the magic they had drained from the core.

Walking on the wall, jumping to get through doorways, Min made her way to Abalendu's study.

"There you are!" the scholar shouted as Min pulled herself through his doorway. Abalendu was curled up in the corner of his bed, purple pillows pulled around him, as if they would somehow protect him from impending disaster. As always, his dragontoad had its long tail curled around his neck, claws locking it tight to his shoulder, the beast looking moronically at Min as she entered, as if this was just a regular day at sea.

"What in Master Aarav's name have you done to my ship?"

Min did not acknowledge the noble's greeting. She did not have time to rise to his insults, and she was not here for him in the first place.

She was here for Zoya.

Abalendu's bodyguard stood in the middle of the room – in the middle of the wall, really, such was the angle they were tilted at now – her harpoon at the ready. The traditional weapon was more ceremonial than anything else. Zoya's real strength was in her right hand.

Specifically, in the stony glove she wore upon it.

"I need Zoya," Min shouted urgently. "Tell her she can come with me."

The bodyguard regarded Min coolly, but otherwise did not respond to the summons. The deep brown of the warrior's skin – several shades darker than Abalendu's, or even Jedda's – betrayed her identity as a Kisiwian, and Kisiwian soldiers were known for their loyalty. Zoya would not go anywhere without Abalendu's instruction.

"Why?"

"The *Narwhal* is falling. Unless Zoya uses her Parasite Glove to deploy our wings, we're all going to die. You included."

Abalendu opened his mouth to protest, but his jaw slackened as he considered Min's words.

Then, with a knot of frustration on his face – the same look he gave Min anytime he found himself forced to agree with her – the scholar nodded at Zoya.

Not waiting for any further conversation, Min spun around and ran, assuming the warrior would be following her. Goryeoans were shorter on average than most of the peoples New Windward had tempted into its cultural melting pot, but Min did not let that hold her back. She had taken her apprenticeship seriously, always pushing herself physically, never allowing others to take the lead just because they were taller or naturally stronger than her.

Despite her intense training, Zoya overtook Min in seconds. The bodyguard was built for this, had dedicated herself to this. Even without the Parasite Glove, Zoya was formidable. Indeed, that formidability was exactly why she had been chosen for the Glove in the first place.

"Where are we going?" Zoya said as she leapt to a high door frame, waiting for the seconds it took Min to haul herself up. The warrior's braided hair held firm in a tight bun at the back of her head, giving the impression of a statue, standing stoic, waiting for Min to pull herself puffing to the top.

"Wings," Min said, swiping her own messy bob out of her eyes. "The guidance wings. Got to force them open. Hope it'll give us some lift."

Still running, Zoya shot her a doubtful glance. "That will work?"

Min shrugged, not really wanting to think about the question. "It's the best idea Jedda's got. It's either the wings, or hope we survive whatever we hit."

Not needing to hear any more, Zoya put on another burst of speed. Swearing, Min prayed to the spirit Holamo to give her the strength to push herself further, to catch up with the bodyguard before she missed everything.

Min was so intent on keeping pace with Zoya, she almost forgot to hold on to something when she got back above deck.

The crystals had clearly failed now, and the ship was in total freefall. Jedda was there, right beside the entranceway, trusting her harness to hold her to the deck.

Boramu's noisy hell, the speed they were falling at now made everything feel impossible. Jedda was trying to speak to her, the artificer's eyes wide, but without fear, just surprise. Min could not hear the words.

"Zoya!" Min shouted, mouthing the words exaggeratedly to try to get through to Jedda. "Which side did Zoya get to?"

Before Jedda had the chance to respond, the *Narwhal* shuddered. Unbelievably, slowly but impossibly, the ship's bow was beginning to rise.

As quickly as she dared, Min swung portside using Jedda's harness, just in time to catch a glimpse of Zoya at work.

The warrior was standing on the side of the ship. She had leapt over the railing, and was now planted on the *Narwhal's* outer hull. Oddly, she did not seem out of place. Zoya had a reputation for achieving the impossible when the situation called for it.

What was unusual was what was happening right in front of Min. Zoya was tall, she was muscular, but she was lifting forces she should not have been able to. The warrior woman was crouched, straining, the veins in her neck clear, both hands gripping the metal frame of the guidance wings, slowly pulling them open.

The Parasite Glove, its rocky surface normally dull and grey, began to glow, red cracks lining the stones that were permanently bonded to Zoya's arm. With the strength of the Parasite Glove aiding her, Zoya could do the impossible.

Behind Min, the crew began to cheer. Min felt like joining in; as Zoya pulled, the wings continued to open, and the *Narwhal* continued to level out.

However, Min knew they were not out of danger yet.

"Come on, Jedda," she said, tugging on her artificer, beckoning her toward the prow.

"What?"

"We've no power, and we're currently gliding on wings not meant for the job. We're going to crash, no doubt about it. Time to see where we're headed, so we know how hard we have to pray."

As she ran, already exhausted, Min cast another glance upward to where they had fallen from. Other than the multitude of floating objects above her – most just a collection of colours, like blobs of paint speckled over a night sky – Min's attention was once again drawn to the purple sun.

The sight of it gave her an uneasy feeling in her belly, and given the situation she had recently found herself in, that was saying something.

The *Narwhal's* prow continued to rise, tilting the deck almost horizontal again. Reaching the railing, Min leaned over to get a look at where they were headed.

Just like earlier, she could see nothing down there. Blackness, stars, nothing.

Min narrowed her eyes.

Wait a second...

"Brace!" she shouted, waving behind her for attention. The rushing of their fall had lessened, as had the roaring of the air around them, so Sung's head shot up, as did a number of other deckhands.

"We're about to land! Brace yourselves!"

Jedda, finally catching up, leaned over the edge to see what Min was talking about.

"But it's just more sky. We're falling into space, Min. There's nothing for us to hit."

Min said nothing, but gritted her teeth. The artificer had not yet spotted what Min had just noticed.

It looked like nothing below them. It looked like a sea of stars.

But that was not quite true.

It was just a sea.

"Brace!" Min screamed, just before the *Narwhal* hit the water.

For a brief moment, Min experienced weightlessness. Her hand gripping the railing close to the prow, she slammed into the deck, and then, as the ship's movement below took the surface away from her, she felt as though she were floating, the spray of the water they had just impacted adding to the dreamlike sensation, taking her back in time.

Even though her eyes were open, taking in the chaos of the *Narwhal's* deck, Min's mind was elsewhere. When she was a young girl, not yet ten years old, a sickness had taken her, and she had almost died. Min remembered her grandfather's healing hands, under her neck, keeping her head above water as he lay her in a bath of iced water, to steal the fever away. The cold spray of water, and the floating sensation of the ship – especially when her fingers slipped, and she lost her grip completely – brought her back to that part of her life.

Hitting the deck a second time drove all fond memories away, replacing them with pain.

Min moaned as the *Narwhal* shook again, tilting almost on its side, sending Min sprawling helplessly along the deck until she was finally caught by the port railing before being pitched overboard.

Then, blessedly, the *Narwhal* began to calm.

They had done it.

Despite the fall, the ship was – as far as Min could tell – in one piece, and judging by the shouts of pain from behind her, at least some of the crew were still alive.

Gritting her teeth, hoping to put on as brave a face as possible, Min got to her feet, steeling herself to survey the damage.

She spotted Zoya first. If Min had been an Eshak player, she would have bet on the warrior as one of the first to be killed on impact; to keep the wings level, Zoya would have to have been standing on the hull when the *Narwhal* hit the water. However, Min saw the Kisiwian climbing back onboard the ship, one leg over the railing as if she had just taken a dip in a calm New Windward cove. Zoya had indeed been on the hull when the *Narwhal* had hit the water. She had simply survived the experience.

"Sung," Min shouted, forcing herself to tear her eyes away from Zoya as the Kisiwian made her way below deck, presumably to check on Abalendu. "Sung, give me a count. Make sure we're all here. And find Holtz."

Hiding her satisfaction at the first mate's immediate jump to attention, Min forced herself to move, making her way to the quarterdeck, daring to hope that there was enough of a wind for her to take control of the ship. Min's heart sank, however, when she raised her eyes to the *Narwhal's* triple masts. They were ruined, the sails hanging in ribbons, and the foremast had lost its top third. Grabbing the spokes of the helm, Min gave it a test, and swore.

It was broken. The rudder – or at the very least, some of the mechanism that allowed her to control it – was damaged.

No core. No sails. No rudder.

They were adrift here. Wherever 'here' was.

Heat radiated from her cheeks as she imagined the eyes of her crew – particularly those who had made it clear they did not appreciate an academy whelp in command – boring into the back of her head, blaming her and her perceived inexperience for their predicament. She snarled, shaking her head, chasing those doubts away; she had proven to herself long ago she was more than worthy of a ship of her own, and her superiors had recognised her excellence on more than one occasion. It was just this bloody crew that still needed to be shown why she had graduated at the top of her year's intake.

Hungry to find a way forward, to start steering them out of this mess, Min latched on to the sight of Jedda crawling above deck, her goggles back over her eyes.

"Jedda!" Min shouted, beckoning the artificer over. "I need options here. How long to get the core back up and running? The sails and rudder are dead, so I'm going to need some magic to pick ourselves up with."

Jedda looked at Min as if she were stupid. "Get the core running again? It's dead, Min. The core's totally drained. I've no way of filling it back up again. This should never have happened."

A commotion erupted from beneath the deck. Min rolled her eyes, swallowing with a suddenly dry throat.

By the hells. The last thing I need is him up here.

Abalendu strode out from below, pushing a younger deckhand out of the way. Zoya marched behind him, unmoved by the destruction on the deck.

"You!" Abalendu shouted, pointing at Min and marching over to her. His dragontoad was still perched on his shoulder, its long tail wrapped lazily around his neck. Abalendu wore a pale yellow embroidered robe, popular with the Zadzerjian nobility, but with all the commotion below deck, his finery had been ruined. In particular, the front of it was now covered in a giant ink stain, and its overly-long sleeves were torn, giving him the comical look of an angrily flapping parakeet.

"Just what in Master Murhk's name are you playing at, recruit?" Abalendu demanded with a sharp finger jab at Min's chest.

Min pursed her lips, her own eyes flicking to Zoya as Abalendu poked her. Zoya was Abalendu's bodyguard, this was true, but the woman was a true soldier, and had proven herself to be a stickler for the rules. Min wondered how much mistreatment Abalendu would be able to dole out before Zoya took it upon herself to intervene.

"Well, Mister Seekwalla," Min said, casting her eyes over the deck, as if performing a routine inspection, "we're just taking stock of things right now. Been a bit of an eventful morning, don't you know, so we've got our work cut out for us just now—"

"Your work? Your work cut out for you? I'll say you have! I'll say so, and a little bit more!" Abalendu's eyes were wide, and he turned to look at the nearby crew, Zoya in particular, to see if they were going to join in, as if he expected everyone else to be as outraged as he was.

Min was used to most of the crew not taking Abalendu seriously. Even his fellow Zadzerjians, separated from him by his nobility and lack of naval experience, smirked behind his back whenever any attention was drawn to his ridiculous dragontoad.

Nobody was smirking at the moment. In fact, Min noticed a few nodding at his words. Taking deep breaths, huffing and puffing like a child preparing for a tantrum, Abalendu turned back to Min. "Where are we? What have you done with my ship?"

Min raised an eyebrow, and was pleased to see a number of the nearby crew – Sung in particular – react unfavourably to the nobleman's statement.

Your ship, Abalendu? You're just a passenger. Your father might be admiral, but to the rest of us, you're just a particularly obnoxious bit of cargo.

Min looked to the crew again. Her people.

The Narwhal *is our ship.*

My ship, damn you.

The only thing that stopped Min from saying all of this out loud was the memory of Abalendu's father, first notifying her of her command of the *Narwhal*. The look on his face, the knowing glances as he gave her this mission, told Min the man had known exactly the burden he had placed on her by putting his son aboard. But she was expected to take Abalendu on his quest anyway, and treating the spoiled scholar with disrespect in front of the others would not go down well with command.

Min swallowed her pride, and her retort.

"Not a bad question, actually. Been a bit busy up here, but from what I can tell, a lot of us don't seem to have any memory of what went wrong."

She raised her voice, allowing all nearby to hear. "What's the last thing any of you remember?" she asked. "Does anyone have any idea how we actually got here?"

There was, for a brief bit of time, silence.

"The Rhineholt Sea," someone finally said. It was Zoya, her voice confident, if not puzzled by her own words. "The last thing I can remember, we were in the middle of the Rhineholt Sea. It was midday. There was nothing at all on any horizon. No ships, nor islands. Just clear blue."

Min nodded, chewing on her lip. She could remember that scene, all right. But how could they have moved from there to… here?

The rest of the crew seemed to be agreeing with Zoya's statement. Nobody could remember anything past the Rhineholt.

Abalendu spluttered. "But that makes no sense. How can we go from day to night? And just what in Master Bartholtocrat's name is that thing up there?"

He pointed above the ship, where the purple orb floated in the distance, casting its violet glare over the land around them.

As one, the crew of the *Melodious Narwhal* turned their gaze upward. Beside Min, Jedda worked at her goggles, turning some kind of lens she had fitted upon them.

"I think…" Jedda said, finally, "I think it's really far away. It's big, Min. That thing up there, it's big. I mean, country-sized big."

Min shook her head.

"Can't be. These waters are well mapped. Something like that? We'd know about it already."

"Unless it's new," Jedda countered.

Min nodded grudgingly, her eyes moving to the stars above the purple orb.

"The stars," she said, lowering her voice so only the nearby officers could hear. "Does anyone recognise the stars?" Silence, again.

"Is anyone else getting the feeling we're no longer in New Windward waters?"

"Capt'n!" came a cry from the railing, causing Min and those close to her to run to follow it. It was Ole, a blond-bearded Iceman that Min had spoken to maybe five times in the month she had been in charge of the *Narwhal*.

"What d'you see?" she asked, pushing her head over the side, straining to catch sight of whatever had alarmed her man.

"The water, Capt'n," Ole said, again forgetting Min's actual rank. "The stars in the water. They're moving."

Min had forgotten about the stars she had seen below them. Sure enough, through the water the *Narwhal* currently floated on, an endless weave of stars moved underneath, dancing just below the water's surface, mesmerizing the crew as they stood there.

"They aren't stars," Jedda said eventually, adjusting her goggles again. "Min, those are fish. Those are fish, swimming down there."

As if on cue, one of the lights – fish indeed, Min could now see – leapt from the water, washing the *Narwhal's* crew briefly with its luminous light, before diving below to join its school once again.

Min had never seen anything like it. Never heard of anything like it, either. She looked at the black water, at the countless twinkling objects moving underneath her. The glimmering sea extended all the way to where the horizon should be, but Min was struggling to find it in the night, the line between fish and stars impossible to judge at this distance.

How many of those fish were there? There was no way something like this could exist without Min having ever heard of it before.

The luminous fish in the distance seemed to blend with the stars in the night sky above, and Min found her gaze drawn back to those stars, hanging high over that purple orb.

Min studied those stars for a few seconds, her eyes narrowed.

"Jedda," Min said, nodding for the artificer to look up as well. "Jedda, those stars up there…"

"Yeah?" Jedda said, adjusting her goggles again, compensating for the vast distance between her and the celestial bodies.

"They're not stars, are they?"

Jedda's mouth opened in a large 'O'. She glanced down at the fish shining below them, then looked back upward.

High above them, well beyond the purple orb that lit the featureless sea, countless luminous fish swam their way along the water that somehow, impossibly, formed the sky.

"Oh," was all Jedda could manage as she took in the sight. "Oh, my."

Day three of solitude

They left.
They all left me.
Looks like I'll be taking over these notes, for all they're worth.
The rift the others finally chose was swallowed by the Darkstar today. Nobody had bothered to mark it on the map, they were so excited to be gone. Guess it's my job to keep the maps updated now, to see if I can figure out when they'll be back.
If they'll be back.
I did a few quick sketches of the rift once I'd pulled myself together, although by then it was pretty far gone; hopefully I got enough details to spot them when they return.
Clara didn't think I'd stay, even though I spent the last week telling her otherwise. When she walked through, walked away, she...
I don't think I'll share that, not in this book. Some things are best left to memory, where they can fade, without feeling the loss when the memory disappears or distorts entirely.
If I commit her words, her face, to the page, the only way of getting rid of them will be to tear the writing up, and I don't think I could bear that.
Stickle doesn't seem to understand what's going on, although she knows I'm low about something. Can't pass my misery on to her. I'll have to pull myself together.
They were decent enough to leave me some food, at least. I reckon it'll last for the next forty days or so, although I might take my own life if I'm forced to endure many more of the brown roots we took from the last world we visited.
Got my first task, then: sort out some supplies.

TWO

Of all the problems Min was currently dealing with, one in particular was starting to get to her.

It was not the strange floating orb that hung above the *Narwhal*; the object that Jedda swore was the size of a large country, the object that painted the scene around them with a purple hue.

It was not the sea of luminous fish that the *Narwhal* currently rested upon. The sea that seemed to extend all around them, and somehow turned upwards in the distance, forming the sky as well.

It was not even the fact that neither Min nor any of her crew had any idea where exactly they were, nor how exactly they got there.

No, Min's big problem was that she was meeting with her officers in their saloon, and Abalendu had yet again invited himself to the table.

There were five who reported directly to her, not counting the apprentices from the academy. The Idlers – Jedda, Aditya and Hertha – rarely took part in major decision making, and the three of them were not here now. Jedda was tending to the helm and rudder using her carpentry skills, since she was adamant the core was dead and gone. Aditya had a number of patients waiting to have their wounds looked it, and Hertha was working on getting the sails back into a workable condition. That left Holtz and Sung, the two shift leaders. Holtz, the senior Iceman on the crew, was second officer, and he was that rare gift of a quiet leader, a lit tobacco stick never far from his yellow-stained fingers. Unlike Sung, Min had no idea how Holtz felt about her leadership, but the pale-skinned man seemed content to nod and get on with his job, making prudent suggestions only on rare occasions.

If only Sung had a similar gift. She still could not stand Min as her commanding officer.

Min had expected as much. In her first term at the academy, before her apprenticeship had begun, her tutors had not shut up about how Min and the rest of her cohort would be treated with animosity, especially from the older sailors. New Windward was, as the name suggested, new. They were a bright star in the darkness of their world, a utopia in which people from different cultures could come together to make the world they lived in a better place.

That, and learn to protect each other from those bloody pirates that kept attacking all the time.

Min was of the first generation that had been born and raised in New Windward, in this community that fostered togetherness and worked towards ideals other than survival of the fittest. However, most of the older crew members of the navy did not truly subscribe to New Windward's ideals. Sure, they had taken the appropriate pledges when they signed their contracts. They knew who they worked for, they knew all about the naval academy that would be – as the older sailors put it – spewing out indoctrinated exceptional young men and women who would take the navy to a better place.

Problem was, most of the old guard regarded the ideals of 'unity' and 'peace among all' as a steaming pile of albatross droppings.

For most of them, they were used to a world in which people climbed on top of others to come out ahead. When they looked at Min, they did not see a highly trained, specially selected and skilled individual who would do everything she could to protect them and to protect the New Windward ideals. They saw an inexperienced brat the powers that be had put in charge, to tell tales if anyone did anything wrong.

They saw Min's heel in their faces as she rose above them.

As soon as Min had met her crew, she had suspected Sung was going to be a problem. Traditional Goryeoans valued the wisdom of elders, and Sung's rough features spoke of the many storms the older woman had weathered during her time on the waves. It had not taken Sung long to show that she did indeed resent being ordered around by a younger commanding officer.

"So, nobody has heard of anything like this happening before?" Min asked again, trying to ignore Sung rolling her eyes for the dozenth time during the meeting.

"Anything like this?" Abalendu squawked.

By the many hells, that man was getting on Min's nerves, and she could tell she was not the only one – even Holtz looked as though he was almost ready to punch the scholar.

"I demand you explain straight away: just what exactly is this situation you've bungled us into?"

Min took a deep breath. "We've got a few theories," she began, thinking over the spitballing she and Jedda had done in the half hour it had taken to make a count of what and who they had lost in the plummet from the skies.

"So," Abalendu sneered, with a dismissive wave of his hand, "out with it, then. I can't wait to hear what you've come up with, recruit."

Holtz shifted again, unsettled by the insult Abalendu had made. Min made a small motion with her hand to indicate she did not want him to take it further. She was fairly certain Abalendu had not noticed, just as she was certain that Zoya, standing behind the gathering like a silent sentinel, would have caught every small action.

Min indicated above. "The stars aren't familiar. In fact, we – artificer Jedda and I – reckon they aren't actually stars at all. They form no pattern we can discern, and, from what we can tell so far, they seem to be moving."

Abalendu snorted in derision, but otherwise said nothing.

Ignoring him, Min continued, focussing on the rest of her officers. "We're pretty certain now that the light above us comes from the same source below: from those strange fish that seem to populate the waters."

"That's impossible," Sung said. "Fish in the sky?"

"Exactly," Abalendu said, the smug satisfaction on his face practically inviting Min to hit it. "Impossible, and moronic. Do please continue, however. If I'm going to die, I'd rather do it while being entertained."

"We're going to die?" one of the apprentices said, and Min felt the tension rise in the room.

Quelling the red that rose inside her, Min blamed herself for this. The time to cut Abalendu down would have been when he had invited himself in the first place. If she got rid of him now, it would look like she was just trying to silence any dissenting voices.

"Nobody said that," Min said, raising her arms to reassure the assembly. "Nobody who matters, anyway," she added, gaining a small amount of satisfaction from how Abalendu's nostrils flared in response.

"There doesn't seem to be a horizon," she said, pointing out the porthole at the blanket of stars they currently lay upon. "From what we can tell – and I know how mad it sounds – the water seems to curl up at the end. The way Jedda explained it to me – she's got the best handle on it so far – is that it's almost as if we're sailing on the inside of a giant bubble. Keep going in one direction long enough, and we'd end up there," she said, pointing directly upward.

"No horizon?" Sung said.

Abalendu added, "Preposterous. Never heard anything like it. Just wait till the sun comes up, and then we'll see it."

Min shook her head, steeling herself. This was going to be a difficult pill for them to swallow.

"The sun's already up," she said, pointing at the purple orb – the purple star – hanging in the sky.

As one, the assembled crew, including Abalendu and Zoya, raised their heads to catch a glimpse of the purple light source through the saloon porthole.

"What're you saying?" Sung asked, after a few moments taking the sight – and Min's theory – in.

"I'm saying," Min said, taking a deep breath, "that we're not in New Windward waters anymore. I'm saying that we've travelled – or been pushed or taken – to somewhere totally different."

"I'm pretty sure this isn't our world anymore."

As Min had predicted, the crew erupted. Abalendu was, to Min's complete lack of surprise, the loudest.

"A different world? You think this is a different world? Preposterous! Ludicrous! Master Bartholtocrat wrote countless articles on why multi-dimensional theory is just poppycock, and his theories are upheld as fact in most respected circles. You're just trying to cover your own mistakes with this fanciful fiction! Admit it – you've no idea where you've taken us to."

Min took a deep breath and cast her eyes over the assembled crew. This was not every person on board the *Narwhal*. Hells, it was not even every officer. However, Min was familiar enough with her crew to know these men and women represented the hopes and fears of all who worked underneath them. Their expectant gazes weighed upon her, and she felt the pressure like a physical burden.

"You're right," she said, eyes locked on her officers instead of on Abalendu. "I've no idea where we are."

The crew began to shuffle, some opening their mouths to protest.

"But we have a plan," she continued, interrupting any commotion before it turned into outright uproar. "The ship's core has been drained, somehow, and it looks like any other crystal-tech we had on board is dry as well. Jedda reckons it has something to do with the purple star up there, that it drains any magic from the area inside this massive bubble—"

"My dragontoad is fine." Abalendu stood, as if it was his right to interrupt Min at every opportunity he got. He turned to the crew, grinning smugly at being able to contradict Min. With a wave of his hand, he activated his Bond with the creature lazing on his shoulder, and three sickly-green bubbles floated in his palm's wake.

Min was pleased to see some of the assembled crew stifle a laugh when Abalendu mentioned the dragontoad. The noble was as chuffed as a seal catching a fish that he had formed a Bond with a magical creature, and Min had to admit that it was something she did not have the smarts nor the patience to pull off, but why in Boramu's name would anyone want to Bond with that?

"What about you?" Abalendu said, indicating Zoya. "Does your Parasite Glove still work?"

In response, without breaking her gaze, Zoya thrust her left arm out to the side, bursting a hole through the cabin wall.

The hairs on the back of Min's neck straightened into hackles.

"I'll ask you not to damage any more of my room than needed, thank you," she said curtly, daring to look the warrior in the face.

"It's not your room, it's the captain's," Abalendu said, "and we don't have one of those. Not important enough for one, as far as my father seems to be concerned. We've had to settle for you instead, and look where that got us."

Min's eye started to twitch, and she had to clench her fists to contain her anger. Why, that effing little—

Abalendu's nose started to bleed.

"Seekwalla?" Zoya said, grabbing Abalendu by the arm. "Are you all right?"

23

"What do you mean, 'all right'? Other than being stranded out here—"

Abalendu raised his hand to his nose, and his face slackened. "The stress," he muttered, "the stress of all this. The indignity. No wonder. No wonder..."

"Come. Come and lie down," Zoya said, leading her charge away.

The rest of the crew seemed suitably subdued after Abalendu's exit.

"We're getting on top of things," Min said, preparing to dismiss everyone. "Priority is to get control of the *Narwhal* again, get repairs underway. Once we're sailing, then we'll figure out where we are, and how to get back to familiar waters. Holtz: starboard watch are up first. Keep things ticking over, as best you can. Not much we can really do until the Idlers have time for some proper repairs, so give the crew something familiar to raise their spirits. Hertha could use some rigging monkeys to help get the mainsail down, so if anyone gives you attitude, you know where you can send them. Hopefully Jedda can sort whatever's up with the rudder soon. I'll feel a hell of a lot better once we've got a helm that actually works again."

The officers nodded in agreement, but did not look convinced. Min couldn't blame them, and it was not because of her lack of experience. She didn't think even a seasoned captain could get them through this, so how could she blame them for doubting the mere first officer they were saddled with?

Through it all, there was the inescapable fear that Abalendu was right. Could this all be Min's fault? Nobody could remember exactly how they got here. Sure, Min suspected foul play, but the fact remained that she could very well have made a decision that resulted in... whatever exactly had happened to them.

She stood up straight, dispelling the doubt that lingered around the thought of Abalendu like a foul odour.

No, this was not her fault. Whatever could be said about her, Min lived for her job, lived for her crew. If she had the choice, she would not have let this happen to her people.

Time to fix things.

Time to see if Jedda had made any headway.

Jedda had not made any headway.

In fact, when Min descended to the belly again, Jedda was initially nowhere to be seen. Min eventually found the artificer crawling inside an armoire, apparently having sawn a hole in its back after finding she could not lift it from where it had fallen.

"Bloody hell, Jed, you okay? What's going on in there?"

"Can't find it, can't find it," the artificer muttered from inside the piece of furniture.

This was not good. Jedda got like this sometimes, obsessed with something, working herself up to an almost frantic level. Normally it was when things were turning particularly pear-shaped. Min dreaded to think about what else might have gone wrong.

"What's up, Jed? What've you lost?"

The artificer's goggle-adorned visage popped out of the hole in the wardrobe.

"Metal cylinder, about this big," Jedda said, using her hands to show an object roughly the size of a person's head. "Haven't seen it since we fell. If I've lost that…"

Apparently the outcome would be terrible indeed, as Jedda failed to finish her sentence, and instead dove back into the wardrobe.

"Anywhere you've not looked yet?" Min said, desperate for a win after everything that had befallen them.

Jedda was becoming increasingly flustered, muttering to herself from inside the furniture. "Small box. Like a cylinder. Place is a mess, could be anywhere. Can't be lost."

Min was really worried now. The crew had found their theory of being in a different world – how was that even possible? – hard enough to deal with. Having to report another problem could break them.

Min dove into the paraphernalia that had accumulated at the bow end of the room when the *Narwhal* had taken its nosedive. The belongings Jedda had amassed in this room were a peculiar mix of artificer tools, and different board or card games; seemingly the only pastime that could hold Jedda's attention long enough for her to get passionate about it.

Throwing aside some boxes holding different playing cards, Min uncovered a tube resembling Jedda's description.

"Think I've got it, Jed."

The artificer was up like a shot. Min was convinced she would have burst through the wood of the wardrobe if she had been able to, to get to the cylinder quicker.

Finding the cylinder did not seem to fully quell Jedda's agitation.

"Don't be drained, don't be drained…"

Min's heart sank. As well as the ship's core being drained of all magic, the few other pieces of crystal-tech they had on board – an enhanced telescope, an heirloom timepiece Abalendu had inherited from his grandfather – had also been drained dry. If Jedda was hoping for another tool to somehow have retained its charge, Min was certain they were in for a rude disappointment.

However, when the artificer unscrewed the box and unloaded its contents, two board game pieces fell out.

Min stared at them in horror.

"Eshak pieces? You've had me worried sick looking for stupid board game parts? Jedda – how long have you been wasting time looking for these?"

Jedda seemed not to hear Min, still looking at the Eshak pieces in concern. Like most Eshak pieces, these resembled weapons of war, or places of military importance – from Min's sparse knowledge of the game, these seemed to be a Sword and a Temple. That was of little concern to her right now; she was furious at her artificer's priorities.

That changed slightly when Jedda rubbed the Sword, and it began to glow with a silver light.

"Wait – is that magic? Are these things magic?"

The second Eshak piece began to radiate a dull green, confirming Min's suspicion.

Seeing hope blossom before her, Min reached out for the objects. Jedda surprised her by shooting a look of anger over her shoulder and jealously pulling the playing pieces away.

"Don't!" she growled, but then seemed to calm, realising what she had done. "You don't touch someone else's pieces," she muttered.

"Jedda," Min began slowly, urging herself to ignore the outburst for fear of distracting the artificer further. "These pieces. If they have magic, can they help us? Can we use them to power the *Narwhal*, somehow?"

Jedda burst out laughing. "They're ascended," she said,

removing a goggle to wipe a tear from her eye, "but just barely."

Min knew that Eshak players were rewarded for particularly high-quality games by having some of their playing pieces absorb magic. It seemed to happen automatically, somehow, but had very little effect on Min's life. A countless number of fans and crackpots – Jedda included – dedicated their lives to the game back home, but most well-standing New Windward citizens dismissed it as an unusual phenomenon, at the very best. Some high-level Eshak pieces had absorbed enough magic to pull off some actual magical moves during their games – moving around the board themselves, sometimes even destroying other pieces – but most were like Jedda's; they glowed, showing off their owners' prowess, but that was that.

"Why the rush, then?" Min asked. "Why d'you need them so bad? Got a theory about them?"

Jedda looked at Min again as if she were a first-class fool. "I worked really hard for these, Min. Do you have any idea how many games I had to play, the stakes I had to put down?"

For a brief moment, red clouded Min's vision. When it cleared, she found she was shouting at Jedda, her hands reaching out to grab the artificer's overalls.

"—need you to save the *Narwhal*, to get her up and running again! Stop messing around with your stupid games, and get back to your job!"

"But Min," Jedda said, her voice quiet, eyes dim, "they're ascended. Do you know how long it takes?"

Min did not know. She did not care. All that mattered to her now was saving the *Narwhal*, and the people on it.

All that mattered was proving to Abalendu and the other, older crew members what Min already knew, deep inside: she was the best person for this job. Even though she was no captain – yet – she was still in charge.

One of the Icelanders burst in. "Capt'n, I mean, First Officer, you've got to see this."

"What is it, man?" Min said, brushing past him, leaving a stunned Jedda in her wake.

"Land, sir. We can see land."

It was indeed land, out there in the blackness, and the *Narwhal* seemed to be drifting toward it. Min gritted her teeth as she looked through her eyeglass, aware of the weight of the crew's eyes upon her. The approaching island was basically a rocky hill, from what she could tell; the landmass rose towards its middle, but was covered in smaller bumps all the way around, jagged outcrops that Min assumed created a network of mini-chasms all around the island. There were a few tall... things towards the left-most shore that Min assumed were trees, although at this distance they appeared to sport purple feathers instead of leaves. In the middle of the island, at its highest point, was a large brown mass that she could only assume was a building. From what Min could tell, the structure looked as if someone had taken a jumble of room-sized boxes and stacked them together in a haphazard way, ending up with a child's puzzle-cube that did not quite fit together properly.

She put the eyeglass away, and turned to look at her crew.

"Looks like someone's home," she said.

"And we can make it there? We're still drifting, right? How soon until we can steer the *Narwhal* toward the land?"

"That's the funny thing, Sung. Looks like we're drifting towards it."

Min looked back at the unusual structure, and took a deep breath. Others in her situation might be fearful, suspicious of who or what was out there. For Min, that brown building meant possibility. It meant hope.

"I'm putting a team together. We're going to find out who lives here, where in Holamo's lonely hell 'here' is, and – most importantly – how to get our arses home again."

Day Fourteen of solitude

Visited the strangest world today.

It was pouring when I arrived. That's nothing new; at least this time the rain didn't start burning my clothing off me.

All I saw was jungle the whole time I was there. However, as I explored it, the weather started changing. And I mean really changing. It went from raining to sunny five times in the space of as many minutes. At one point there was even snow, and the winds would pick up and die within seconds of each other.

I was getting ready to quit when I came across some kind of stone temple, basically just a large pyramid built in the middle of the jungle. There were people there, and these guys weren't too far away from looking like what I class as people; they had bright red skin and no noses, but otherwise they were similar to those from my world.

However, at the top of their temple was a giant toad, and there were thousands of natives queuing up to visit the thing, taking it in turns to bow before it and say a few words.

They didn't have a problem with me walking up to have a look (as long as I didn't threaten to skip the queue — that particular play almost got me killed). Marching up to the top of the temple, the weather continued to change, and I was buffeted by gales at one point, roasted alive the next.

It took me a while at the top to figure out what was going on. The natives weren't just bowing to the toad; they were telling it stories. Couldn't understand them myself, of course, but the way they were speaking, and their hand gestures — it was pretty clear what was going on.

The strangest thing about this, however, was what happened when the stories were over. The natives told a sad story? The toad started to cry. That was odd enough in itself, but when the toad started to cry, it began to rain. Next person tells a funny story? The toad starts to chuckle, and the sun comes out. Toad gets angry? That's when the gales pop up. You get the picture.

I had no idea why changing the weather was so important to these people. I could see why a farmer would want rain to come after a scorching day, but by the time these people made it to the bottom of the temple steps, the next supplicant would already have changed the toad-god's mood.

I stuck around and watched for a few hours, but then began to get hungry. On my way out, found a clutch of hairy brown fruit the size of my head. Tried them out after I got home and they gave me the runs.

Can't see myself visiting again anytime soon.

THREE

The *Narwhal* bumped against the island's coast about forty minutes after sighting land, causing Min to have conniptions about the extra damage running aground would do to the hull, but there was no helping it. As it was, they were lucky the island happened to be in their path.

If you can call it lucky. Min preferred 'suspicious', but she decided to keep that particular nugget of joy to herself.

"I'm coming." Abalendu emerged from his cabin, an overlarge scarf swaddling his neck, the dragontoad's head protruding from it like a pimple poking through a beard.

Min almost barked with laughter at his words, before dread settled in.

"You're not serious? You want to go out there, into the unknown?"

"I didn't say I wanted to come. I said I *am* coming."

Despite knowing the stench of the hole this line of conversation would take her down, Min could not help herself. "But why? Why take the risk?"

Abalendu rubbed his nose, looking away, almost bored at having to answer the question. "After some consideration, I've come to wonder whether or not this place," he indicated the purple void around them, "might have something to do with my quest."

Inside, Min sighed, and several of the crew audibly groaned.

"This isn't Glimmerwrought, Abalendu. This is nothing like it."

"Oh, you've been there?" He snapped his fingers before she could respond. "Don't answer that – of course you've not. Nobody has. That's what makes Glimmerwrought so special."

That's what makes it non-existent, Min thought, but again, in her wisdom, decided not to share the thoughts she had been happy to vocalise when originally told the goal of her first command.

Abalendu Seekwalla was a scholar, an armchair explorer of sorts. His area of expertise was lost civilizations. One in particular, as a matter of fact. Glimmerwrought.

Glimmerwrought, a place that categorically did not exist. Every sailor, every traveller – by the many hells, every child – knew that. A bit like Jedda and her Eshak games, however, the Glimmerwrought bug bit certain intellectuals, who became obsessed with proving its existence.

Abalendu, poor bugger, had been bitten hard, and unlike most similarly afflicted, he had the family background to actually pull off a search for it.

Min could see how someone as self-obsessed as Abalendu could decide that this strange land they found themselves in now had something to do with him. However, it did not, and she had no interest in him tagging along just to endanger the rest of the team.

"Besides," Abalendu added, indicating with his thumb behind him, "you'll be wanting the Parasite Glove to come. Zoya stays with me. You want the Glove, you get me as an added bonus. I get to find my lost civilization, and we're all happy."

Min bit her tongue against the retort she almost spat out. She was far from happy, but could not argue that having Zoya along would take the edge off the unknown.

The things she would endure to save her crew.

"On top of all that, the success of this mission is paramount to getting me back home. You've proven well enough already that this particular fix we find ourselves in is beyond your… talents. I won't put my faith in you again, recruit. I'm coming."

Min glared, but otherwise said nothing. She had already chosen Kristairn and Jeet to accompany her for the task. Both were big, seasoned seamen, and both had plenty of experience in brawls. If things came to blows, as they so often did, the seamen could deal with most mundane disturbances. Having Zoya and the Parasite Glove seemed like overkill, really.

"We'll not be more than three hours," Min told Holtz, who as second officer would have command in her absence. "Keep the repairs going, focus on the physical parts – sails and rudder. I'm starting to believe Jedda when she says there's no chance of starting the core up again, but don't let her stop trying. That brain of hers will find the solution eventually, if one exists. If you don't hear from us, gear for war, and get the hell off this island as soon as you can."

Holtz, ever the emotional one, nodded, said nothing, and got back to work.

∞

"Try not to lead us to our deaths, yes?" Abalendu said as the *Narwhal* disappeared behind them, her bulk obscured by the rocky outcrops that littered the island.

Min decided to ignore him. She was fairly certain the stream of constant insults thrown her way was more than just Abalendu's regular demeanour. Yes, she was confident he was a total arse, and he would like nothing better than to spend his days reminding those around him he was better than they were. Still, in their month travelling together, Min got the distinct impression he had singled her out for special attention, to make her life a particular misery with the constant insults and put-downs. It was fairly obvious to Min that Abalendu was carrying some serious daddy issues on his shoulders, and he had taken it as a personal slight that his research vessel had a new recruit in charge, instead of a proper captain.

Hells, perhaps it was meant as an insult to the scholar. Min had never actually seen the two of them together, but she could not imagine the admiral having a particularly close relationship with his arrogant son.

Min had dealt with bullies before. Since she could not beat this one to a pulp – not with his Kisiwian bodyguard along for the ride – she would ignore him instead.

The landscape before them was unusual, alien. When Min was a child, she had contracted salt fever. It had nearly killed her, and took a year of her life from her; once the fever finally broke, her muscles had wasted away. It was for this reason that Min's grandparents – her mother's parents – had travelled to New Windward, giving up their homes in Goryeoa to help nurse her back to health. Min supposed the rocks of this island were somewhat reminiscent of the mountains that surrounded New Windward city, reminding her a little of the walks her grandfather had taken her on when she was fit enough to get out of bed again.

However, the purple light of the star above coated these protrusions, shrouding them in otherness, stealing away the sweetness that any recollection of her family might have given.

Min took a glance at the seamen accompanying her. Kristairn was particularly nervous, his hand with the club in it visibly shaking.

Blast. If she had not been distracted by Abalendu earlier, she would have noticed the Iceman was not the right choice for the job. Better keep an eye on him. Thankfully, Jeet seemed in better shape. Hailing from the same group of islands that Abalendu's father came from, Min supposed the woman must be made of stern stuff if all Zadzerjian men were half as prattish as Abalendu was.

Min had almost decided to send the two of them back to the ship when Zoya, scouting a few steps ahead, stiffened.

"We're here," was all the warrior said, although the ready position she adopted, with her harpoon pointing forward, told Min much more.

Not wanting the first thing any natives saw to be an aggressive Kisiwian with a long, pointy weapon, Min made her way to the front of the party, to the entrance of the building she had noticed when approaching the island.

It was an unusual construction. What struck Min first was the sheer size of the thing. It was big, much bigger than the sketches Min had seen back in the academy of the various dwellings of indigenous people New Windward explorers had come across when travelling the seas. The building before them reminded Min more of the harbourmaster's office at the New Windward docks. She was confident there were at least two, possibly even three floors to the structure, and it was almost as long as the *Narwhal* herself.

Definitely more than just a simple hut, despite the material it seemed to have been made from.

Mud. From this distance, Min got the distinct impression the building had been pieced together from large mud bricks. Which was funny, because so far the island had been rocky, without even sand at the cove where the *Narwhal* had beached.

"Ever seen anything like this, scholar?" Min asked Abalendu, her curiosity overcoming her enjoyment of the Zadzerjian man's silence.

Abalendu wrinkled his nose at the sight. "Rudimentary construction," he said. "An impressive scale, I suppose, if the size of a dwelling is of particular importance to you, but there's no art here. We're clearly dealing with some primitive people."

People, Min thought. That's optimistic.

Beside her, Kristairn gave a low moan.

Great Spirit Gorya, that Iceman should never leave the water again. He would be worse than useless inside.

"You two," Min said, pointing at Jeet and Kristairn, "stay here, keep an eye out. Come and get us if anyone – or anything – approaches."

The relief from Kristairn was palpable. Jeet was less enthusiastic at missing out, and Min was certain the seaman shot her some dark looks as she turned away, a result of being one of Sung's watch crew.

"Well, lead the way, Zoya. Time to go and meet the neighbours."

Zoya, harpoon still pointing forward, glanced at Abalendu for confirmation, then followed Min's order. Min took up position just behind the warrior, her own sabre staying in its sheath. If they met someone or something dangerous, they would be receiving a Parasite Glove to the face much quicker than Min would be able to achieve anything with her own weapon.

The warrior stayed on point as they entered the building, and Abalendu actually started being useful. His dragontoad kept belching forth dimly-glowing green bubbles, the only source of illumination available to them since the crystals in the *Narwhal's* lanterns had been drained of their magic.

"If anything happens," Min heard Abalendu say to Zoya, doing little to disguise his volume, "remember your directives. I am the priority."

Min heard Zoya grunt in acknowledgment, but otherwise the warrior kept her eyes forward on the dark corridor. Min had never been able to tell exactly how Zoya felt about Abalendu. Sure, she had accepted the mission to guard him. And sure, the woman – like so many military types – seemed to attach an unhealthy amount of honour to following orders correctly. But to have to spend that much time around Abalendu Seekwalla? Min was convinced Zoya would happily use the Parasite Glove on him, if given the chance.

Given the dirt-based structure, Min had wondered if the

building was a kind of insect-like construction, and half-expected a warren of tunnels worming its way through the dirt, eventually leading them to a hungry queen at the centre, ready for Min to shove Abalendu into her mouth.

Instead, the building seemed horrifically mundane. It was just a regular corridor, with empty rooms off of it, and nothing of interest in view.

Nothing of interest, until the corridor opened up into a much larger room.

Abalendu gasped before Min could properly see anything, and the scholar pushed forward to Zoya's side instead of cowering behind her.

"Well, I'll be a crustacean's wetnurse," Min said, as she managed to squeeze her head between the two.

The room before them was large. Massive, even. What was more, it was full, brimming with… stuff.

Abalendu began to make his way forward slowly, hesitant – Min assumed it was because of the threat of danger – but his hands subconsciously reached out, wanting to get a closer look at the treasure trove.

The room, more like a warehouse than anything else, was full of oddities. It distinctly reminded Min of walking into an antique store with her parents, the walls decked with paraphernalia the shop owners had accrued over the years. From what Min could tell, this was a large square room with only four walls and a roof, but everywhere she looked, she saw something new. A wide variety of furniture (a chair that seemed to be carved entirely of faces, each wearing a different expression; an upside down four-poster bed, which Min could swear had a bed of suspended soil instead of a mattress), weapons (there was a sword three times larger than even Zoya could properly wield, along with what looked like an assortment of silver crossbows attached to the wall, although Min could not see the limbs nor any bolts), and even toys littered the vast space before her. Suspended from the roof, paper dragons chased what seemed to be a family of flying snails, forever petrified in their pursuit, never to complete their movements. On a blue chest of drawers close by, a toy monkey sat staring at them, its left and right hands resting gently on its knees, a third arm rising from behind its back, holding what looked like a frying pan.

"What is this?" she said aloud, not really expecting an answer.

"Look," Abalendu said, awestruck, pulling off one of the many white cloths that covered the forgotten wares of this place. It unveiled a statue carved from a substance not unlike marble, depicting a trio of young girls, each with two mouths, fixed forever in a singing pose. "Such beauty. Why would anyone cover something like this up? Who would own something like this, and keep it hidden so?"

Min's heart leapt when she saw a jar of crystals sitting on a pedestal nearby. She ran over to it, hoping to find something that she could use to repower the *Narwhal*; some more crystal-tech Jedda could somehow siphon the energies from. However, all of the stones within the jar were dull, dead – either drained like the magic from the *Narwhal's* core, or never having been imbued in the first place.

"What a load of junk." She scanned the rest of the room, unimpressed. Most of the belongings here were either hidden by large white cloths, or were covered in a generous layer of dust. "If the owner hid these things away, they must be worthless, not worth our time. Can't see us finding anything to help the crew in here."

Abalendu shook his head, having moved his attention to a painting he had found on the wall closest to the door. It was a landscape, but depicted a scene completely alien to Min. It was, as far as she could tell, a city, but one that clung to a protrusion of rock that resembled a stalactite more than anything else, the bedrock of which was the ceiling, and the point of the city suspended above a pit of inky blackness far below.

"This," Abalendu said, "is a cave of wonders. First Officer Choi Minjun, can't you tell? These objects, they are not of our world."

Min raised an eyebrow. "You believe in Jedda's theory now? That we're no longer anywhere near New Windward?"

The scholar gave a snort of derision. "Believe some crackpot theory you and the hired help came up with? Hardly. This was a conclusion I reached by myself, using facts, not fanciful supposition."

"Seekwalla, stay back," Zoya said, moving in front of the scholar when he got too close to the image. "If we don't understand these things, they may be dangerous."

"Don't be ridiculous," Abalendu said. "If there is anyone here qualified to explore, to understand this collection of oddities, it is me."

"Nevertheless, stay behind."

"Fine, fine," Abalendu said, resuming his safe position behind the warrior. "Best protect the goods, eh?"

"Finally, a bit of sense." Min relaxed, leaning on the pedestal beside the empty jar of crystals. Unfortunately, she was so caught up with Abalendu's attitude she did not notice the pedestal was already occupied.

The small glass orb atop it rolled off. Min turned, but her movement felt slow, useless. Try as she might – despite both Abalendu and Zoya shouting behind her, somewhere distant – Min could not move fast enough to catch it.

The orb hit the floor with a twinkle, a gentle introduction to a piece of music before the calamitous orchestra joined in, time speeding up again as the glass of the sphere fragmented, shattering across the ground before her.

For a breath, all of them froze.

"You fool!" Abalendu screamed, and Min struggled to debate with him. "How many priceless artefacts are you planning on wrecking before this travesty of an expedition is through?"

Min felt her face redden. "Sorry, everyone. Sorry," she mumbled, crouching to start picking some of the pieces up. It galled her to be apologising to Abalendu, but this time he was right – she was an idiot. Hopefully, whoever owned this mud building would not mind one small breakage.

She picked up a piece of glass, held it between her thumb and forefinger, and looked at the rest of the mess on the floor. Shards decorated the hard surface like the fish in the black sea beneath the *Narwhal*. She was not going to get far cleaning this up without a broom.

Min turned to Zoya. "Maybe we should just move on, and I'll come back later to sort this out? Could take a while."

The glass piece fell from her fingers.

Abalendu rolled his eyes and swore. Zoya turned away, but Min looked at the shard of glass on the floor, fixing it with a hard stare.

This time, it had not been her fault. She could almost swear the glass had jumped from her hand.

"Master Murhk, save me from the idiots I have to work with," Abalendu mumbled.

"Look, everyone," Min said, pointing at the glass on the ground. The shard she had held between her fingers was trembling, vibrating like a silent gong. Then the rest of the shards on the floor were vibrating too, their movements becoming more pronounced. Min stood and backed away from the glass, drawing her sabre. Zoya went straight to Abalendu, placing herself between him and the unusual activity.

"I think you are right – it is best we move on," Zoya said, not taking her eyes from the glass on the floor. But before she could say or do anything else, the glass began to move.

It gathered together first, the pieces that had tumbled furthest away jumping across the compacted dirt of the floor, bouncing toward each other. Then, like a school of dolphins seeking out warmer waters, the rest of the glass moved as one, clumping together in a ball, then spreading out, working itself into its own facets, building a structure out of the pieces Min had broken.

In the end – after a few seconds of construction, during which the *Narwhal*'s crew looked on with morbid fascination – a figure stood before them. A knight. A glass knight, just a little bit taller than Min, but considerably wider, its fractured surfaces glinting green from the light emitted by Abalendu's floating bubbles.

"Surely there wasn't that much glass in that tiny ball," Min said in a low voice, waiting to see what the figure would do.

Abalendu shook his head. "The bauble was solid. Now that some idiot has broken it, the pieces have spread out, formed a shell. It looks to be hollow inside."

"If it is hollow," Zoya said, tensing, "then it should be easy to shatter."

"Zoya, no!" Min shouted, but it was already too late.

The Kisiwian took a few steps toward the glass creature.

Perhaps it was Zoya's readied harpoon; perhaps it was always the creature's intention. Whatever the reason, the glass knight took one look at Zoya, then held its arm up. The shards of glass that formed the limb reconstituted themselves, the pieces tinkling off one another as they changed from the shape of a hand into that of a long blade, fixed to the creature's elbow.

Zoya did not wait for the knight to attack. Seeing the blade, she jabbed at the thing's chest with her harpoon. There was a crunch as the knight's chest shattered, the weapon easily piercing through, its tip bursting out the other side.

"If it's hollow," Min shouted, circling the knight as it focussed on Zoya, ready to dash in with her blade when the opportunity presented itself, "then what good will stabbing it in the heart do?"

As if in response, the construct twisted, ripping the harpoon shaft from Zoya's grip, and then kicked at the bodyguard. The glass knight was clearly more powerful than it looked; the blow catapulted Zoya through the air, causing her to disappear in a crash of paraphernalia, the precariously stacked, covered items folding in on the hole her flight caused in the jumble.

Min's eyes widened. If that thing hit her in the same way it hit Zoya, she would be dead before she reached the floor.

Not giving the knight time to refocus, Min lunged at it, holding her sabre in two hands. If stabbing it did not help, perhaps a cruder approach would be more effective.

Min sliced at the knight's blade arm, not yet employed in this fight, cutting at it just above the elbow.

It was – shock of all shocks – like cutting through glass. The arm shattered; the blade fell to the ground, again disintegrating as it hit the floor.

Min's triumphant grin was cut short when the creature's other fist swung at her. She managed to dodge it, but sacrificed her footing to do so, falling on her arse as the glass creature stood over her.

"Seekwalla," she said, eyes fixed on her approaching doom, "I could really use some help here."

The scholar was skulking in the shadows close to the entrance. He was backing away slowly, face grim, showing no intention of joining in.

Her gaze flitted back to the glass knight. The creature held up its left hand, forming this one into a replacement blade.

The glass knight's head exploded.

In its place was a fist. Specifically, a glove.

"Zoya!" Min sighed with relief. "Bugger me, that was close."

The Kisiwian warrior, fist still poking through the glass creature's head, thrust downward through the thing's chest and groin, spraying Min with tiny shards as she tore her opponent apart.

"You'll be stripped of command!" shrieked Abalendu's shrill voice from the other side of the room. "I'll see you in the stocks! You bring us to this… this place, somehow, then you set this creature on me by smashing a stupid glass ball—"

"It was hardly on you," Min said, pulling herself up into a sitting position. "You did your best to make sure that never happened."

To Min's surprise, Zoya held a hand out to help her up. The warrior's face was otherwise dispassionate, but Zoya hauled Min up all the same.

"Don't help her," Abalendu continued, his confidence returning as the tension of the attack faded. "This is all her fault."

As Min's longcoat began to vibrate, she felt a coldness bloom in the pit of her gut.

"Abalendu," she began.

"No, I'll have my say, thank you very much, recruit. After the second time you've tried to kill me today, I'll have my say."

Min picked at one of the glass shards on her jacket. It was definitely trembling.

"Listen—" she began.

"Don't 'listen' me," Abalendu said, almost screeching now. Min was surprised the man was not foaming at the mouth yet. "You don't get to 'listen' me. Nobody gets to 'listen' me!"

"Shut up," Min ordered, holding the vibrating shard out for Zoya to see.

The warrior had just enough time to widen her eyes before the shard, and all the other glass detritus that had collected on Min's jacket, shot away from her, combining once again into a molten lump from which the knight began to reform.

"Does it seem bigger this time?" Abalendu asked as the three of them backed away.

"It's just because you're closer," Min said. "You know, instead of running away."

She was, tragically, lying. The glass knight was at least twice the size it had been before. Its surface seemed thinner, more brittle, as if the substance it was made up of had to spread out even more to create this larger form, but the cracking of the floor beneath its feet as it marched towards them showed it was no less deadly.

Abalendu sneered at Min. "Just you watch, recruit. You don't know the power of someone with a fully-forged Bond."

With that, Abalendu stepped forward, pointing a finger at the approaching construct. In the palm of his hand, a garish green bubble formed. He took the expanding sphere in both hands and pulled at it, straining, stretching it until the bubble was almost the size of him, and difficult to grip properly. Then, Abalendu thrust the bubble forward, his dragontoad giving a petulant roar as he did so, and the deadly sphere impacted upon the glass knight.

The green bubble coated the creature, hissing as it touched the glass.

However, the damage Abalendu caused, heralded by the burnt smell of the decaying glass, did not seem to do anything to put the creature off.

Instead, it took another step forward, and swung with its blade arm towards Abalendu, standing alone before it.

Except he was no longer alone. At the moment she was needed, Abalendu's bodyguard was there. The creature's blade shattered once again as Zoya grabbed at it with the Parasite Glove, showering herself and the scholar behind her with another hail of glass.

Min took the moment to duck in at the creature's left side, where it no longer had an arm to defend itself with.

"So," she said, grunting as she carved a wedge of glass from the thing's side, "are we sure this is a great idea? Smashing it into pieces again?"

Close by, Zoya grunted as she engaged the thing's remaining arm, already re-forged into a replacement blade. The knight seemed to have learned from previous encounters, and was now thrusting at Zoya, trying to pierce her from afar, instead of letting the Kisiwian destroy its last remaining weapon.

"It's just, the last time you smashed it – and I did love your work – it came back twice the size. We're going to run out of room if that keeps happening."

Another grunt as the knight opened up a slice of red on Zoya's shoulder. Despite the blood that began to run down her front, the warrior did not seem to notice.

"I do love our chats, Zoya," Min said, dancing behind the glass creature to hit at it from a safer spot. "We should talk more often."

Taking another chunk from the creature's back, Min finally got its attention.

She gulped as the knight turned on her, but it was exactly the opening Zoya needed. The warrior grabbed the glass construct from behind, and with a single yell she hurled it beyond the tight circle of curious objects they were fighting in, flinging it somewhere into the empty darkness of the rest of the room.

There was a cacophony of shattering as, out there in the gloom, the thing once again splintered into fragments.

Min turned to Zoya, her eyes fixing on the warrior's wound. "Was that really the best idea?" she asked.

In response, a giant arm – the length of the *Narwhal's* shortest mast – reached out from the black beyond their circle. The glass that made up the arm was so thin it was almost invisible, but that made the knight's grip no less effective when it plucked Abalendu from behind them, holding him high in the air.

Min stared at the scholar – a man who had earned so much of her hatred – as he was suspended above her, struggling in a translucent grip. Despite how much she loathed him, her blood ran cold at the thought of losing anyone on this mission.

Zoya's first reaction was to leap up to smash at the fist that held her charge. From the darkness where the rest of the creature hid, a second limb – a club this time, instead of a blade – erupted, slapping Zoya down from her leap and smashing the warrior into the wall.

Cracks ran from where Zoya cratered into the masonry. More broken bones, for anyone except the wielder of the Parasite Glove.

Baring her teeth, Zoya changed tack. She glared at the darkness where the thing waited, and leapt into it.

There was a shattering of glass, and Min's heart pounded in triumph at the sound. However, moments later Zoya flew back into the light, landing crumpled on the ground beside Min.

Min ran over to the warrior and shook her. "Come on, Zoya, we need you. I'm completely outclassed here."

Zoya rolled onto her back. She was conscious, but her eyes were threatening to roll back in her head.

She was hurt, badly.

Min lay the warrior down, turning to look at where she guessed the knight must be standing, the gloom around it broadening as Abalendu's garish spheres began to fade away as the scholar began to lose consciousness in the creature's grip.

Taking a deep breath, Min stood up, holding her sabre in one trembling hand. Her only saving grace was that Abalendu, now unmoving, could not see how much she was shaking.

"All right, you ugly bugger," Min said, pointing at the knight with her sabre. "You've earned my attention."

"Just what in the star's shadow have you done?"

Min was caught off guard by the voice to her right. She turned in shock to see a lit lantern move around one of the piles of tarp-covered furniture.

The lantern was held by a man. He was old, that much was clear from his mad shock of grey hair and his long, matted beard. His skin was as black as Zoya's, and Min noticed his step had a vitality that did not match the wrinkles of his face. He was dressed in a swaddling of grey robes, with bandoleers crossed over his chest, various pouches hanging from them, a personal collection as varied and eclectic as the objects in this room. In his hands, the old man held a long staff of what seemed to be polished driftwood.

The man gave Min a glassy stare, raising an eyebrow at the sight of her.

"What do you think you—"

The old man's words were cut off as the glass knight swiped at him from the gloom. Min tried to cry out, but it was just too bloody fast. Luckily for her, the old man's reactions were better, although not as good as Zoya's; he managed to get out of the way of the blow, but fell on his arse in doing so.

"A Flagonknight? You let a Flagonknight loose in my home?"

The man's eyes were twin balls of fury, fixed on Min.

She realised the glass creature – the Flagonknight – had left its club in a vulnerable position, and leapt at it with her blade. She was not as strong as Zoya, so the weapon did not shatter, but cracks ran all along its length from where she struck it.

The club withdrew, and in the dark the Flagonknight rumbled, moving toward them.

"It wasn't on purpose," Min said. "Never seen one of them before."

"You make a habit of breaking into people's homes and poking around stuff you don't understand? Damned idiots…"

Min began to grumble an apology, but the man turned and scrambled away from her.

Above, the Flagonknight rumbled into view. It was huge now, bent double in order to fit itself inside the old man's warehouse. The lantern light filtered through the thin glass of the Flagonknight, making it seem Min was facing down a creature composed purely of flames.

"Don't leave us!" Min shouted as the man moved away. "How do we fight it? Can it be stopped?"

The club swiped at Min. She rolled out of the way, and heard the weapon crack as it hit the ground. At this rate, it would batter itself to pieces, but Min was getting tired.

Also, Min could not pull herself together after falling apart.

"Won't achieve anything by smashing it to pieces," the old man grumbled, searching around in the boxes close to the pedestal the orb had originally perched on. "What kind of idiot keeps hitting a Flagonknight after it pulls itself together? Was the first time not a good enough hint of what was going to happen?"

The glass club swung for Min, missing her, instead embedding into the ground behind. She hammered at it again, shattering the weapon.

The old man's head shot up.

"Are you serious?" he shouted. "You aren't listening to a word I'm saying?"

Min, puffing heavily now, readied herself to get out of the way of the next club swing. "Just doing my best not to die right now, thanks."

"You're doing a poor job of it," the man said, resuming his rummaging. As if it heard him, the shards of the club shot through the air, back to the Flagonknight's body, reforming.

Convinced she was staring her death in the face, Min struggled to catch her breath, her eyes darting around the room, looking for anything that could save her.

"Here we go," the old man said, jumping up with a rod in his hands. "Time to clean house."

It was a poor weapon, Min could see straight away. It was too short. The rod was almost black, made of a dark metal that seemed to drink in any light that touched it. Min was certain the rod was engraved with symbols of some kind, but she was too far away to see them properly.

The man clutched the black rod in his hand like a schoolmaster marching across the playground to meet with the parents of a disobedient child, and tapped the Flagonknight's foot with it.

The effect was instant. The glass of the creature's leg compacted, clumping up into the collection of shards that had originally been part of the orb.

Of course, with its leg taken out from under it, the creature fell, dropping Abalendu as it flung its remaining arm out to break its fall. Min ran to the scholar as the old man continued to beat upon the fallen Flagonknight, causing more glass to compact, the creature shrivelling up in response to his assault.

Min was certain Abalendu was dead, but the pitiful croak of his dragontoad told her otherwise. The scholar suddenly coughed, then lay there, gasping like the fish her father brought back to port every morning.

"You'll be discharged, recruit," he said, between his agonised gasps. "When my father hears of this, you'll be discharged."

Min suspected she was indeed in line to lose her job, but that loss had nothing to do with Abalendu's brattish request.

A few steps away, Zoya groaned. Not only did Parasite Gloves grant immense strength, but their wielders healed fast. The Kisiwian would be on her feet in no time.

Abalendu sat up. He was looking straight at the old black man, who in turn had reclaimed his driftwood staff. The old man placed the Flagonknight — now returned to its original form as a glass orb — back onto the pedestal Min had knocked it from.

"Don't touch," he said to them both, the same way Min would tell a dog to sit.

"Who in Master Wellflek's name are you?" Abalendu asked.

"He saved our life, Seekwalla," Min said.

His lip curled up in consideration of the pair, the old man moved forward, the various pouches attached to his bandoleers clinking as he walked.

"They call me Brightest," the old man said. "Welcome to my home."

"Welcome to the Darkstar Dimension."

Day thirty-six of solitude

Today, the rift I've been keeping an eye on finally came low enough for me to reach it.

It has been over a week since the rift appeared, and waiting for it to descend has been a frustrating experience. I can't help but feel there must be some way to use the floating rocks in the sky to get access to more of them. Will keep experimenting.

Unlike most worlds I've visited, I didn't see any ground in this place. Instead, I was surrounded by a labyrinth of stairs, running in all directions, turning on small landings, splitting into multiple paths, extending into the distance.

I spent a short time exploring before coming across a much larger landing, which held a market of some kind. The natives — some green-skinned humanoids about half my height who seemed to be closely related to lizards — were not particularly surprised to see me, and a number of them were willing to trade, which was lucky, as food stores have been running low.

Getting home was more difficult than I expected. It appears the stairs in that place can shift, and although I had marked my trail when first exploring, the chalk lines I made on the ground eventually broke.

I spent an hour running blindly up and down staircases before coming across some of the traders with whom I had exchanged goods earlier. They were much more familiar with the ways of this place, and also appeared to know exactly where I wanted to go.

I'm hoping this world will be a regular traveller around the Darkstar, and will save up trading goods accordingly.

Will have to figure out a better alternative to chalk for marking my way up and down those shifting staircases; I can't imagine a more boring existence than looking at nothing but steps for the rest of my days.

FOUR

"Zoya, take him down."

"Do not," Min said, stepping forward, sheathing her sabre. She could see the whole situation breaking against the rocks quickly, especially if Abalendu kept forcing himself in charge.

However, Brightest, as the mysterious man had identified himself, did not seem the least bit concerned that he was being threatened by the idiot scholar. In fact, it seemed Brightest was still getting over his anger at the mess they had made of his home. Just below Brightest's left eye, his cheek was twitching uncontrollably, a tick Min assumed had been brought on by their intrusion.

Abalendu, limping after his encounter with the Flagonknight, sneered. "Your orders are to report to me, not to her," he said, speaking directly to Zoya. On his shoulder, the dragontoad belched, a small, ponderous green bubble floating lazily from its mouth. "This man almost killed me. We have no idea who he is, or what he is capable of. Take him down now, before he tries to harm me again."

Min spoke before Zoya was able to act. "Under New Windward protocol, a ship's commanding officer is the reporting officer in all away team missions. As I've not been incapacitated, Zoya reports to me. After me, Zoya – as military personnel – is in charge. Abalendu, you're a civilian. Nobody is taking orders from you right now."

Abalendu looked as though he'd been slapped in the face with a wet fish. Min was certain he was about to order his bodyguard to take her down instead when Zoya spoke.

"She is correct, Seekwalla. The only orders I've been given that supersede her own are to protect you from harm. That does not include attacking people who you think might harm you."

Brightest gave a mirthless chuckle. "Well, pretty kettle of fish you've got here. I guess you lot are from that wreck beached up east?"

Min nodded. "That's our ship, the *Melodious Narwhal*, yes." "When are you leaving?"

She pursed her lips. Not the response she had been looking for. "Our ship has sustained damage. We're going to need to repair her before we can set off again. Any help you could offer in that regard would be much appreciated, and would certainly make the process quicker."

"What've you done to the ship?"

"Not sure yet. We crashed from the sky when our core was drained. Our craftsmen are inspecting her now for any structural issues, but the bigger problem is the empty core."

"A core? What's that, then? You were in the sky?"

Min frowned, confused by the man's questions. "Yes, the *Narwhal* is a skyship. The core is where we store the magic that keeps her aloft."

Brightest shook his head matter-of-factly. "Nope, that won't work here. Not going to get her working again anytime soon."

"And what makes you so sure of that?" Abalendu's tone was challenging. It was obvious he did not think Brightest had a clue what he was talking about.

Brightest looked at them, face stern, his head bobbing up and down, his jaw working as if chewing something tough. After a moment's consideration, he indicated the doorway with his head.

"I'll show you."

Uncertain, the trio followed him, making their way up a tight spiral staircase, lit by the conflicting glows from Brightest's lantern and Abalendu's green spheres. Underfoot, the stonework felt almost hollow to Min as she stepped, giving her a sense of uneasiness as she climbed higher.

Then, finally, the staircase opened out onto the structure's roof. Above them, in the light-studded darkness of the sky, Brightest waved an arm towards the purple star, seemingly a permanent fixture of this place.

"That," Brightest said, indicating the celestial object, "is the Darkstar."

"Not the most ambitious name," Abalendu said. "I suppose you came up with it yourself?"

Brightest seemed disgruntled. "The group I came here with called it that, yeah. Never had any complaints before."

Min wished Abalendu was still unconscious. Finally they had found someone else, someone who seemed to have knowledge of this place, and the scholar was doing his darned best to wind him up at every turn.

"What has the Darkstar got to do with the *Narwhal?*" Min asked. "You said you wanted to show us something about the core."

Brightest, shooting Abalendu a glare, nodded at the Darkstar again. "Best I can gather, it drains magic, if it can. Never really had any myself, but it seems to have a draining effect on anything being stored, sucking it dry. Items that are actually magical, that make their own magic inside them, like the Flagonknight? It doesn't seem to be able to take it from them. But good luck trying to get your crystal topped up again. Even if you found a source you could draw from, the Darkstar would suck it dry within minutes."

Not good, Min thought, trying to ignore the yawning pit she felt opening up beneath her. Without that core, they were grounded.

Not good at all.

"You said you came here," she asked, not letting herself wallow in her inability to get the *Narwhal* flying again. "You weren't born here?"

Brightest chuckled. "Does it strike you as the best place to raise a kid? Nah, I came here, long ago, same as you. From another world."

"You're from New Windward?"

The old man shook his head. "Name's not familiar. No skyships where I come from, either. I'm from somewhere else."

"Across the Rhineholt Sea? Are you some kind of descendant of the Kisiwians?"

Brightest tutted. "Listen to me, girl. I'm from another world. Not from your little chunk of rock, not from the other side of your planet, not born here in the Darkstar, either. I'm from somewhere else."

"Preposterous," Abalendu said, regaining some of the bluster the Flagonknight had beaten out of him. "Multiple dimensions? That fanciful notion was disproved long ago; anyone who raises the idea now is denounced for quackery. The idea of being from another world is absurd."

"Well, then, I'm quacking. Star's shadow, we're all quacking here. Most people work this out by now – you're not in your own world anymore."

Abalendu fumed, and Min felt an inner warmth at hearing this man confirm Jedda's suspicions.

"Did you really think this looked anything like your New Windward?"

"The world is a large and mysterious place," Abalendu said, taking on the rigid stance Min assumed he used when lecturing students. "No need to make up fairytale lands in our heads when the one before us is an interesting enough place to explore."

Brightest rolled his eyes, then turned back to regard the Darkstar. "Fine," he said, his voice resigned. "I don't really care. Will just be happy when you head on, and leave me to myself again."

"Yourself?" Min said. "I thought you said you came here with others?"

Brightest did not turn around.

"I did. And now I'm by myself. And happy about it."

Min saw Abalendu and Zoya glance at each other, raising their eyebrows. There was a story here, but Min could not help feeling that its telling would ruin the small bond they had forged with this stranger.

"Brightest, can you help us understand what's happening? How did you get here? How did we get here? We can't remember anything about what happened to bring us to this place."

The old man turned to her, and she got the distinct impression her question had pulled him out of some particularly dark thoughts.

"The Darkstar," he said. "Don't really know what it is, why it's here. Just know that it's hungry, hungry for magic. It takes anything brought to it, and if it can't find anything in here… well, then it does exactly what it did to you, and what it did to me."

"And what is that?" Abalendu asked.

"It punches a hole between worlds, pulls people and places to it. You've figured out what this place is yet?" Brightest asked, indicating the fish-lit sky above them.

Min nodded. "It's like we're floating on the inside of a bubble."

Brightest chuckled. "I like that one. My… I've heard others say it's like a world turned inside out, and we're left floating on the inside, stuck in here, while everything else around us is mad."

"And are we?" Zoya asked, stepping forward, speaking to Brightest for the first time. Brightest looked at her appraisingly, taking stock of the warrior. "Are we stuck in here?"

The old man smiled, shook his head, and pointed back up into the sky. "Punching holes between worlds ain't an exact science, I guess – look." He pointed up at one of the collections of coloured gas that Min had spotted orbiting the Darkstar earlier. She could see dozens of them up there, close to the purple star – clouds of red, green, one purple, all seeming to orbit lazily around the miniature sun.

Brightest's finger wandered, and Min started to notice other objects floating up there, in the dark. Mostly rocks, some of which she reckoned were the size of buildings, perhaps even small villages. Many of the floating objects were far away from the water's surface, close to the sun, but others hung surprisingly close to the black sea.

There were a few distant objects, suspended too far away for Min to properly make out. Was one of them… was one of them a tower, sitting on a plinth of bedrock, but floating hundreds of miles off the ground?

Min reached for her telescope, but recalled she had left it back in her quarters on the *Narwhal*.

"Are they… are they different worlds?"

"Ways between them, most of them. Certainly the glowing ones. Don't know how the Darkstar punches through, but a lot of the rifts never really close again. Sure, they wander off, most don't stick around all the time, but there seems to be a pattern between most of their movements."

"Ludicrous," Abalendu spat. "A purple sun that steals people from different worlds, sucking up their magic, abandoning them here in some sort of… wasteland dimension? Preposterous. Why would such a thing even happen?"

Brightest shrugged. "Beats me. I always reckoned it had something to do with the dragon."

Abalendu burst out laughing. "As if we hadn't wasted enough time with you. First multiple worlds, now dragons? They are fairy stories. We first realised dragons weren't real when we learned how to make maps. With all the journeys we have made around the world – all the people of New Windward, long before we banded together under one flag – after all the crackpots have tried and failed to prove their existence, it is categorically clear that dragons – real dragons – do not, and never have, existed. So stop trying to fool us again, old man."

"Dragons don't exist, eh?" Brightest said, giving a half smile. "Well, you seem like a smart guy who knows what he's talking about. Guess you must be right. You can be the one to tell her that, though."

A chill ran up Min's spine. She realised Brightest was looking behind her now, upward. She turned her head, to find herself partially blinded by the Darkstar above.

Min squinted to get a better look, to see if there was anything flying between the objects that drifted around the distant star. She had to agree with Abalendu on this one: everyone knew dragons only existed in stories. Perhaps this Brightest did not really know what he was—

Min gasped as she saw what Brightest had motioned toward. The reason she had not seen it earlier was that she was looking for something small, some detail she had missed. But her first clue as to the dragon's location was when the Darkstar itself shifted above her.

Min's legs turned to jelly. She took a step back, reaching out for anything close that would support her. To her surprise, she found Brightest, who clutched her arm tight, holding her upright. She turned to look at the old man, who returned her gaze with a grin, almost excited, seemingly oblivious to the alarm on her face. He nodded encouragingly back to the Darkstar.

Slowly, nervously, Min looked up again.

Something was moving on the side of the Darkstar. On both sides. Min knew that bright object, the one that coated Brightest's home in purple light, was close to them, relatively speaking – certainly closer than the sun that beat down upon New Windward. But still, it must be huge. And anything that was able to wrap itself around such an object must be immense as well.

For a moment, it looked as though the side of the star was cracking, and Min wondered briefly if the Darkstar itself was the dragon Brightest was talking about.

But then she saw it.

What she thought were cracks forming on the star's side unfurled, and Min realised they were wings. Colossal wings, each of which must be the size of…

Boramu's filthy hell, each wing was easily larger than the island New Windward called home, and that island contained a city, two large towns, and innumerable villages.

"It can't be…" Min said, just before a long neck craned from behind the Darkstar. The purple maw at the end of it – still bathed in the violet fire of the light source the dragon clung to – opened, and the Darkstar Dragon let forth an almighty screech.

It took a few seconds for the sound to reach her ears, but Min knew it was coming. She caught herself waiting, and started to count the seconds, as her grandfather had taught her when thunder and lightning warred along New Windward's coast.

One.

Two.

Three—

When Min was five years old, New Windward had been assaulted by the worst storms in her lifetime. She distinctly remembered the hours spent in the cellar, her father holding her tightly, hunched protectively over her as the winds outside ripped their home apart. That was what the dragon's cry reminded her of, now.

The rooftop shook. In the distance, Min heard echoing screams, and she realised they belonged to the crew of the *Narwhal*, reacting to the impossible sight above them.

See, Minjung, her grandfather would have told her, *three seconds before the thunder reaches you. That means it is three miles away. It would take a long time to reach us, this storm, even if it wanted to. But the seconds will grow longer next time, and you will see the storm is moving away.*

Above Min, the dragon pulled itself from the Darkstar, gave another silent cry that Min expected would assault her ears any moment now, and began to glide.

"It… it's coming toward us," Abalendu said. Min glanced at the scholar, and would have found humour in the goldfish-like look on his face if she hadn't been wearing the exact same expression.

Beside the scholar, Zoya stood tall. The warrior, gripping her harpoon tight, did not have the look of helplessness on her face that Abalendu did, but the Kisiwian's rapid blinking betrayed her own shock.

"It's coming toward us!" Abalendu screamed it this time, his shout punctuated by a weak cry from his dragontoad, which started to waddle from one of his shoulders to another, the only movement of its own accord Min had ever seen the creature make. *Bugger me,* Min thought, her mouth suddenly dry. *Bugger me, we're dead.*

The distant cries of the *Narwhal*'s crew reached her ears, and Min decided to take action. If this was it, if her fate was to be eaten by a dragon, then she would bloody well go down protecting the people she had promised to look after. It had taken them about twenty minutes to reach Brightest's place from the *Narwhal*, but if she ran to them—

Brightest put a gentle hand on her arm, steadying her. Her panic drained when she saw the excitement on the old man's face.

He isn't afraid. This crazy old coot isn't afraid.

"But it's coming right for us," she said, her voice a question.

Brightest nodded, still smiling, his eye twinkling in the purple of the Darkstar.

He isn't afraid.

"First Officer," Zoya said, and Min was surprised at the tremble in the warrior's voice. "First Officer, what are your orders?"

Brightest turned to look back at the dragon, as casual as a fisherman on New Windward's wharf watching a passing sharkbird. Those creatures could tear a household apart in seconds, picking the flesh clean from any bones they found, but they had long ago learned to stay clear of New Windward and her harpoons. This was routine for Brightest. That was why he was not scared. There was something Min was missing here.

She looked back at the Darkstar Dragon. It had doubled in size since leaving the star, its monstrous wings outstretched, almost dwarfing the purple sun behind it, causing a great shadow to fall over Brightest's island. Still, Min got the impression the creature was still very, very far away from them.

Bigger than a city, she thought. *Bloody hell, there must be countries out there smaller than that thing.*

Abalendu was quivering on the ground a short distance away. He had simply given up, no doubt realising he had no chance of fleeing from such a creature.

"So big," she heard him muttering. "Should be impossible, for something to be that big."

The dragon opened its mouth to roar again.

One.

T—

The blast reached her, considerably louder than before.
Grandfather would have been picking her up at this point, trying to make his voice sound easy as he led Min and her brother to the cellar below their home, doing his best to distract her from her grandmother's paling face.

"Why is it coming?" Min asked Brightest. "Is it friendly?"

The old man, face still fixed on the dragon, shook his head. "Friendly? No. It is hungry. But don't worry – won't be long now."

Min looked back, the dragon now fully silhouetted by the Darkstar behind it, a black shadow surrounded by a violet sky peppered with glowing fish.

Then the island began to move.

It was too much for Min. The entire experience of being pulled to this place, the sight of the beast coming at them from above, and now the idea of something else going wrong threw her to her knees.

Zoya, fortunately, still held strong, even though the warrior was more scared than Min had ever seen her before, her ebony forehead coated in sweat that ran into her eyes. "What is going on?" She shouted to be heard over the rumble of the land around them.

Min knew that if it was an earthquake – not unheard of in New Windward territories, and certainly a plague upon her ancestral home of Goryeoa – then the building beneath them could quickly fall apart under their feet.

Brightest, though, had a full grin on his face now, his hands grasping the banister at the edge of the rooftop.

He was not looking at the encroaching dragon anymore. He was looking at something else, something on the far end of the island.

Desperate to make sense of the situation, to clutch at any hope of surviving the demon in the sky above, Min threw herself beside the old man, grasping onto the handrail like a drunkard.

Brightest was staring at the peninsula with the funny looking tall trees, the only unusual sight Min had noticed when first approaching the island. The peninsula began to buckle, rippling with the tremors that were rocking the entire place.

Then the peninsula began to rise up.

It took a few moments for Min to comprehend that the stretch of land was actually a head.

The head, with the trees atop it – no, not trees, Min realised;

ears, or some kind of insect-like feelers – turned to regard the dragon, and Min looked in wonder at the thing's face. It was, from what Min could tell at this distance, made of something that might have the texture of rock, and captured a range of colours from muddy brown to a deep green. The thing's face – the island's face, she corrected herself, recognising that Brightest must have built his home on this creature's back – reminded Min more of a lizard than anything else, perhaps even a newt. Its smooth face curved in the slightest suggestion of a beak just above its mouth, and its black, emotionless eyes faced the Darkstar Dragon.

The island creature opened its mouth. Instead of a roar, the very air around it rippled, seeming to vibrate. The ripples poured out from the creature in waves, finally knocking all of them – Zoya and Brightest included – to the ground.

The vibrations in the air focussed, their pitch intensifying. Then, with a turn of its head, the island creature threw those painful vibrations at the dragon, the agonising sound buffeting into the approaching harbinger's chest like a waterfall upon stone.

The Darkstar Dragon roared, and it was close enough now that there was no delay between the creature's movements and the sound reaching Min. The sky was all dragon, and when its maw opened, her ears bled.

However, the Darkstar Dragon clearly had second thoughts about approaching them after the rippling air faded. Giving no other hint that it was annoyed, scared or angry, the dragon's head turned, its wings tilted, and the creature redirected its course.

The dragon roared one more time as Min picked herself up again.

One.

Two.

The beast's cries were moving away from them. The storm was over. Grandfather would open the cellar hatch, his relief clear behind his forced smile. Time to make repairs.

Min stood, mouth open, looking at the head that remained above the water at the other end of the island. The thing's neck had twisted around, and the creature was staring right at them.

A soft cooing sound came across the wind, so foreign to the abrasive noise it had made only moments ago.

Her jaw slack, Min moved her gaze from the island creature to Brightest's face. The old man was grinning like a king's fool.

"Meet Stickle," Brightest said, his voice warm and proud. "My best friend."

Day sixty-four of solitude

Okay, I'm starting to get the hang of this.

Over the past few weeks, I've explored dozens of the rifts available to me, and have built up quite the food store.

It'll last for a few months, but I'll work on keeping it topped up.

Most of the worlds I took food from are out of reach now, but when the others were still here we found out that the worlds cycle through, so I should be able to visit most of them again at some point.

Thought it would make sense to have a list, to remember which ones are worth heading back into when they come around:

Purple-green oblong #2 — Rift opens onto a mountain that seems to be alone on a green sea. Tried fishing from it and caught a pink fish that looked a little bit like a human foot. Tasted amazing. Head back to this rift as soon as it returns.

White swirl #5 — The natives here come up to my knee, don't wear clothes, and I'm pretty sure have absolutely zero bones underneath the flesh that pillows around them. However, they are friendly enough, and taught me how to whistle and convince the trees to lower their branches for me. The nuts of the trees can be ground together to form a pretty tasteless paste, but it is filling; reminds me of porridge. I collected several bags of them before leaving that world. Unless I find something to mix the nuts with, I'll be using these as my last resort when it comes to cuisine.

Collection of blue dust that looks a bit like a sock — the city this rift opens up in appears to be caught in a state of perpetual feasting. However, entry to the whole affair seemed to be pretty high — they wanted me to donate one of my body parts to them for scientific research. One of my eyes would have bought me a spot at the highest table, and they weren't joking — even from the barrier I could see a bunch of one-eyed fools in togas kicking over wine glasses as they danced across a loaded banquet. I passed on the offer, but will keep the place in mind if things get desperate. Or if I get particularly bored.

FIVE

As Min predicted, the crew of the *Narwhal* had lost it on sight of the dragon.

When she made her way back to the ship, Abalendu and Zoya not far behind, half the crew were outside of it, running around like maniacs.

Jedda was there, shouting at the top of her voice, trying to get people close by to listen to her, but clearly the majority of the crew had other ideas.

Holtz was screaming at the deckhands to get back in line. However, most of the seamen, Sung included, were down by the side of the *Narwhal*, doing their best to push the ship back into the water. Clearly going against Holtz's directions, but not really caring.

"Everyone just bloody well calm down," Min shouted, jumping atop a barrel that had been pushed off the *Narwhal* at some point.

The relief on Holtz's face at her arrival was evident. The crew turned to her, but those who had already chosen to ignore their orders did not relax.

"Calm down?" Sung shouted. "Did you not get a good look at that thing? That dragon? I mean, I'm glad Zoya is back, with her big fist and all, but what good is she going to be against something like that? No, we're getting out of here as quickly as possible."

"I know you are," Min said, fixing Sung with a steady glare. "You're getting out of here as quickly as possible, because I'm going to get you out of here."

Min had to be careful; the crew were spooked bad. Some of them had clearly been going against Holtz's orders. That was a small side-step away from mutiny. The last thing Min wanted to do was push them over the edge, especially the ones who had not learned to trust her yet.

"But if you manage to launch the *Narwhal* into the water now," she continued, "she'll be adrift without power or sails, never mind any damage the hull might have sustained when she was grounded. Which I'm sure is what Jedda's been trying to tell you."

"Yes! That's exactly what I've been saying," Jedda said, her frustration clear, "but these—"

Min raised a hand. "That's enough, Jedda. It was scary, damned scary, that dragon. I near enough shat myself. But it isn't as bad as it seems, and we've got a plan, and an ally. So calm down, stop doing something you'll regret later, and get with the bloody plan."

Min could see Sung considering her options. The first mate glanced at Zoya and Abalendu, who were not directly conflicting with what Min was saying, and that seemed to calm the first mate a bit more. Sung walked away from the *Narwhal's* hull, and the members of the port watch soon followed.

Inside, Min breathed a sigh of relief, but was careful to not show it.

"What do you mean, you've got an ally?" Jedda asked, running up to Min. "They can fight dragons?"

Min smiled at the artificer. "He can't, no. But his island can."

Jedda walked beside Min, captivated by her story as she caught the artificer up to speed.

"He's happy enough to help us?" Jedda asked, shaking her head in disbelief at Min's tale.

Min chewed her lip. "Don't know if 'happy' is the word I'd use to describe him, but he isn't running after us with pitchforks. Yet. Come on, time to head back there. Brightest said he's got something to show us, and I want the officers to see."

Leaving Sung in charge, and making it plain – with Zoya standing glowering close by – that any further deviations from their commands would result in immediate sanctions, Min led a small assortment of her officers back to the Mudhut; the name they had already adopted for Brightest's place. On their faces, she could see the amazement she had felt first walking along this alien landscape. However, their wandering gazes contained more than just amazement. Fear? Helplessness? Many of them reminded Min of children, walking alone in a part of a city they had never been to before.

Strange that she did not feel that way.

At one point in her life, Min thought she would get to see nothing of the world around her ever again. When she had been sick, her grandparents had looked after her, nursed her back to health, but there had been a price for their love. Min's grandparents were traditionalists, Goryeoan through and through, and had made it clear to Min's parents they did not approve of their granddaughter's integrated upbringing with the other New Windward children. Instead, her grandfather had opened his own school, exclusively for those living in the Goryeoan quarter, so the children there could be brought up properly, the way the spirits had intended. Min had been pulled away from the friends she had made. Even now their faces in her mind were only ghostly remnants, memory of them forever shut off to Min, as the world of her childhood had threatened to close everything off.

Min loved her grandparents – she still did – but their control of her life had been stifling. Was it any wonder she had applied for the academy as soon as she was old enough, despite their intense disapproval?

Her grandparents would have balked at the notion of Min being trapped in the situation she found herself in now, cut off from her home and from the world the great spirits had made for them.

Min, however, was in her element; she had almost lost her access to the world once. That little girl – who stared out of her grandfather's school window at the friends she was no longer allowed to have carrying on their lives without her – would never have dared imagine she would find herself lost in a strange land, hoping for a crazy old hermit to help guide them back on their way.

Brightest was waiting for them, and led Min and her small troupe through the warrens of his home. Min noted the old man had spent the time they were away trying to rearrange his warehouse – his treasure trove, he called it – sweeping away anything too broken to repair, covering the rest in the old tarps, hiding them in plain sight.

Not hiding them well enough, however, to keep a nosy artificer at bay. When Jedda let out a high-pitched squeal, Min panicked. She thought that perhaps a seaman may have knocked something else onto the floor of Brightest's trove – maybe even the Flagonknight again, which she had spied a few moments before, back on its pedestal. Even worse, it could very well have been the sound of Abalendu, finally coming out of the silent stupor he had lowered himself into since the irrevocable appearance of the dragon, despite his assurances that it could not exist.

However, when Min turned, she saw it was just Jedda. A really excited Jedda.

Min ran over to the artificer, who was shaking like a landlubber experiencing their first squall. Jedda's eyes were fixed on something glowing golden down one of the tributaries off the main path through Brightest's towering hoard.

"Jedda, what's wrong?" Min asked. She had never seen the artificer like this before. Showing her emotions was not something Jedda was particularly good at; she would often head back to the relative solidarity of the *Narwhal's* belly if she got upset about something during an officer meeting, and rarely had smiled about anything.

"There," Jedda said, her hand outstretched towards the golden object down the side path. Her pointing finger was trembling. "I've never..." She paused, swallowing, as if her mouth was dry. "I've got to see..."

And with that, Jedda was off, marching briskly towards the golden light.

"No, wait—" Min had almost brought ruin upon them in here with her own clumsiness earlier. After only a month together, Min knew Jedda was capable of much worse.

As they got closer, Jedda increased her speed, causing Min to have to jog to catch up.

"It is," Jedda shouted, almost reaching the object now. "Ancestors' ghosts, it is!"

The artificer stopped short, as if coming into contact with an invisible wall. Trembling, Jedda stood in wonder, almost cowering before the golden object.

It was an Eshak piece. A gold Eshak piece, glowing as bright as a burning brand, floating in the air before them, encapsulated by a glass dome.

"Really?" Min said, thoroughly unimpressed. "More of this game? Jedda, don't you think about anything else?"

Min was used to Jedda looking at her as if she was an idiot, and fully expected that the artificer would be shooting her the same look right now if only she had been able to take her eyes from the game piece.

"But, Min, don't you know what this is?"

"I don't know. An Eshak piece? Looks like it has some power in it. A bit like the ones you showed me earlier." A bit more, probably, based on how brightly this piece was shining. And mysteriously floating.

Okay, a lot more power, then.

"A golden Eshak piece, Min? These things... these things are legendary. And I mean that – they only exist in legends, nobody has ever seen one before."

"Like a dragon?" Min asked.

Jedda did look at Min then, and Min was unnerved at how sweet the normally awkward engineer looked with the small smile on her face. "Just like a dragon."

They stared at the golden piece together, Min aware she would have a fight on her hands if she tried to pull Jedda away from this moment. Still, Min was anxious to get back to the other officers, and to Brightest. She felt her relationship with the old hermit was tenuous enough, and that one more bit of snark from Abalendu – snark that man was eminently capable of – was all it would take for Brightest to demand they leave. Or order Stickle to shake them off.

"Jedda," Min said after a while, allowing herself to study the Eshak piece subconsciously while she worried about getting them back to New Windward. "Jedda, are you sure this is an Eshak piece? Doesn't look like one I've seen before."

There were a few different combinations of Eshak pieces, based on where a particular set originated from. Min had never really been into the game, unlike so many of her peers back at the academy, but she had played casually enough to recognise most of the common game pieces found at New Windward – the rook, the barge, the queen, the peacock. From what little Min knew of the game, the pawns that made up the front row were the only constant between the regional variations, but she was certain she had seen most of the sets in circulation.

This golden piece was unfamiliar to her. It was a simple, monolithic pillar, made up of rigid lines, as if it had been smelted into existence, instead of carved.

"Never seen it before," Jedda confirmed, "but there's no doubt. This is just a piece used on different worlds, that's all."

A game played across dimensions? *Inconceivable,* Min thought, then squirmed as she realised it was Abalendu's voice speaking inside her head.

"We've long thought it," Jedda said, her yearning hand reaching out to the piece, but still keeping a fair distance away. "Those of us who play, those of us who are really into it. Isn't it weird that Eshak pieces seem to attract magic, even those you carve yourself?"

It was weird, but was a well-known phenomenon back home. Like any peculiarity, Eshak had attracted its fair share of conspiracy theories, and a crackpot culture of Eshak fiends – of which Jedda was clearly one – had latched onto those theories, running with them to their full extent. Most Eshak pieces, those owned by the most successful players back home, eventually attracted enough magic to glow when in use. At the highest level of tournament play, some pieces were able to move of their own accord.

What Min saw before her, the levitating, radiating monolith, was well beyond that.

A thought came to her.

"Jedda," Min said, her voice tentative, "Jedda, how much magic do you reckon this piece has? Do you think it could power the *Narwhal*?"

Jedda looked at the golden piece quizzically, as if seeing it for the first time. She opened her mouth to speak.

"Don't touch that! Get away from it."

She turned to see Brightest waddling up the alley of junk that she and Jedda had made their way through, his driftwood staff stamping into the floor with every step he took.

Their host did not look happy.

"Stop touching my things."

Although Jedda had never met the man before, she did not wait for formal introductions.

"You're a collector too?" she asked, rushing over to him, indicating the glowing Eshak piece behind.

"Couldn't give a stuff about you fanatics and your little games. But don't touch my things. Especially not that thing."

Min stepped forward, anxious that curious, awkward Jedda not become the ambassador for the crew. Still, she had questions that could really do with being answered.

"Brightest," Min began slowly, aware of how wound up their host seemed to be at them finding the game piece, "we were wondering: our ship has lost its magic, you know, its power. Could something like this Eshak piece have enough in it to power a flying ship?"

For a split second, something like fear flitted across Brightest's face, but his perpetual scowl chased it away.

"Can't be done," the man said, grabbing them both by their sleeves, pulling them back toward the main path. "Just can't be done."

Unsatisfied with his answer, but also wary of upsetting him further, Min decided to save further enquiries for later.

Jedda looked back longingly at the golden piece, but Min caught her eye, urging the artificer to do what their host wanted.

Still, Min thought, casting a final glance at the umbra of gold as it was swallowed up by the mounds of other artefacts. *A powerful source of magic that is not being drained by the Darkstar? Very interesting.*

The doorway Brightest took them through led to a short corridor, unlit except for the lantern their host hung from his driftwood staff. Holtz was waiting for them, a thin tobacco stick hanging from his lip. The man's hand was trembling as he put a light to it.

"Captain," he said, rolling his eyes as he fumbled over his address. "First Officer, sorry. Have you seen this? You've got to see this."

He stepped aside, giving access to the room behind, a room which already held most of the *Narwhal's* command, even the Idlers. The assembled personnel, however, were not what drew Min's eyes.

In the centre of the room hung a purple ball, a sphere roughly the height of Min herself. It did not glow, but it was clearly meant to represent the Darkstar, with a detailed drawing of a dragon curled about its surface. For a moment, as her eyes adjusted to the brighter light of the room, Min thought the purple ball was levitating, like the golden Eshak piece she had just left. However, she quickly noticed a sturdy black rod that descended from the ceiling, piercing the model Darkstar at its pole, holding it in place in the centre of the room. Dozens of other objects were attached to this model, some held close, spinning around the purple ball at speed, some suspended on a complex network of metal rings that radiated from the central Darkstar, spinning slowly, dancing around the room in a slow but orderly fashion.

"It's an orrery," Jedda said, standing at Min's side. Min had seen only one orrery before, in the academy's library, where she had spent a lot of time in her first term of study, but not paid any attention to it at all once she started to go out on apprenticeships. However, whereas that device – a miracle of engineering and design, so they claimed – showed the regular orbit of the celestial bodies over New Windward and the rest of Min's world, the device they were all looking at now was a working model of Brightest's Darkstar Dimension.

Min looked at the old man. "You made this?"

For once, Brightest broke eye contact with her, looking at his feet and scratching his beard. "Well, you know, I've had time. And it's fascinating, don't you think? This place."

"But what is it?" Holtz asked, the question almost like an explosion, a wave that had been building since arriving in this place finally breaking upon the shore. "What in all the Ice Flats is this place?"

"We called it the Darkstar," Brightest said, indicating the purple ball hanging above. "Seemed appropriate. It's the main source of light here, the only natural source, other than the fish."

"And the water?" Jedda asked. "Does it really go all the way around?"

Brightest's smile twinkled. "Took us months to realise that was what was going on. But then, we weren't sailors like you lot. I was just a boy…" Brightest's concentration slipped, his eyes drifting.

"You said you were pulled here, like us? That's what the Darkstar does? Why?"

Brightest shrugged. "Why is water wet? Would you try to explain a force of nature? Back in my world, the sky is stone, and we live in cities carved into great stalactites that cling to our stone ceiling. Why was my world like that? Certainly no other world I've been to works that way."

"You've been to other worlds?"

It was Abalendu who asked the question, to Min's ongoing irritation. This was meant to have been a meeting of the *Narwhal*'s officers. Yet again, Abalendu had decided to include himself in that number, despite his role as passenger, as human cargo.

Brightest looked at Abalendu as if he were stupid. "Of course. How do you think I survived out here all my life?"

"What do you mean?" Min asked, properly curious now. Her

one trip between worlds had been a bad enough experience; being torn apart and reassembled like that. She struggled to contemplate someone going through that torture more than once.

"Other than the dragon and the Darkstar itself, this place is just water, mostly. Even the fish, and the turtlemoths like Stickle here, I can't imagine they're native to this place. More like they got sucked in at one point, and thrived. No, there's nothing here, except for the crap the Darkstar pulls in. If you want something solid, something you can live on – like food – you've got to nip outside for a bit."

"Nip outside?"

Brightest grinned.

"The shapes you can see in the sky, the different colours, floating all around the Darkstar? They're worlds. Holes between worlds. Rifts. And this here contraption is how I keep track of them."

Min's eyes widened as she took in the orrery again. With the majority of this place, this dimension, being a bubble of water, there was not a lot of land to map out. Instead, Brightest was surveying the movements of other worlds.

Jedda stepped forward, adjusting her goggles, studying the objects above.

"They're moving differently," she said. "Some of them, anyway. There's no regular pattern here."

Brightest raised his eyebrows, impressed. "That's about the height of it. Some of the rifts are permanent enough," he said, pointing out a few of the different objects rotating around the Darkstar. "From what I can tell, they've settled into a regular orbit, and they're always here somewhere. Sure, some of them might go under the water for a while, or get so close to the Darkstar as to be dangerous to reach, but they stick around. Most though, they come and go."

He gestured over to a collection of chests at the corner of his map room. One of the chests was open, and Min spied an assortment of models inside. Some were detailed pieces of art, which seemed to be chiselled out of wood, or a material like it. Others appeared to be household objects, given a quick lick of paint. She was fairly certain she could spy at least one green boot poking out from the box.

"Started off with good intentions," Brightest said, noticing Min's gaze.

He walked over to a leather-bound book sitting close to the chests, and opened it. "The good news is, even after they disappear – mostly when their orbits collapse and they fall into the Darkstar – most rifts reappear, after a while. I reckon they all do, at some point; there are only a small handful I've never seen pop up again, and I reckon it's because I've just not been waiting around long enough. The trick is figuring out what the pattern is, and how long until they reappear. Can be handy if a particular world has got something in it you'd like.

"Take that one, for example," he said, pointing at a small pink object whose orbit was dangerously close to the Darkstar. "It only appears every four months, and it sticks around for three or four days at a time. From what I can tell, it's a world with nothing but shrimp in it. You'd get tired of spending time there pretty quickly, but for those days Stickle and I feast like kings if I can get a few nets up to the rift."

"Are you trying to say you're some sort of... scavenger?" Abalendu said. Min did not have to look at the scholar to hear the disdain in his voice.

Brightest glowered. "I prefer the term 'survivor'. Or tradesman, most of the time, now. Take my home, for example. Didn't think I built it myself, did you?"

"You traded for your home?"

The old man's eye twinkled. "Let's just say I outsourced my workforce, yeah."

Min had been silent this whole exchange, her mind whirling through the facts Brightest was giving them.

"Brightest. These worlds, the rifts – have you been to all of them?"

"I try to visit any new ones that pop up, long as they aren't in danger of vanishing anytime soon, yeah. What of it?"

"Do you know which one is for New Windward?"

Min held her breath as the old man thought. Then Brightest shook his head, causing Min to almost choke in disappointment. "Not a name that's familiar to me, sorry. That's your home, is it?"

She nodded quickly, not willing to give up just yet. If he had visited home through the same rift they came through...

"You'll have seen mostly water, if you've been there. In the middle of the ocean, somewhere."

Brightest pursed his lips, looking at the whirling objects on his orrery. "You'd be surprised how often that happens. A whole chunk of worlds out there have a crap-ton of water in them. Still… not too many of them orbiting the Darkstar at the moment. Maybe that one," he said, pointing to a green hair comb that seemed to be almost touching the water on the far end of the dimension from them at the moment. "Never got a name for that one, so I call it… well, I call it Green Comb. Could be up there, as well," he said, pointing to a more artistic blue-green carving of a rift that was slowly rotating its way closer to the Darkstar. Brightest flicked through a few pages of his book. "Yeah, met some locals who called it Jigu—"

"That's it!" Jedda shouted, stepping forward. The artificer then became aware of the room's eyes upon her, and lowered her gaze. "My people," she said, her voice meeker, "that's what we call the world, in our language."

Brightest's gaze darkened as he looked at the suspended carving. "That's no good. Rift's almost disappeared, too close to the Darkstar already."

Min's heart sank. Brightest looked back at his notes.

"It's a regular, though," he said, his smile returning. "Lucky enough, it's one that appears enough that there's a bit of a pattern to it. Shouldn't be too long until it comes around again, close to the surface, and should be easy enough for you to hop back home."

Min fought the grin that was threatening to break out on her face. "How long, Brightest? How long till we can get back?"

He looked through his notes again, then looked back to her, smiling. "Three years. Three years, give or take a month or two."

There was stunned silence in the room.

Three years?

Min struggled to move, rigid with shock. They were stuck here, in this awful place, for three whole years?

The stunned silence was shattered by a scream.

It was Zoya.

The warrior fell to her knees, wailing uncontrollably, burying her head in her hands.

Day three hundred and sixty of solitude

Stickle spoke to me tonight.

Okay, that's not quite right. Technically, she's been speaking to me since I met her.

Today, however, I understood her for the first time.

She has grown a lot since the others left; she's almost the size of a large sailing ship, now. Don't know how much longer I can keep the dragon from her, at this size.

I had been thinking about that hooting sound she keeps making. It's really been the only speech I've listened to in all this time since being left here, and I was certain there was more to it than a normal animal's growls or grunts.

Stickle has a language. It's hidden there, within her voice, once you get used to the subtle modulations in it.

Admittedly, her size (and the deepening of her voice) have made her a little bit easier to understand as well, a lot easier than the other turtlemoths we've met on the Darkstar Sea.

I'm certain it has nothing to do with how long I've been out here on my own.

We had a delightful conversation about the last rift I entered, some kind of forest world where the trees have mouths and bicker constantly.

Now that we can speak, I think it is safe to say that Stickle has fully replaced the companions I lost all those moons ago.

In some ways, she is better. She is large enough now to carry me across the sea, and never complains about travelling long distances with me on her back.

I hardly think about them at all, now.

SIX

Min was exhausted. All day she had been overseeing the *Narwhal*'s crew, organising her people into making the ship seaworthy again. She could not deny that the loss of the ship's mobility was getting to her; standing at the helm, turning the wheel and feeling none of the familiar resistance from the mechanism that moved the rudder, she could not help but recall being stuck back in her grandfather's school, that feeling of having lost control of her destiny.

News had spread fast about the events in Brightest's map room, and the crew's spirits were low. She had reckoned heavy work would be enough to keep their minds busy – a tactic Captain Bolvar had employed during her apprenticeship on the *Seadragon*, effectively keeping the crew from despair when their mainsail had torn loose during a summer squall. On the *Narwhal*, the ploy worked well, for the most part. However, Min was aware of whispers between the crew members, especially from the port watch, Sung's people. They had fallen for Abalendu's rhetoric, and appeared to be hanging the blame for their current situation firmly around Min's neck.

She tried not to let it anger her. It was common nature, to blame your superior for anything that went wrong. It also appeared to be common practice for old sailors to rally against academy officers, especially in tense situations such as these. It was frustrating, because Min had clearly already proven her credentials to herself and to her superiors – why else would she have been given a command like this? However, she had long ago realised she needed to prove herself anew every time she worked aboard another ship, every time an unfamiliar crew came aboard.

She represented the new, and people still rallied against it, especially when that new seemed to be steering them into trouble.

Min knew, however – again, thanks to Captain Bolvar – that she would soon be called on to crack some heads. The crew were too wound up, and they would be looking for a way to release their frustration. It was Min's job to remind them exactly who was in charge, so the ill-feeling that caused the small disagreements voiced after the dragon attack did not fester and manifest as something far worse. This was not a part of her job she relished at all, but after a few days Min was at the stage where she was just waiting for someone to step out of line, so she could exert her authority in front of the rest of the crew.

That tension came to a head just after lunch, when the majority of the port watch, off shift, were still milling about on the beach after eating the stew Runako had served them.

Min, on the quarterdeck, going over Hertha's progress with the sail repairs, caught wind of the commotion when two of Sung's Icefolk started to shove each other, gathering a crowd below. Sung was there, and did nothing to stop it. In fact, she seemed to be supporting blond-bearded Ole.

"Keep at it," Min said to Hertha without looking at her, moving to the gangplank. "I've got some heads to pound."

Within a minute, Min reached them, shoving herself between the warring Icefolk. Trude already had blood running from her nose, but Ole was the one whose left eye was swelling shut.

"Have you two lost the plot?" Min pushed them both back, actually making Ole stumble, raising a laugh from an idiot in the crowd when he lost his footing. The last thing Min needed was for the Iceman to lose his temper at being humiliated. She needed to put this fire out, fast.

"Things are bad enough around here without you idiots making life harder for everyone else. Look at Ole's eye," she said, focussing on Trude now. "Who's going to do his rigging work for him, now that he'll be no good to us for the next few days?"

"I'll do it," Trude said, voice low, having the good sense to lower her eyes in humiliation.

"You're bloody right you'll do it. Along with your watch officer."

"What?" Sung said, standing in the crowd of port watch observers.

Min turned on the first mate, not worried about hiding the

redness of her face. She was angry with Sung, and wanted everyone else to see it.

"You didn't have a problem with letting these two have a casual scrap? Don't see a problem with Ole's swollen eye? What if he'd lost it altogether? How long do you think a broken leg would have taken him out of commission for?"

Sung snarled. "I happen to think Ole was right, though. Maybe if he hadn't won, I'd have finished the job for him!"

Min should have punished Sung there and then; maybe even demoted her for suggesting she would have attacked another crew member. But Min could sense the agitation in the gathered port watch, and became aware of a number of others nodding around her. The watch was with Sung on this one. They wanted Ole to win.

Min turned back to the two combatants, Trude now pinching the bridge of her nose to stop the blood flow. "Just what exactly was going on here?"

"Ole wanted to steal from the old man," Trude said, nodding in the direction of Brightest's Mudhut.

"And you didn't see a problem with this?" Min said to Sung, incredulous.

"Boy talks sense," Sung said, not losing her cool. "What he wants to steal sounds like it could solve all of our problems."

Min tried to ignore the tingling inside, already worried about where this was headed. "Explain," she ordered Ole, although she was pretty sure she knew the answer.

"Artificer Jedda," Ole said, "she told us she saw something inside, something that might be able to power the core again. Something like that could get us home."

Jedda. You wonderful idiot.

"That's not all she told you, is it, Seaman Ole?" Sung said. The first mate's tone was relaxed, confident, completely at odds with where Min wanted her to be.

"No?" Min said.

"Er, no, First Officer," Ole said, looking away from her. "She also said you didn't want us using the old man's stuff. Said it would be no good asking you, because you already told her to stay away from it."

"So, knowing this, you thought it would be a good idea to take it from behind my back?"

Ole, face red, plucked up the courage to look her in the eyes again, his shame clear.

Again, this confession would normally be clear grounds for confinement, but there was nothing normal about what they were all going through.

"Listen to me, everyone," Min said, raising her voice so that all on the beach could hear. "We've been dealt a rough hand. Tensions are high, so I'm going to pretend that was the root of this scuffle down here, not that a small bunch of you were willing to directly defy your commands. So, take some time to calm down, shake and make up, and we'll hear no more about it."

A few of the assembled crew smiled, their relief clear.

"Is it true, though?" Sung asked, punching through that relief like a needle through leather. "Does Brightest have something in that big room of his that could get us home?"

Min looked around again, and was surprised at the hunger she saw there, on those faces. They had obviously been mulling over this information for a while.

She was slow to respond, choosing her words carefully.

"As Jedda seems to have already mentioned, Brightest has made it clear he does not want us interfering with his belongings. He specifically mentioned the golden Eshak piece, the item in question. I'm sure I don't have to remind you we are guests of his, and the only reason we survived the dragon is because of his island, the creature he calls Stickle. If he doesn't want us touching his Eshak piece, we won't touch it."

"But could it take us home?" It took Min a moment to find the source of the voice, as she had assumed it would be Sung who spoke next. Instead, she found Uj, one of the apprentices in the port watch. Although he must have been sixteen, as the navy would not have accepted him any younger, if Min had come across him in the Goryeoan quarter back home, she would not have put him as any older than twelve.

"Could the golden Eshak piece take us home?" he asked again, nodding as he spoke, a sort of pathetic desperation in those movements.

She paused before speaking again. "We honestly don't know," she said. "The *Narwhal* was built to be powered by a crystal core, and Jedda has no idea if she would be able to modify the core mount to accept any other power source. It's a moot point, though;

the Eshak piece doesn't belong to us."

"We could take it," someone else said. Min, struggling to believe what she was hearing, eventually found Jeet in the crowd, the older sailor studying her intently. "Even with all his fancy toys, he's just one man. We could just take the Eshak piece."

It was not just Jeet, or Uj, or even smug Sung, waiting like a self-satisfied devil in front of everyone else. More than half a dozen of her crew were gathered around them now, and most of them were nodding, agreeing with Jeet's statement.

"I'm only going to say this once," Min said, eying up the whole crowd, her fists clenched, "so listen very closely. We will not steal. We will not steal from this man who has helped us, we will not steal from anyone. New Windward – the whole reason we're all here together – was founded to fight against piracy, because we were sick of being stolen from, so we could band together against those evil people. There's no way in Gorya's frigid hell I'm going down in history as the captain who turned to piracy to save my own skin."

"But you're not captain—" Sung said, but Min did not give her time to finish.

"I know I'm not the bloody captain," Min snapped, spittle flying from her mouth. "I'm not a bloody captain, but I've served under the best New Windward has to offer, and you'd better bloody believe I'll be seen among that number before my time is up."

Sung raised an eyebrow at this.

Min should have stopped. Her point was made, the crowd had been put in its place.

But Min was angry.

"You know what your problem is?" she said, eyes moving from Sung to the other older sailors close by – Jeet, Ole, even Trude who had spoken against the notion of theft. "You're too stuck in the old ways. You started learning your trade when nations fought against other nations, as well as the pirates. When stealing from your neighbour to survive was a way of life. Well, we're better than that, now, and you need to learn and catch up."

"So we need someone better, do we, to show us the way? Someone like you?" Sung said. There was no smile on the first mate's face now.

"Yes, you smart arse, you do need someone to show you the

way. And yes, in this case, it is me. You take the mickey behind my back about my academy education, but that isn't because it makes me a bad sailor, a bad commander. It's because it makes me a different sailor, the kind of sailor New Windward needs, one who will stick by their morals when things get tough. Well, guess what? Things have gotten tough, and it looks like you need me to remind you how to do your job.

"Better than you? I seem to be the only one here not wanting to rob an old man to help myself, so I guess that does make me better than you today.

"So – and I mean this to the lot of you – shake yourselves out of this notion of nicking whatever you think you need, and start acting like New Windward navy again.

"And try not to get too put out that you needed an academy whelp to remind you how to do your bloody jobs. Now, disperse, and shut the hell up. That's an order."

The port watch did as Min said, but it was clear by the dark looks on many of their faces that she had made a few new enemies today.

Fine. Idiots. If you would lower yourselves – the name of New Windward – to piracy, then those are enemies I would happily make.

Min walked away from the crew, up a small hill nearby – a growth on Stickle's back, perhaps? A knob of shell? – giving herself time to recover from the encounter. As she did so, she imagined the look her grandmother would be giving her now if the old woman could see how she had just treated those people. There would be hurt and disappointment in the old woman's eyes, and possibly shock at how Min had left her crew's disposition, leaving them angry and frustrated, the fact that Min was willing to leave behind dozens of people who clearly hated her. Min supposed her grandmother would be able to count off a good number of hells that would accept Min right now.

But it needed to be done, Min told herself, as well as the memory of her grandmother. *That's what happens, when you become a leader. You focus on keeping people alive, instead of trying to make them all like you. Yes, the crew is angry at me right now. I'd rather they direct that anger at me than try something against Brightest, and jeopardise the only friendly-ish face we've met here so far.*

She felt as if she was going to drop from exhaustion. Min had been working almost as hard as the crew, and had not stopped during the watch shift a few hours ago. She had wanted to keep her mind from the inevitable thoughts that were coming now as she sat down to observe the *Narwhal* from afar.

They were stuck here for three years. At least.

And poor Zoya. Of course that revelation meant more to Abalendu's bodyguard than anyone else aboard the *Narwhal*.

Min narrowed her eyes to see if she could spot the Kisiwian among the bodies that milled around on the *Narwhal's* deck, but Zoya was not there. The warrior had remained confined in her own quarters since Brightest broke the news yesterday.

"If you've got a few moments, I've something to show you."

The voice from behind made Min jump. She quickly got to her feet, turning around to see Brightest standing not ten feet away, leaning on his driftwood staff.

"Think you can spare the time?"

Min did not think so. The native man – well, the closest there was to a native in this place – had been helpful enough over the last day, but Min was under no illusion that Brightest wanted rid of them just as much as they wanted to be able to leave.

"I was only catching my breath," Min began, eyes moving back to the crew below. The starboard watch was active right now, coating the holes in the hull with tar and planks salvaged from the unused bed in the captain's room. Stickle had no trees growing on her back, so despite Brightest's insistence that they could nip into a neighbouring dimension to find whatever they needed, Min had instructed the crew to start stripping away any non-essential uses of wood aboard to begin the most necessary repairs. As before, anything to keep their minds occupied. Also, Min was wary of putting the lives of her people into the hands of this stranger any more than she had to.

"They'll be wondering where I am; time to head back."

"I've been watching you all day, girl," Brightest said.

The heckles on Min's neck rose at the word 'girl'.

"You've done more than your fair share of the work, and I also get the impression some of your people would prefer to get the job done without their captain breathing down their necks."

Min chewed the inside of her lip. She struggled to disagree with him on that point. "First officer," she said, absentmindedly. "The *Narwhal* doesn't have a captain. I'm in charge, but I'm only first officer."

"Odd," Brightest said, frowning. "That happen often back on your world?"

"Never, actually," Min said, not able to keep the pride from her voice. "I'm the first of my rank to be given a command like this."

Brightest considered her words. "The first? I wonder—"

"Oh!" Min exclaimed. A thin trickle of blood had started from Brightest's nose.

Brightest touched the trail with his finger, licked the blood, and considered it further. For a brief moment, it looked as though he were going to continue talking about it, but then he looked up at her, his confusion gone.

"Stickle wants to meet you."

"The... the turtlemoth?" She tapped her foot on the hill to emphasise her question.

In response, there came a low, distant hooting from where Stickle's head had reared in response to the dragon.

Brightest chuckled. "I told her about you, and she didn't believe it. Told her she could meet you herself."

Min had a dozen questions, but her brain decided upon the most useless one to ask. "Stickle's a girl?"

Brightest shrugged. "Don't really know, I guess. Not sure what to look for. Feels right to call her 'she,' though, and she's never objected. That's worked well for the last fifty years or so, so why stop now?"

Min looked over to the peninsula that was Stickle's head, and then back to the busy *Narwhal* crew.

"They'll be fine without you for half an hour or so," Brightest said. She could sense the irritation beginning to enter his voice. "Probably need it, I reckon. Also, isn't this supposed to be your job, First Officer – to make contact with any locals? Isn't that what you guys say when you discover a new land – take me to your leader?"

"She's your leader?"

Brightest smiled. "If that's what it takes to get you over to her, I'm sure she'd be more than happy to play the part."

He turned and began to walk down the hill. Min went after, trying to shake the feeling that this felt distinctly like the many walks she had taken as an apprentice, when her superior officers welcomed her to a new ship, filling her in on the particular oddities of her new vessel.

"So," Brightest began as they reached the bottom of the first hill, "how come you all hate the bookworm, then?"

It took Min a few moments to figure out who he was talking about. "Abalendu? It is that obvious?"

Brightest chuckled. "Clear as the star itself. Caught wind of it within minutes of meeting you all. Is it a race thing?"

Min looked at him, caught off guard by the suggestion. "I'm sorry?"

"A race thing. Pale skins hate the black skins, everyone hates the brown skins, that sort of thing?"

Min stopped walking, her brow furrowed. "I'm sorry, what?"

It was Brightest's turn to stop moving, regarding Min with a raised eyebrow. "Well, I noticed you all… well, you all look different. Must be from different parts of your world, right? Just wondering if that's where the hate comes from?"

Min shook her head in disbelief. "No. Hate each other because of our skin colour? That's… no. That sounds ridiculous. Back home, as long as you aren't a pirate, you're a potential friend."

She did not miss the surprise on Brightest's face at her response.

"Is that… is that not normal, on other worlds?" she asked.

He smiled, shook his head, and returned to walking. "It's refreshing, that's what it is. Forget I asked." They reached another rise on Stickle's shell, and Brightest stopped to catch a deep breath. "So, why do you all hate him, then?"

"Well," Min began, picking her words carefully, "Abalendu's from a very well-off family—"

"Ah, so," Brightest interrupted, "where you're from, all the rich people are assholes?"

Min took a moment to contemplate his assessment, thinking about the melting pot that was New Windward, and the wealthy families that had been placed in charge of it. "That's about right, I guess."

Brightest chuckled again. "And some things never change…"

Not long after that, they reached the edge of the island, the part Brightest had indicated as Stickle's head. This was also the place Min had spotted those tall growths when first approaching the island, assuming she had been looking at some kind of vegetation. Drawing near to them now, Min was still not certain what they were; they were purple in hue, much lighter than the Darkstar sky, and were tall yet thin, like a pair of seaweed strands reaching from the sea floor to the sunlight far above. When the growths moved as she approached them – rippling, not fully bending – accompanied by the soft hooting she had come to recognise as Stickle's call, Min recognised the 'trees' for what they were.

"These are... antennae? Are we standing on Stickle's head?"

Brightest smiled at her, but it was the turtlemoth itself whose broken hoots – was it chuckling? – confirmed Min's theory.

The old man took Min down to a beach that lay just beside Stickle's head. If Min had not been looking for signs of life, and if the creature had decided to stay perfectly still, Min would have mistaken Stickle's face for the side of a cliff.

As it was, even though the area Brightest pointed out to her was more than twice the height of the *Narwhal's* main mast, Min was able to make out the turtlemoth's facial features – a ridge that might be a brow, a definite beak, the clear dip of a chin. Min could not spot where Stickle's mouth might be, though the lower half of the turtlemoth's face was such a collection of what looked like barnacles and seaweed that Min was not surprised she found features difficult to spot.

What was apparent to Min, however, was Stickle's eye; it was an area of smooth blackness that stood out distinctly in the rough crags of her face.

Min got the impression the turtlemoth was staring at her intently.

The cliff face moved, and Stickle's hoots echoed around the bay, the sound accompanied by a spray of surf just below her chin.

"I was wondering about that myself," Brightest said, his volume making it clear he was speaking to the island, not to Min.

"What's she asking about?" Min said.

"She wants to know why you look so different from me."

Min raised an eyebrow. "She's never seen a woman before?"

Brightest smiled. "Oh, she's seen women. But they looked like me," he said, indicating his face, but then frowned when he noticed Min looking with alarm at his wild beard. "No, my skin, they were all black skinned. I told her you were different, that your crew are all different from each other. Stickle wanted to see for herself."

Min nodded, taking the information in. Then she turned to the turtlemoth, and spoke.

"Where I'm from, New Windward, this is normal, to see a

collection of different people, working together. It's kind of the whole point of where we live. It's why it was made. My world, the one we're trying to get back to, it's plagued by pirates. Selfish men and women who are happy to ruin lives to keep themselves fat and in power. Pirate lords collect the weaker captains, becoming stronger than some of our countries. New Windward was created to stop all that. It was proof the people of my world could work together, to bring peace back to the seas. So, you see, although we may look different, and our families come from different places, we're all together, keeping the seas safe."

"Even the rich ones?" Brightest asked.

Min shot the grinning man a glare from the corner of her eye.

"So," Brightest asked, reaching out to pat what was probably Stickle's cheek, "was a bit surprised at your big woman squealing back there. Got the impression she was a bit of a toughie, but I guess you can't always judge these things by just looking at people."

Min looked at Brightest, to see if he was about to have a laugh at Zoya's expense. If he was, then protocol be damned, Min was ready to punch him. No matter that he might be the key to survival in this place for the next three years – he was going to get it right in the face.

However, there was no malice in the man's expression. Brightest was paying more attention to Stickle's cheek, speaking about Zoya's outcry in the same way he might speak about the weather.

Min's eyes narrowed. Not callous, then, but not particularly concerned either. At best, he was being nosy, which Min could cope with, as long as he did not pry too deeply.

She shook her head. "No, you don't understand. It's different for Zoya. The rest of us learned we were about to lose a huge chunk of our life, wasting it while waiting in here. Zoya, though…"

Min sighed. She felt a little guilty for speaking about the warrior behind her back, but it was best Brightest understood now, instead of putting his foot in it in front of Zoya later.

"You saw the thing on her arm? The Parasite Glove?"

Brightest raised an eyebrow, glancing at Min from the side. "Noticed there's power in that thing, yeah."

"So, Zoya chose to bind herself to it. Well, 'chose' isn't strong enough a word. She fought to get that Glove. New Windward – the nation we all come from – only has a few of them, and they go to our best warriors, to those who can use them to the greatest benefit of the rest of our people."

Brightest nodded. "It makes her really strong, yeah? Not unusual. Seen a few magical items in my time that did similar. Once owned a pair of socks that let you kick like a volcano, but lost one of them, and it turns out you need the pair for the magic to work."

"The Parasite Glove makes her strong, yes. But there's a price."

She had Brightest's full attention now.

Min continued. "She can't take it off, you see. And it's moving up her arm. When she first put the Glove on four months ago, it only came up to her wrist."

Brightest looked back in the direction of the *Narwhal*, as if expecting to see Zoya there, looking at him. "It's up past her elbow now, right?"

Min nodded. "And it won't stop. Eventually it'll reach her head, and when the Glove infects her brain... Well, Zoya won't be Zoya anymore."

"It'll kill her."

Min shrugged. "I guess. Depends what you mean. She'll still exist. She'll be able to hear people, she'll still be strong, be able to follow orders. In fact, she'll be great at following orders, as there won't be anything left inside her head to debate with them."

"The perfect soldier," Brightest muttered. His eyes flicked away, unable to lock with Min's.

Min nodded. "And all it cost her was her soul."

"But why would someone do something like that? Give up so much?"

"Would you believe she had to fight for it? Whenever a Parasite Glove becomes available – normally when its host dies, and believe me that isn't an easy achievement for anyone – they are clambering over each other to be the one to claim it."

"But why?"

"Instant fame. Instant elevation. Power. For Zoya, and – probably more importantly, I'd guess – for her family."

"Her family," Brightest muttered. Then his eyes shot open, and he looked at Min intensely. "You mean her parents, right? Her brothers and sisters?"

Min shook her head, and the light in Brightest's eyes dimmed. "She has children, Brightest," Min said, closing her eyes as she admitted the truth to him. "Back home, in New Windward, she has a little boy – three years old – and a girl who is almost one."

"By the star's naked flame, no."

"From what I gather, before putting on the Glove, Zoya shared a home with at least two other families. Now, they have a three-storey apartment overlooking the sea, and she knows they'll be looked after for the rest of their lives."

"How long does she have?"

"This was supposed to be a short mission," Min said, letting it all spill out now. "Three months at the most, to disprove Abalendu's theories. It was part of Zoya's agreement to get the Glove in the first place; she promised Abalendu's father, the admiral of New Windward's entire fleet, she'd accompany his spoiled brat of a son on his little adventure. After that, it's traditional for those bonding with a Parasite Glove to get their remaining years to spend with their families, before the Glove takes over."

"But now..." Brightest said, the look on his face reflecting the sickness in Min's belly. The sickness that had been there, that she had been trying to ignore, ever since Zoya let out her wail yesterday.

Min let her eyes unfocus as she spoke, trying to detach herself from the reality of the situation. "But now, by the time Zoya sees her boy and girl again, there'll be nothing left of her."

And they blamed it on Min. So many of them thought it was her fault they were here.

Perhaps Zoya did too.

How many of Min's grandmother's hells would open their gates to her, this woman who had let down the people who trusted her, who deprived a pair of children of their mother?

Beside Min, Stickle gave a dull hoot, its forlorn cry echoing lonesomely across the Darkstar Sea.

Second year of solitude, day fourteen

I'm not alone out here.

That sounds pretty obvious, but some might look at the Darkstar Dimension and think of it as empty, as a stopping-off point between worlds. Even without Stickle and me living here, they'd be damned wrong.

There's an island about half a day's travel from where Stickle and I normally spend our time; one of the few permanent islands of the sea. Every time we visit it, Stickle and I both hear voices. We can't understand what they're saying, but we're both confident someone is speaking to us. Thing is, the island is empty. Barren, not even any vegetation. I'd like to say I'll figure it out someday, but if I'm being honest, that place freaks me out, and I'd rather not go back.

The shopkeeper comes by too, sometimes. He can be summoned, if you've got the right supplies, but that process is dangerous enough in itself. The guy – I reckon he's a guy, under that mask he wears – has a pretty high opinion of himself. Reckons because he's amassed such an impressive collection of stuff, that junk makes him something. Anyone can gather up bits and pieces from different worlds. I've been doing it for years, even before I was left alone here. Still, the shopkeeper can be handy sometimes, if you can cope with dealing with a complete weirdo, but be warned; his prices are always ridiculously unfair.

I'll not speak about the castle that floats about halfway between the sea and the star. It's not that I don't think it's important (it is), or that I don't think people living in the Darkstar Dimension need to know about the three who live in that castle (you do, you really do need to know). It's just that I promised them I wouldn't. They seem to know all about this book, all about my life, and they've proven to me they are not to be messed with. They made me promise, and that's a promise I'll keep; other than the dragon, they're the thing in this place I fear the most.

SEVEN

"Wake up, Zoya," Min called cheerily, rapping on the warrior's door. "Opportunity knocks!"

"I don't hear opportunity," Zoya grumbled, stirring in her cot. "I hear an irritating superior officer."

Min raised an eyebrow at one of the longest sentences Zoya had ever uttered, but chose not to draw attention to it. At least Zoya was talking to her. That was something Min could work with.

"We need to eat," Min said.

"I'm not hungry," Zoya replied.

"I didn't say you needed to eat. But the rest of us do. Brightest's been giving us some of his supplies for the past few days, but he's used to feeding one person, not twenty-four. We need to get more."

"Then put out a line and cross your fingers," Zoya said. "Plenty to eat down there."

Min shook her head. "No good, Brightest said. They taste worse than Stickle's leavings. Not too sure how he knows that particular fact, but I'm happy to let that one pass. Still, we need food. Brightest reckons there's a rift close by that should sort us out, but we need some muscle to come with."

Min was concerned that bringing Zoya's attention back to her Glove by mentioning the word 'muscle' would upset the Kisiwian again, but that did not appear to be the case. The warrior sat straight up in her bed, eyes now fixed on Min.

"We're going into a rift?"

That got her interest?

"Seems that's how he's survived in here, by visiting other worlds and taking what he needs. Should be plenty of food to keep the crew going for the next few weeks."

Zoya mused. "I'll have to speak to Abalendu. I'll need his permission to leave him for a few hours."

Min's hackles rose at the idea of asking Abalendu permission for anything, but she nodded.

The best part of an hour later, Zoya met with Min and Brightest a short way along the coast from where the *Narwhal* was beached. Jedda was there as well, anxious to see Min off once she had learned about the plan. To Min's ongoing irritation, Abalendu had accompanied Zoya down to the beach.

"Glad you decided to join us," Brightest said to Zoya, considerably kindlier than she had heard him speak to any of the other crew members before. Min noticed Zoya's eyes flick to the trio of harnesses that hung over the old man's shoulder. "Ready for an adventure?"

Zoya looked at him, expressionless. "I'm here to get food for the crew. Nothing more."

Brightest nodded. "Well then, the adventure will be an added bonus for you. Not every day you get to jump between worlds."

With that, the old man looked up. Min followed his gaze, and as she drew her neck back, her concern grew.

"Brightest," she said, "is that the rift we're going to?" The old man was looking at a pale blue cloud, the tones of which were undulating between a summer sky and oceanic depths. "It's almost a mile away. How can we reach anything that high?"

Brightest said nothing, but gave Min a wolfish grin that made her shiver. He fished around in the bandoleers that criss-crossed his old robes, and eventually found a purse, from which he pulled out a small silver flute.

He put the flute to his lips, turned to face the emptiness of the Darkstar Sea, and blew.

There was no sound.

Min looked at Brightest for a moment, then at Zoya standing beside her. There was no emotion – not even concern – on the warrior's face.

"I can't hear anything," Abalendu said, the impatience clear in his voice. "Did you all hear something? I can't hear anything."

The scholar was voicing the words in Min's own head, but she chose to keep quiet, more to disassociate herself from Abalendu than because she did not want to know the answer to the question.

"I'm guessing it works like dogs," Jedda said. "Some sound human ears can't hear, but others out there can pick up."

It appeared Jedda was correct. No sooner had she said it than Min spotted a collection of green luminous lights moving in the blackness of the sea, getting closer to the shore.

Her first reaction was alarm. The source of the lights was unknown, and they were moving toward her. All the instincts honed during her years of study and practice were telling her to get away from them. Beside her, Min sensed Abalendu and Jedda moving backward at the sight of the approaching objects.

However, Zoya and Brightest did not move, although Min could sense Zoya tensing. Brightest seemed unconcerned.

Fear of the unknown. In a place like this, that was a fear that could overcome you, as the unknown was turning out to be an everyday occurrence.

Instead of succumbing to it, Min chose to place her trust in the people around her, particularly in Brightest's experience.

The moving objects broke the surface some distance from the shore, and continued to move toward Stickle. They were, Min realised, fish. Luminous green, massive – about horse sized, she reckoned – flat fish. More than anything else, they reminded Min of the manta rays that frequented the New Windward docks during the springs back home, when bread was plentiful, and the city children would drag their families to watch the large fish move in and out of the pier supports. The approaching creatures were much larger than those familiar sights. Also, with a start Min saw these green rays were not swimming any more. They were gliding, hovering a few feet from the surface of the water, their passage still carving out furrows in the dark liquid.

"Astounding," Abalendu muttered from somewhere behind Min.

She struggled to disagree.

The rays swam right up to the shoreline and then raised their fronts, as if sniffing the air, or like a dog looking for attention. The creatures were almost circular, except for the stubby tails that stuck out behind them. They had no distinct facial features where Min assumed their heads should be.

"Perhaps," Abalendu said, his gaze fixed on the new creatures, "perhaps you could spare one for me? For research purposes."

Min shuddered at the thought of what that might entail.

Ignoring the scholar, Brightest walked straight over to the rays, and scratched the closest one on the top of its raised 'head'. After cooing to it for a few seconds, Brightest slung a harness from over his shoulder and fitted it onto the lead creature.

"You're not seriously suggesting you're going to ride those things?" Abalendu spluttered.

Brightest looked at him, gave a knowing smile, and went back to his work.

"And you're all right with this?" the scholar said, not directing his question to anyone in particular.

Min, unsure of how she felt about the idea herself, looked at Zoya. The warrior caught her eye, shrugged, and looked back to Brightest.

He flung one leg over the back of the lead ray, grabbing hold of the reins to stop himself from sliding off its back.

"Come on, then."

Zoya stepped forward first, getting herself into position on her ray.

Min turned to Jedda. "Holtz is in charge. I've filled him in on what to do if anything goes wrong. We should only be a few hours." She smiled. "Nothing to worry about."

Although it was Jedda she was speaking to, Abalendu was the one who responded.

"We're not worried," he said, putting his hand on Jedda's shoulder from behind. Min could sense the artificer's tension straight away – Jedda did not like to be touched.

"We've got complete faith in you," Abalendu said, smiling.

Min almost cancelled the mission there and then. That, or confine Abalendu to the surgery – she could not recall seeing him smile at all before, and the curved lips that graced his face now did not fill her with ease.

"Come on, First Officer," Brightest shouted, moving his ray from the shore. "The sky won't wait for you forever."

Min took one last glance at Jedda. "It'll be okay," she said, hoping she was as good at faking confidence as she was at manning a ship's helm.

Turning around, Min sized up her ray, which Brightest had already harnessed for her. Min had some small riding experience, but that was horses and orax, basic beasts of burden, none of which travelled on water. Or flew. Still, Zoya seemed to be doing well enough. The warrior was wobbling a bit on top of her mount, making exaggerated turns as she tugged on the reins too tightly, but she had not yet fallen off.

Min was determined not to be the first to tip. She could not see the Parasite Glove giving Zoya any advantage here. In fact, she hoped her own smaller size might favour her as a rider, but Min held little hope of besting Zoya in any physical activities.

Brightest gave a yell, which caught Min off guard. She almost fell into the water, but managed to catch herself on the reins at the last second. She turned in her saddle to see what was the matter. Brightest's face held an expression of pure joy. He was looking across at Min and Zoya, his elation clear, and gave another whoop.

He was so far removed from the grumpy curmudgeon Min had been introduced to, and his smile was infectious. Boramu's noisy hell, even Zoya was cracking a half grin.

The old man gave another whoop of excitement, turned in his saddle, and pulled on the reins. His mount took off, in only a few seconds reaching the speed it needed to hover over the water's surface, not breaking the liquid below it at all.

Gritting her teeth, but grinning through the grimace, Min did her best to follow.

She squinted, looking for signs of Brightest's mount touching the water's surface again, but it did not seem to do so. The old man took a right turn, and Min and Zoya's rays did so automatically.

Ah, his is the leader, Min thought, somewhat dismayed that the control she thought she had over her mount might simply be the ray following orders. She tried giving the reins a small nudge to the left. The ray tugged on the harness, pulling her back, not changing course.

A growing unease bloomed in the pit of Min's stomach when she realised how little sway she had over things. Behind her, Stickle and the *Narwhal* dwindled into the distance. To her left, Zoya hunched low over her reins, fixed on Brightest far ahead. The warrior seemed either unaware or unconcerned at their apparent lack of control over their destinies.

Min glanced above, to the blue umbra of light that Brightest had indicated as the rift they were making for. The man had been frustratingly coy as to how they were actually going to reach it. Min silently cursed herself for not forcing the issue.

She was trusting this stranger with far too much, not least her own life.

It was at that moment, when Min was distracted by her thoughts for the briefest of seconds, that Brightest disappeared.

Min first became aware when Zoya started yelling at her.

Startled, Min looked to the warrior shouting off to her left. Automatically, Min pulled on her ray's reins, trying to urge it closer to Zoya. Like last time, the ray refused to follow her lead. Her fingers felt numb, gripping the reins so hard, doing her best to effect some change upon her mount.

She was helpless.

Squinting, Min tried to make out what Zoya was shouting.

"He's gone under! He's gone under!"

Min's eyes widened, especially when she realised that her ray would in seconds be following Brightest's lead.

"We'll have to jump," Min shouted back, well aware of how far away Stickle was now. If they abandoned their mounts, they might never make it back to land again.

The second before Min threw herself off her mount, the water exploded in front of her. It was Brightest, still atop his ray, whooping like a mad idiot as he shot from the Darkstar waters like a harpoon from a cannon.

Min gaped as the old man sped upward.

There's no way he'll make it, she thought, looking from Brightest to the rift much further above. A field of floating rocks still lay between Brightest and their goal, and his ascent was slowing already, not having made it a third of the way to the blue light.

However, as Brightest's ascent slowed, something unusual happened. Min was prepared for the man to drop back to the Darkstar Sea; that did not happen. Instead, at the apex of his ray's leap, Brightest hung there in the sky for a few seconds longer than should have been possible, before he began to fall. But instead of falling back in the sea, Brightest began to fall upward.

What in Gorya's frigid hell?

He was not falling all the way toward the blue rift. Instead, his ray seemed to be pulled toward one of the larger rocks that was floating between the water and the rift, the way a person was normally pulled towards the earth.

Min did not have time to fully appreciate what was going on before her own ray plunged under the sea.

She swore. Min was not ashamed by the fact that she swore out loud, the fury of bubbles that left her mouth accompanied by a string of unheard expletives. It took all her might to grip onto her mount's reins as it pulled her down, under the black, the pressure of the water above and around her squeezing at her skull.

In the seconds she had under the water, Min became aware of a few things. Most importantly, she realised the water was clear, almost perfectly so, and did not taste of salt. Unlike the seas back home, this water did not appear to have any sediment suspended in it, affecting neither the taste nor her visibility. She could see for miles in every direction, including down. All around her were families of luminous Darkstar sea life, most of which were taking no notice of her. Off to her left, a few seconds delayed from herself, she saw Zoya's ray take the same plunge. Zoya, seeming more secure on her mount than Min felt, wore a face that would strike fear into any foe. Brightest would regret meeting Zoya now, if they managed to catch up with him.

Min sensed her ray was slowing, getting ready to propel itself upward. Min took a second to glance down, to try to judge how far the Darkstar Sea descended, or if there was any sign of a bottom. The assorted lights of the sea life seemed to end some distance below, maybe the same distance again as Min's ray had taken her under the water. After that point, there only seemed to be blackness.

For a brief second, Min fancied she could see something moving in that blackness. Something huge.

Then her ray took off.

Min had the wherewithal to expel all the air in her lungs as her mount tore upward. Then they broke through the water, and Min gasped, taking in joyful breaths.

The excitement did not last, however. Just like Brightest's ray before her, Min shot up, lancing into the sky far above the sea. She looked up and saw the purple Darkstar, hanging far above, and was aware of the variety of celestial objects that shared the sky with her – floating rocks, yes, but also the strange luminous lights that represented the doors to different worlds, and other unusual shapes that Min did not have time to fully comprehend. Was that a tower drifting on its own somewhere close to the Darkstar? She looked below, and was able to make out a shape in the distance that might well be Stickle on the Darkstar Sea. However, there was an assortment of islands out there, and Min found it difficult to decide which one her ship was beached upon. Looking at the other islands in the water, Min wondered how alone Brightest really was in this place.

Soaring through the air, travelling at dizzying speeds, taking in all the sights of this weird, beautiful world she had found herself in, Min could not help herself.

She screamed, an equal mix of terror and elation.

Like Brightest before her, Min's ray slowed, and she found herself pulled towards a rock suspended above in the sky. As she gathered speed toward the massive stone, she wondered briefly what would happen when she made contact, considering there was no water on that small landmass. She need not have been concerned, as her ray never actually hit the floating rock itself. Her mount did not slow down at all, but instead angled itself to use the speed of its upwards fall to start circling the rock, hovering just off the surface, spinning around the lifeless chunk of earth like a small moon orbiting its planet. Min was distantly aware of Zoya making the same journey, her ray circling a different rock. For a few minutes, as Min's ray circumnavigated the floating boulder at an increasing speed, she lost all sense of her surroundings, and could not figure out where Brightest had gone.

Then a whoop from above clued her in to her guide's location. Brightest was much higher now, his ray just having made its way to a small rock whose orbit of the Darkstar seemed to line up perfectly with that of the blue rift they were making for. The old man dismounted, turned to look at the women below him, and gave a cheer of encouragement.

At that moment, Min felt a bump beneath her that almost threw her from her mount. She was not certain if her ray had actually hit off of the rock itself, or if it had somehow compressed the air beneath it into a pushing force. What she was aware of was the fact that her ray jumped into empty space.

She flew off from the rock they were orbiting, and Min was convinced they were destined to fall back to the black sea below. Then, however, they got caught in the pull of another object some distance above. Min had to close her eyes to give her brain a moment to adjust to the fact that her notion of 'down' had once again been changed, and when she reopened them her ray was already beginning to circle this new rock, again building up speed.

We're jumping upward, she thought. *We're not flying directly to the rift, but the rays are using the pull of these rocks as a ladder to climb above the water.*

Amazed, Min looked out at the expanse of the Darkstar Dimension with new eyes, taking in the floating objects that had originally seemed unreachable to her with the *Narwhal's* crystal array no longer working.

So many worlds, she thought, eyes wide, reflecting the variety of lights within reach of the floating rocks. *Has Brightest visited them all already? Surely he can't have fully explored them yet.*

What wonders this place must contain.

Her ray took another leap, and Min shouted again, but this time the joy in her cry was pure.

She wished her grandfather could see her now.

Min lost all track of time, as well as all concept of up and down. With a thrill, now that they were airborne, she found the ray was responding more to her movements, and she could exert a bit more control over the creature. A small nudge of her knee made the ray budge a bit more to the right. Min hunkered down on the mount's back, her teeth gritted in a grin an equal mix of elation and fear. How far would the creature let her guide it, she wondered, before it allowed her to send them both to its doom?

Eventually, a familiar face flashed past on her right, and Min saw she had landed on the same rock as Brightest. Her ray, however, did not slow down, instead beginning to twist and turn around the rock, just as it had done with the others, building up speed. She realised, with a thrill, that it was waiting for her command. She glanced upward, seeing more rocks to climb, more new worlds to visit – she was not restricted by the one Brightest had chosen for her. If she so desired, Min could forge her own path here.

Instead, she pulled on the reins, and her ray came to a gradual stop beside Brightest, Min grinning madly as she met her host's face. Brightest, for his part, seemed confused.

"Why did it keep going?" he said, indicating the ray. "I thought it would stop as soon as it reached me."

Min just kept grinning, and shrugged as she dismounted.

A glimmer of delight twinkled across Brightest's face. "Well, all right," he said, smiling, then turned to the maze of floating rocks below them. "Wonder if your friend is getting on just as well."

Zoya was not. Her ray was only two rocks away from where Min stood, but Min could tell from the warrior's face that Zoya was not enjoying this experience. The Kisiwian's eyes were focussed, dark, and her body was rigid.

Zoya's ray made the final leap, and stopped beside Brightest and Min straight away. She tumbled from her mount with a grunt, nostrils flaring as she came to her feet, the intensity of the look she shot Brightest making it clear she blamed him for the indignities she had just suffered.

"You okay?" Min asked. Part of the reason for this trip had been to alleviate Zoya's mood. So far, they seemed to be having the opposite effect.

"Fine," Zoya nodded, her glower not fading.

"So," Brightest said, turning from them – although Min was not sure if he was turning to show them where they were headed, or if he was avoiding Zoya's stare – "time to head inside. You two are going to love this."

Min somehow doubted that Zoya was in any state to love anything, but she could not argue against the skipping she felt inside her own breast as she approached the blue rift. It was directly adjacent to the rock they all stood upon, seemingly orbiting the Darkstar in perfect synchronisation with the more solid object. As Min stepped toward the rift, the dancing blue of it capturing her eyes, she felt her body pulled toward the mysterious energy she had been assured was actually a route between worlds. Remembering her experience coming to the Darkstar Dimension in the first place, it struck Min she was a bit like a moth, attracted to a candle flame.

"Will it hurt?" she asked. "Last time it hurt."

"Of course it will hurt," Zoya said, shouldering past. "Otherwise, you wouldn't have asked me to come along. We've got to head in there?" she asked Brightest, nodding at the lights before her.

The old man nodded.

Waiting for no further words, the warrior jumped into the rift.

Min stood for a moment, frozen. She looked to Brightest for reassurance.

He shrugged. "It stings, I guess. You get used to it. Probably the same way people keep going back for tattoos, if you know what they are."

Min did. She had always fancied the idea of having one, but had never found an image that meant enough to her to keep it on her skin forever.

"After you," Brightest said, aping a gentleman's bow, indicating the rift before them.

Licking her lips, which now seemed incredibly dry, Min stepped forward.

Last time, the pain had been incredible.

This time, the pain was incredible.

Just like before, Min screamed.

The transition did, at least, seem shorter this time. For one moment, the agony of having her very being torn apart polluted her thoughts. A second later, the pain was gone, and Min was lying in a ball of hurt on the ground. Beside her, Zoya was already struggling to stand. The warrior was not, of course, screaming, but a heavy sheen of sweat decorated her forehead.

Behind them, Brightest was stepping out of the tear. Min saw a slight grimace grace his face, but nothing more.

"Well," Brightest asked, after taking a moment to compose himself, "what do you think?"

"Pretty much as bad as last time," Min said, finally bringing herself up to a full stand.

"No," he said, tutting. "I meant, what do you think of all of this?"

He gestured wide, and for the first time Min got a proper look at the world they had tiptoed into.

She could not believe how green it was. Far off toward the horizon – and there was a proper horizon this time, unlike back in the Darkstar Dimension – rolled wide, gently undulating grasslands. At least, Min was certain it was grass she was looking at, although the blades of green that sprung up from the ground were wider and thicker than any grass Min had seen before.

"Where's the water?" Zoya asked, and Min realised she had been subconsciously looking for the same thing. Both of them came from island nations, and water was such a key feature of their lives. Same with the Darkstar Dimension. It felt odd to be able to see so far and not have any hint of it.

Brightest's forehead crumpled. "You know, I've come here at least a dozen times, but I've never even noticed the lack of water before. I've always been too busy looking at the bubbles."

Min followed Brightest's gaze upward.

"What in the..." Min began, but then trailed off as she took in the pink bubbles floating above, like dandelion seeds caught in the wind.

They were bubbles of all sizes, from as small as Min's fingernails, to one or two the size of a yacht. The lowest ones were only twice Min's height from the ground. Some of them soared as high as the clouds.

"They're..." she found herself unable to find an adjective to properly describe them. She had been about to say 'beautiful' – and indeed there was a beauty in the unusual collection of pink objects that floated above – but the word caught in her throat at the last second. There was beauty here, but something else.

"They're pink," Zoya finished for her, looking at Min with a deadpan expression. "You can see that they're pink, correct?"

Min turned to Brightest. "What are they? I mean, I can see that they're bubbles, but where do they come from, what do they do? Are they all over this world?"

Brightest nodded. "Now, those are much more familiar questions to me. I'll be honest, I don't know the answer to most of them. Never seen where they come from, can't really figure out what's going on with them. Have seen a few come down to ground level, and I almost reached out to touch them, but..."

That queer feeling that had stolen the word 'beautiful' from Min's mouth flared into life again. "But something stopped you. There's something wrong with this place, isn't there?"

Brightest nodded slowly, one eyebrow raised, as if inviting Min to continue.

Puzzled, she looked around, scanning the bubbles for some key information she had missed.

Then her gaze lowered.

"There's nothing else here. Nothing alive, I mean. Not even trees or bushes or flowers, nothing except this weird grass."

She looked to Brightest, and caught him looking at her, eyebrow still raised.

"How common is that, for one of these worlds to not have anything alive on them?"

"Oh, it happens," Brightest said, his eyes returning to the bubbles, "but normally there's a story behind it that you can figure out. Dead civilization, leaving nothing but ruins or dust. Warzones, where two sides clearly blew themselves out of existence. Here, though? Far as I can see, there's no story here."

"Except for the bubbles."

Brightest nodded. "Except for the bubbles. So, I'll be standing here, keeping an eye on those pink bubbles, and you two can dig."

It turned out, although the thick grass was a particularly boring piece of vegetation above the ground, underneath its brown roots were particularly chunky, and Brightest assured them they would provide all the nutrition the *Narwhal's* crew would need for the next few weeks. Brightest did not seem to have any issue with Min and Zoya doing all of the grunt work, the women working together to fill the hessian sacks they had taken with them for just this purpose.

Zoya grunted as she dug. The Kisiwian opted to not dig with a shovel, but instead used her Parasite Glove to scrape great furrows out of the dirt.

At one point, Zoya cursed, rubbing at the place on her arm where the Glove melded with her elbow. The join between the Glove and Zoya was not a perfect one, and it was clear that something was distorting Zoya's skin where it touched the Glove, presumably putting it through the process that eventually turned more of Zoya into more of the Glove.

Zoya rubbed at the join with her ungloved hand, and Min noticed the warrior's skin was particularly raw, as if she had just burnt herself.

A new piece of the Glove was forming.

Brightest, still looking at the pink bubbles that hung ominously above them, moved over to Zoya, doing a very bad impression of someone walking casually.

"You know," he said, eyes still upward, "I've not heard of a Parasite Glove before, but I have heard about a few items with properties not dissimilar from yours that take over their hosts the more they used them. I wouldn't want to get your hopes up, but it could be the same for you. Might be worth trying not to use that Glove again, and see if the growth stops."

He raised his arm, holding a shovel out to Zoya. "Fancy trying things the old-fashioned way?"

Min thought Zoya was going to take the old man up on his offer. For the second time since Min had known the warrior, Zoya's stern facade dropped. Min was not sure what emotions she glimpsed behind it in the brief moment that door was open – Hope? Fear? – but Zoya closed herself off almost as quickly, looking from the shovel to Brightest's face, doing little to hide her disdain for the man.

"If I didn't have this," Zoya said, raising her Glove in front of her face, "what would be the point of having me here? I made many promises to get this gift, promises I plan to keep. I can't keep those promises if I refuse to use what I fought for."

With that, Zoya went back to digging.

It took the best part of two hours for all the sacks to be filled, with Zoya tossing them back through the rift once they were ready.

"You know," Brightest said as they prepared to leave, "this has got to be the most pleasant trip I've made to this place. I should come back more often."

As long as you have some lackeys around to do all the digging, Min thought, but said nothing about it.

"Stickle always liked the sound of this world," Brightest mused, collecting his shovels back in. "Was too big to make it through the rifts by the time I first found it, but she always liked hearing about it."

A lazy smile settled on the old man's face when he talked about the turtlemoth, one that hinted at true affection there. From nowhere, a memory of Min's grandmother resurfaced. When her grandparents had travelled from Goryeoa to look after her in New Windward, one of the few belongings her grandmother had brought with her had been an oddly coloured porcelain cat. Min had thought the statue to be childish and stupid, but her grandmother had doted on the old thing, and it had brought her real joy. Just as Stickle seemed to do for Brightest.

"What do you call it?" Min asked. "If there's nobody living in this world, what do you call the place?"

Brightest shrugged. "Oh, I've named dozens of worlds, but it gets kind of boring after a while. I'm sure it won't shock you to know that this goes by the exciting title of 'Pink Bubble World' in my ledgers. Feel free to change it to something more inspiring."

Min could not hide her enthusiasm, but realised Zoya was the member of the party who really needed the pick-me-up that naming a new world might bring.

"Zoya?" Min asked. "Got any good ideas?" She almost suggested Zoya name it after one of her children, but was unsure how the warrior would react at them being brought up.

"Pink Bubble World works for me," the Kisiwian said before

jumping back through the rift.

Min looked at Brightest, took a moment to gulp, to sum up the will to tear herself apart again, and threw herself after Zoya.

Travelling through a rift was not any easier a third time.

Back through, once she had recovered from the transition, Min noticed how much gloomier the Darkstar Dimension now seemed. The bubble world had had a blue sky, like back home. Here, although most of the place was illuminated by the purple glow of the Darkstar, the 'sky' was mostly black, with the water's surface not reflecting the Darkstar's light. It was like being out at night, with a peculiar bright purple lantern providing illumination. She could see well enough to get on with tasks, but Min knew it would not be long before she craved throwing herself through a rift again, just to see daylight, the ripping apart of the fabric of her being be damned.

Zoya had already begun strapping the bags of roots to the rays, which were waiting patiently for them. Min was tempted to begin conversation with Brightest again, to quiz him more about the different worlds he had discovered, but she noticed he was glancing at Zoya, that there was concern in his eyes. Min did not feel her questions would be appreciated at this time.

Despite the mood caused by Zoya, the trip down was just as exciting for Min, particularly because she was becoming more adept at controlling her ray. Once, just before the bottom, she even chose her own route through the rocks, straying from the path that Brightest had taken, squeezing her own mount's sides to let it know that she wanted it to jump early. Sure enough, the small floating rock she had jumped to had no other route down from it, so Min eventually had to urge her ray to backtrack, and then to take Brightest's path, but the ability to choose was liberating.

Eventually, they ran out of rock, and made one final leap to return to the surface of the Darkstar Sea. Back in the water, they headed in the direction of Stickle and the *Narwhal*.

Suddenly, a distant hooting sounded.

Min's eyes widened in alarm, and she saw Brightest stiffen in his saddle. Min knew what she was hearing.

Stickle. Something was wrong with Stickle.

Her mind racing with possibilities – the dragon returning, Abalendu somehow upsetting the turtlemoth – Min pinched her ray with her knees, urging it forward. Still, she was unable to keep pace with Brightest, who seemed to be half standing now, beating on his ray with his hand, funnelling his own anxiety into his mount, using that frustration to spur it onward.

When Stickle came into view, the turtlemoth's head was above the water, and she continued to hoot away, her cries becoming more urgent with each exclamation.

"I'm here, I'm here," Min was certain she could hear Brightest bellow in response. At his increased speed, the old man landed on Stickle at least two minutes before Min, but even at that distance, she could see the place was in pandemonium.

Odds and ends from inside the *Narwhal* were strewn across the beach as Stickle rocked back and forth, and the crew members she could see were running aimlessly, or lying flat on the ground in a fit of panic. Min fancied she could spy Sung doing her best to stand on a rock and shout orders, but the first mate could not catch anyone's attention, nor could she keep herself aloft.

Min spied Brightest taking off toward his home, waving his arms in anger. She did her best to follow him as quickly as possible, not waiting for Zoya to catch up.

Please, don't let this be us, Min thought, praying to her memory of her grandmother's enshrined ornaments. *Please let Abalendu be behaving himself.*

It was Abalendu who greeted her on arrival at Brightest's home.

Well, 'greeted' would be a kind word to use. 'Shouted expletives at' would be more precise.

"Where in Master Murhk's name have you been?" the scholar cried. His skin looked waxen, his face drawn. "Where is my bodyguard?"

Min gestured behind, back to the beach. With a final snort of contempt, Abalendu made his way in that direction.

"Where'd Brightest go?" Min shouted.

The scholar did not even turn around. "Into that blasted treasure room of his," was the only response he gave, before disappearing down the path back to the *Narwhal*.

The treasure room.

Min's heart sank. She knew exactly what had happened.

As she raced through the small, dark corridors, she prayed she was wrong. She prayed she would bump into Jedda along the way, who would be just as confused as everyone else about what was happening.

Instead, Min made her way to the treasure room unopposed. She could already hear Brightest's curses as soon as she stepped inside, but she did not need to hear him to know where he had gone.

The lantern light flickered off the accoutrements that littered the room as Min wound around the pathways towards where the golden Eshak piece had been floating in its glass ball.

The ball was now lying on the ground, smashed.

Empty.

Brightest stood before it, and turned when he heard Min approach.

It was then that Min remembered what had happened to her grandmother's oddly coloured porcelain kitten.

Min had been playing with her brother, throwing a ball in the family room with him instead of working at her studies. The ball had hit the kitten, smashing it to pieces before it hit the ground.

The look on Brightest's face now matched the one on her grandmother's all those years ago.

"She took it!" Brightest shouted, spittle flying from his mouth as he ran toward Min, grabbing her by the lapels with two hands. "That damned fanatic took the one thing that was keeping me alive out here!"

Fifth year of solitude, day sixty-two

I'm getting worried about Stickle.
    She's too big now. I can't believe the dragon hasn't caught her yet; she's larger than anything else I've ever seen on the Darkstar Sea.
    I can only put her survival down to the rules we follow when we travel on the sea. As much as possible, we stick close to land, clinging to it if we can. Stickle is actually large enough now that she can pull off pretending to be a land mass of her own, a small peninsula from one of the larger islands. I've recently taken to camping on top of her, instead of on the nearby islands – saves the bother of taking the tent down all the time, and she doesn't like to submerge anymore, if she can help it. Islands don't go under the water, do they? She feels safer as an island than a turtlemoth at the moment.
    Anytime we reckon the dragon might be ready to take flight, she'll cling to a nearby piece of land, and pray.
    The problem is, unlike so many of the worlds around the Darkstar, there's no pattern to the dragon. It's a fairly safe bet that if the dragon takes flight, once it settles down we have the best part of a week before it goes hunting again. Doesn't always stick to that pattern, though. Sometimes it can be only a few days. Once, the dragon took off only a few hours after last landing. We had already moved into open water at that point, assuming it would be safe to take a longer journey, so we were right out in the open when the dragon flew overhead. Stickle went perfectly still. So did I, for that matter. We must have been lucky; some other unlucky bastard must have caught the dragon's eye quickly, because it didn't notice the new island floating down there on the black sea.
    After that, Stickle latched onto a nearby island and it took nearly twenty days to convince her to move away again.
    She has a point, though. We both know it.
    It's only a matter of time before she gets spotted.

EIGHT

"Now wait a moment," Min gasped, hurrying after Brightest as he stormed through the treasure room's passages. "Fanatic? You mean Jedda? Jedda would never have done anything like this."

Brightest glanced back at her, his face an agony of anger lines. The man who she was beginning to think of as a friend said nothing, but instead bared his teeth at her.

"I'll kill her," he shouted to the random crew members he came across, causing them to cower out of his way. "When I find that little bitch, I'm going to take my belongings back, and then I'm going to wring her scrawny neck."

It was time for Min to take back control.

She doubled her step, and put her hand on Brightest's shoulder. "You will do nothing of the sort."

The man turned, presumably to glare at her again, but he hesitated when he locked eyes on her.

Min saw a reassessment take place behind Brightest's eyes in that moment, as if he were properly seeing her for the first time. Before, to him she had been a lost, frightened young woman, trying desperately to get home. There was a part of that about her, it was true, but Brightest had just threatened one of her crew members.

That brought the other Min into play, the one that had been forged for the best part of a decade through New Windward's naval academy's most intense training.

"You will do nothing of the sort," she repeated, in a voice that held a world of promise behind it.

Instead of storming off again, Brightest gritted his teeth.

"The Eshak piece was mine," he said, still almost growling, despite Min's assertion of control over the situation. "I need it back, now. And then I need the lot of you gone from my home."

The last part stung, but Min tried to not let Brightest see the effect it had on her. They needed Stickle, and the safety she – it? – had given the *Narwhal* for the past few days. Having a safe port had helped the crew start to pull themselves back together. Sure, it seemed as though they had already lost the faith they had fostered with Brightest, but he was speaking out of anger right now. First order of business was to prove Jedda's innocence, find the Eshak piece – Min already had one prime culprit lined up – and then she could work on reforging that trust again.

"You there," Min said, her hand still on Brightest's shoulder, but her head now motioning towards an unfortunate deckhand who had just wandered into the corridor.

The young man – Uj, a Goryeoan apprentice – paled, his hands resting on his chest as if asking, 'Who, me?'

Yes, you, you unfortunate bastard.

"Go to all of the officers, even the Idlers. Tell them we have a situation, and that we're meeting in the orrery room in thirty minutes." As far as they had figured, there was no proper way to measure the days in the Darkstar Dimension, so they had tasked Jedda with keeping the ship's clocks all wound up and running on New Windward time. Min knew most of her officers would get there when she needed them.

She chewed her lip as the boy nodded, making ready to leave.

"Head to the belly first," she told him, "see if Artificer Jedda is there. If she is, just send her. No need to send the others yet if she's still around."

Uj looked at her, puzzled.

"I don't think she'll be there," she told the boy, "but best to be sure. No sense in sending the others to look for someone who isn't actually missing."

The officers convened in Brightest's map room not long after. Min was slightly disheartened that Jedda had not turned up, not because Min thought Jedda was capable of theft, but because she was worried that whoever actually was responsible for this mess might have done something to the artificer to cover their tracks.

Min was not surprised to see that Abalendu had taken it upon himself to join, with Zoya in tow.

Good, she thought. *I want him here, for once.*

"I should've known this would happen," Brightest said, pacing around, impatient. The old man had not been able to sit still since the theft, walking in circles around the room while the officers assembled. "Should have hidden it from her as soon as she realised what it was."

"Hold on," Min said, her voice raised so all assembled could hear her, "you're talking like you know it was definitely Jedda who took it. I know she hasn't turned up yet, but that's still no proof it was her—"

Brightest cut her off with a dismissive 'Pah,' waving his hand and turning away.

"First Officer," Holtz said, raising his hand, "you're going to have to get us caught up on this. What exactly has happened here?"

Min bit her lip, contemplating how much to share. "You're all aware of Eshak, right?"

Everyone in the room nodded, some more vigorously than others. Nobody in New Windward grew up without learning the rudiments of an Eshak board.

"Well, after a few months together, you're probably aware that Jedda's into it. Really into it, lives her life by it."

Again, there was little surprise on any of the faces – each of them had visited the belly at least once – although Min did spot a sneer of derision on a few faces, including Abalendu's. This was not unusual either – the obsession levels some Eshak fanatics could get to was often a strong source of irritation in social situations, and Min had no doubt that many looked down on Jedda because of her fascination with the game.

"Well, it seems Eshak is a bit of a bigger deal than we thought; from what Brightest has told me, it gets played all across different worlds. Between them, sometimes. Probably explains the way magic is drawn to the pieces when you win or lose; Jedda has probably already shown most of you her own ascended pieces. Brightest here had a particularly rare piece, and reckons the temptation would have been enough for Jedda to steal—"

"Rare?" Brightest exclaimed. "First Officer, you have no idea. A thighbone from a Grapfrit would be rare. A jewel from the palaces of Homduru is rare. But that Eshak piece? A golden one? To someone like your artificer, that piece is a holy relic. It's not just something rare that she hoped to maybe have someday. That piece is something she will only have heard about in rumours, like fairy tales about a distant land that you hope exists, but know is too good to be true. To someone like your Jedda, that golden piece is like touching a god – I should have known she wouldn't be able to resist taking it from me."

"Jedda wouldn't do that," Min said, for what felt like the hundredth time that afternoon, but even she could sense there was less conviction behind her voice now. Like touching a god? Would Jedda be able to resist an experience like that?

"Why does it matter anyway?" Abalendu asked, his mocking tone suggesting he had no interest in anything to do with Eshak. "I mean, it all sounds pretty impressive, but for those of us who couldn't care less about moving small men across a tabletop, why should we care about something like that, even as rare as it is? It's not as if we can cash the piece in anywhere, is it?"

Abalendu leaned forward, now more curious, his gaze intense upon Brightest.

"Say, that's a good point, Mister Brightest: why do you care so much about it, anyway?"

Brightest turned to look at Abalendu, suspicion on his face, his tongue worrying at his teeth as he contemplated the scholar.

"It protects me," he said, slowly, eventually. "Or rather, it protects Stickle. Specifically, it's what protects her from the dragon."

"What, most turtlemoths can't do what she did when the dragon attacked?"

Brightest laughed, but there was no mirth in his voice.

"Most turtlemoths don't get much larger than the rays we rode on earlier. I've seen maybe half a dozen the size of your skyship, but that's all, and I've spent most of my life on these waters."

"Then why—"

"It's the dragon, you see. She eats them. Eats anything big enough that catches her eye. No idea why; there's no way anything living here is big enough to fill her belly, so I always assumed the dragon got her food another way, maybe from the Darkstar itself. Still, she seems to take a very particular pleasure in killing things, eating them. Most of the creatures close to the surface don't tend to grow larger than a ship." He shrugged. "Anything bigger than that gets eaten."

Brightest hunkered down and put his hand on the ground. Min noticed the floor of the room was exposed shell, and the old man smiled as he stroked his friend's back.

"Stickle found me when I was at my lowest, when I was much younger, and she was about the size of a… do you know what a cat is? A small mammal about this size. She rescued me when I needed it, when I was alone, and we've looked out for each other since.

"After a few years, it became apparent she was in danger. Fortunately, I had come across the golden Eshak piece—"

"Just like that?" Abalendu interrupted. "How exactly did someone like you get their hands on the playing piece of a god?"

Brightest glared at him. "Are you wanting my entire life story right now? Because that'll take a lot longer to tell than Stickle has left, even if I was willing to tell it. I got my hands on it through a combination of luck, bravery, skill and stupidity – a potent brew that has served me well throughout my life – and can't see myself or anyone else replicating that situation anytime soon.

"Anyway, in order to save herself, Stickle Bonded with the golden Eshak."

Abalendu burst out laughing.

The rest of the room looked at the scholar in confusion.

Realising nobody else was in on the joke, Abalendu stopped, and pointed at Brightest.

"Don't you get it? He's lying to us. Buying time for something. A dumb creature was able to Bond? With a playing piece from a board game? I've never heard anything so ridiculous."

Brightest regarded Abalendu dryly. "After your time here, you still struggle to believe events outside of your experience can happen?"

"I think you will find that I am the only one in this room who truly has the experience to understand how preposterous your tale is," Abalendu retorted, standing to confront Brightest, waving to indicate the dragontoad with a grandiosity that suggested a miniature king was sitting on his shoulder, instead of a slug with warts.

Brightest glanced at the dragontoad, looked back at the scholar, and then shrugged. "I'm not following you."

"This hunk of flesh Bonded with something?" Abalendu said, beating on Stickle's shell with the heel of his boot. "Idiocy. It took me – the foremost scholar of my time at the university – years to train my mind to master the art of Bonding. You are trying to suggest your animal could do the same? I don't believe it."

Brightest looked back at the dragontoad, raising his eyebrow.

"Look, I don't know what passes for impressive creatures back in your world," he said, causing one of the apprentice officers behind Abalendu to suppress a snigger, "but Stickle is more than just a simple beast. She can speak, if you can take the time to learn the language. And it seems that Bonding is possible too.

"But now that Bond has been broken. Someone has stolen the Eshak piece, and robbed her of the power she uses to protect herself. Without that Bond, the next time the dragon has a go at her, Stickle and everyone living on her back are going to be dragon food.

"So maybe now you can understand why I'm a little bit put out that the only thing keeping me and my best friend alive has just been taken from us."

"Preposterous," Abalendu continued, not bending to Brightest's suggestions. "So your giant pet is able to Bond, somehow. I'm not certain I believe that, but there's no way it could have Bonded with a board game part. Bonds are only with certain creatures, magical ones, like my dragontoad. Certainly not with any old glowing item that happens to be lying around."

Brightest stepped forward, with more aggression in that movement than Min had seen from the old man before.

"I told you," Brightest barked, "it's an ascended piece. Fully ascended, as high as it can get. It contains power, so much more than a simple magical object. Something needs to be alive for it to be able to Bond? Maybe it is alive, then, I don't know. All I know is that it has the power to fight off a dragon."

"How powerful is it?" Sung asked, stepping forward. "I heard it could power the *Narwhal* again. Could it do that?"

Min's mental list of suspects immediately expanded to two names.

By Holamo's lonely hell, she thought, eyes widening as the realisation hit her. *Not just two people. All of them. If the crew truly believed the golden Eshak could get them home, then any one of them might have taken it.*

Instead of answering Sung's question, Brightest did something Min had not expected. He paused, backing away, eyeballing all of the gathered crew suspiciously.

He just realised the exact same thing I did. No wonder he didn't want to talk too much about the Eshak piece. Of course he'd think we would take it if there was a chance of it getting us home.

I've got to rescue this situation before it gets any worse.

Min stood, her hand outstretched towards Brightest.

"Look, let's not do anything stupid. Nobody here wants to—"

"He's got something in his hand," Abalendu shouted, interrupting her. "Zoya, stop him!"

"No, wait—" Min shouted, but it was too late.

In fairness, Abalendu was correct; Brightest did indeed have something in his hand. Min spotted it seconds before the situation got thrown overboard. A spherical grey object, presumably fetched from one of those many pockets of his. Where Abalendu was not correct, however, was thinking he had any authority or right to interfere with this discussion.

Zoya, of course, did not care if Abalendu had the right to or not. The scholar had given her an order, and she had to follow it.

And Min suspected that right now, Zoya was just begging for a ripe face to punch.

Brightest acted faster, however, throwing his grey pellet to the floor, where it exploded.

Min was thrown backwards, landing on her arse, ears ringing.

It was not like a cannonball explosion, thank the spirits; those involved flame, random spikes of metal, and considerably more death than one would normally wish for. Brightest's pellet was like a rush of wind, screaming outward, blowing them all – even Zoya – to the ground. Min caught a glimpse of brown overhead, of Brightest using the wind to propel himself across the room, and then he was gone.

"You bloody prat!" Min shouted at Abalendu, straightening her jacket as she got up.

The look on the scholar's face was comical, as if it were the first time in his life anyone had spoken to him like that. It might well have been.

"Nobody listen to this idiot – this civilian – again," Min shouted, looking at the rest of the assembled officers, then glancing to Zoya. "And that goes for you too, if you know what's good for you. Keep your charge under control, or we're going to have some very serious words."

Zoya raised an eyebrow at the challenge, but said nothing more.

Holtz made his way over, clutching his arm, sprained or broken in the blast. "What now?"

"He'll be after Jedda," Min said, making for the door. "And I think he might just kill her when he finds her. We can't let that happen."

Min turned and ran down the darkened corridors of Brightest's home.

He'll make for the Narwhal, she thought, as her feet pounded the shell of the floor. *If he thinks we're all in on the conspiracy, he'll reckon Jedda's in the belly trying to get that Eshak piece to work. Gorya's hell, I half believe she'll be there now, knowing what I know. Jedda probably figured it all out the first time she saw the damned thing. Okay, maybe not the Bonded-to-an-island part of it, but she must have known how much power that game piece contained.*

That it really was a chance for us all to get home.

Exiting the Mudhut, Min dashed towards the *Narwhal*, Stickle's moaning hoots still sounding in the background, reminding Min of the whole reason Brightest was worked up in the first place. Nervously, she glanced up to the Darkstar, the dragon's home. There was no sign of the creature yet. In her last few days here, the dragon had appeared twice more, but had not come back to worry Stickle again. How often had Brightest said they had to ward off attacks from it? She thought of that nightmarish figure, getting so close it became the sky, and her mouth went dry.

They needed to get the Eshak piece back to Stickle before anything like that happened again.

She gained sight of Brightest just as she reached the cove the *Narwhal* was beached in. Min shouted to get his attention, but realised he had already stopped, looking at something else.

By Frathuda's windowless hell.

Brightest was looking at Jedda.

The artificer was standing on the beach, halfway between Brightest and the *Narwhal*. It looked as if she had been hiding somewhere close by, and Brightest had come across her just as she was skulking back into the open.

"Brightest, leave her alone! I'll deal with her," Min shouted, just as he began to break into a run.

As he did, Min saw Brightest pull something long from within one of the folds of his cloak. Something to help catch Jedda? Something to kill her? Min had no clue, and did not want to find out.

Jedda, seemingly realising the stakes that were in play here, broke into a run, still heading for the *Narwhal*.

Min could never reach Brightest in time.

Luckily, someone who could was hot on her heels.

Zoya overtook Min seconds after Jedda disappeared up the *Narwhal's* gangplank, when Brightest still had half the beach to cross before reaching the ship.

"Zoya, you've got to get Brightest! He could kill Jedda if he catches her. I'll sort her out."

Zoya raised an eyebrow at Min, matching her pace, even though Min knew the warrior could be considerably quicker if she wished. "I thought you didn't want me using the Glove anymore?"

Min nodded in frustration. "If he kills her, we lose our only artificer. If we lose Jedda, there's pretty much no chance of us getting home before that rift appears again."

Scrunching up her face in resignation, Zoya threw herself onto all fours, turning her sprint into an animalistic run, bounding from her two feet onto her two hands.

Then, using the power of her Parasite Glove, Zoya pushed against the ground, shoving herself high into the air.

She landed between Brightest and the *Narwhal*, knocking the old man to the ground.

Not waiting to see the outcome of that encounter, knowing Brightest had no chance against Zoya now she was in the game, Min sped past them.

"I can make this better, I can make this better," she muttered under her breath. Sure, being stuck in this place was a bloody awful situation, but things had started to take an upswing for them; they had found safety with Stickle, and the countless rifts orbiting the Darkstar offered infinite possibilities, if they knew how to access them. Whatever madness was going through Jedda's mind right now, Min was not about to let the artificer's oddities screw this up for them.

Racing across the gangplank, it was obvious to Min where Jedda had been, both from the startled faces of the crew onboard, and by the fact that all were pointing toward the place Jedda most likely thought of as home: the *Narwhal's* belly.

Min was not, however, expecting the mallet in her face when she entered the room. Jedda had clearly been waiting for her – for someone, anyway – with a solid metal artificer tool in hand, ready to batter Min as she entered.

Min hit the ground with a thud, her mind casting her back to the stream of stars as the *Narwhal* had first fallen into the Darkstar Dimension.

Dimly, in the far-off distance, someone was speaking to her. Someone was slapping her face.

Jedda.

"...know it was you. I didn't know. You believe me, right?"

Her consciousness snapping back into place, Min jerked her hand up to grab Jedda by the throat. Unfortunately, her motor control had not quite re-established itself, but the violence of her reaction was enough to cause Jedda to scramble back, still speaking. Not shouting at Min, not even really looking at the first officer. Just saying over and over again, "I didn't know."

Groggily, Min got to her feet. She was dimly aware of footsteps not far behind, descending the stairway toward the belly.

Abalendu. It sounded like Abalendu, and maybe one of the apprentices.

By Gorya's frigid hell, that man had a knack for turning up exactly where he was not wanted.

"Bonds of entrapment!" Abalendu shouted as he entered the room, following Jung, the Goryeoan apprentice officer, who was warily holding a sabre aloft.

At Abalendu's command, the dragontoad belched before Min could raise a hand to stop him.

The slime ejected from the Bondmate's mouth splattered across Jedda, and then expanded around her, enveloping the frightened artificer's midriff even as she hit the floor.

Behind Abalendu, Zoya pushed into the room, holding a protesting Brightest with one of his arms pulled forcefully behind his back.

"Jedda," Min said, her tongue questing about in her bloody mouth as if it was hesitant about what it might find, the resulting sentence coming forth in a slur. "Jedda, before they arrive, just tell me: you didn't take it, did you? You didn't take Brightest's Eshak piece?"

The stricken look on Jedda's face said it all.

"Boramu's hell, Jedda, I can't believe it. Can't believe you'd jeopardise everything just to steal a piece to play your bloody stupid game with."

The guilt on Jedda's face disappeared, as if Min had flipped over a playing card. Instead, the artificer seemed offended.

"I'd never steal a piece to play with it. No true player would. That goes completely against everything I believe in."

"Why'd you take it, then?" Brightest asked, the bitterness clear in his voice.

"I was ordered to."

"Who ordered you?" he asked, doing nothing to hide the threat behind the question.

Guiltily, almost apologetic, Jedda raised her finger to point at the person who had given her the order.

"She did."

Jedda was pointing at Min.

Fifth year of solitude, day two hundred and seven

I met myself today.
Except this time, I was a woman.
She arrived not long after I had awoken, beaching a small rowboat on the shore of the island Stickle had been clinging to.
Travellers to the Darkstar Dimension are not uncommon; the rifts continue to pull in people from other worlds, just like I was brought here originally. The manner in which I've encountered these newcomers tends to vary. Most of them are in pretty bad shape mentally; getting pulled through a rift is painful, and the initial experience seems to mess with people's memories, so by the time they come across me, they tend to be in a bad way. I've learned to be careful, and have picked up a number of tricks from my explorations to deal with these people. Only had to actually defend myself once, though, from some kind of jelly person that refused to stop advancing, even after I had fired a warning shot in their direction. Pretty sure the object they were carrying was some kind of weapon, so I'm not letting myself feel too bad about that one.
Sometimes the visitors die on arrival. The rifts can get pretty high up, and the fall... well, most races out there don't seem designed to survive that kind of fall.
This woman, however, she was different. She was me: her name was Brightest, we had the same skin, hair and eye colour, we even had the same history: she was pulled to the Darkstar Dimension from her world when she was a child, and the rest of the people pulled with her eventually abandoned her. Thing is, she hadn't been pulled to this Darkstar Dimension. She was exploring a rift, and the rift had taken her from her Darkstar (which glowed red, not purple) to mine.
I didn't warm to her. She didn't seem to have a Stickle over in her place, and clearly had issues with my explanation of how I can speak to my friend. I eventually pointed out a few low-orbiting rifts that I often use for supplies, and she took the hint and went on her way.
She identified the rift she came from, and I've marked it on the map as a red ball. Even took the time to draw a little dragon face on it.
Don't have any plans to visit anytime soon, though. Unlike me, she clearly isn't a people person.

NINE

Time seemed to move slowly for Min after Jedda's accusation.

The artificer's head dropped straight away, unable to meet Min's eyes.

"What?" Min said. She should have been angry, she should have been authoritative, but she was just too shocked.

Jedda would never lie about something like that. They were friends, weren't they? Close colleagues at the very least. There was no way she would say something like that – Jedda knew how much it would cost Min.

"You did what?" Brightest said. It was a good thing Zoya was still holding the old man, as he had murder in his eyes when looking at Min now.

Min just shook her head, contemplating the room, eyes darting between all in there. Apprentice Jung was slack jawed, completely clueless as to what to do next. Zoya was busy with her charge. Abalendu and Jedda were both staring at the floor. Brightest, though, Brightest's eyes were wide, his pupils pinpricks.

She had lost him.

"First Officer?" Jung asked. "What do we do now?"

"It's not true," Min said, trying to summon as much calm as possible. She looked Brightest in the eye again, and repeated herself. "It's not true, but I understand you can't take my word for it."

"I hope for your sake you are telling the truth, First Officer," Abalendu said, raising his head to look at her. The scholar seemed visibly shaken, almost knocked off his feet as much as Min was by the accusation. "Because you know my father would not take well to a deception of this magnitude."

Min's eyes narrowed. Why exactly was Abalendu acting this way? That smug bastard would love to catch her at something like this, so why so nervous?

Her eyes darted back to Jedda, who was still not looking in her direction.

Min had left them alone together, Abalendu and Jedda, when leaving with Brightest on the rays...

By Holamo's lonely hell.

Min looked to Jung. "I've been accused of a crime. One that I deny, but I can't assume everyone will just take my word for it." She looked Brightest in the eyes as she spoke her next sentence. "I want to prove to you all that something is up, here, that it is not true." Back to apprentice Jung. "Go get the other officers. They'll need to deal with this." *And please, find Holtz before you find Sung.*

Jung nodded dumbly. He seemed to stagger out of the room, a movement which Min – her head still ringing from the mallet to the face, and from Jedda's accusation – thoroughly empathised with.

"Right," Min said, looking at Jedda, "time to sort you out, then."

Abalendu coughed.

Min looked at the scholar, and this time there was a small smile on the man's lips.

"Should you really be the one making that call, First Officer?" he said.

This can't be good.

Zoya stepped forward next.

"In the New Windward military, when a commanding officer is accused of malpractice, she or he is asked to withdraw from command while the matter is attended to. I imagine the navy has something similar in place?"

Min's heckles rose. Her eyes darted, falling briefly on Jedda, and then finally resting on Abalendu, whose smile cracked a little wider.

I'm willing to wager at least one of you knows exactly what is in place for a situation like this.

Slowly, Min nodded, letting out an exasperated gasp of air. "Of course, you are correct." She glanced at Brightest, who was looking at her as if he had never seen her in his life before, seeming altogether puzzled by her presence.

Shaking her head, Min addressed the room. "As per protocol, I will be confined to quarters until the other officers arrive. I will ask, however, that you honour my status as commanding officer – and hopefully my presumed innocence – by making sure that Jedda and Brightest are both treated kindly in my short absence. Brightest in particular has been wronged by us, and his reaction is only natural, especially given the new knowledge we have of his situation."

"Of course," Zoya said, releasing the old man straight away.

Min allowed herself to be escorted to her cabin, which was just off the officers' saloon, beneath the quarterdeck.

Zoya, her escort, did not speak, which suited Min just fine. To her frustration, Min found she was fighting back tears as she was led through the ship.

Accused of misconduct on her first command.

She knew she should not be letting this get to her. After all, situations like this were not uncommon. Frathuda's windowless hell, she had sat through one herself, on the second vessel she apprenticed on – Captain Marya had been accused of selling some of the naval supplies to line her own pockets. Back then, the captain had dealt with the situation calmly, due protocol had been worked through, and proceedings had not lasted twenty minutes before the captain regained command.

Still, Min could not help but feel her situation was different.

For a start, at least one of the officers responsible for clearing her name – Sung – plainly did not like Min. Min had no reason to believe that Sung would act irresponsibly to get rid of a first officer she reckoned was not good enough – or experienced enough – to command her, but Min had not had the opportunity to see how the first mate would act under pressure.

Because – and this was Min's real concern with her present situation – they were well outside the boundaries of normal experiences right now. Captain Marya had been accused of pilfering grain. Min was coping with being stranded in an unknown world. Although it was possible to draw a comparison, the situations were as similar as a hummingbird and a dragon. There were vague similarities, but the differences were colossal.

Min listened at her cabin's door. Sung and Holtz arrived in the saloon not long after she was confined to quarters. Quickly, the group decided to move elsewhere, as Min had expected. To her irritation, however, it was Abalendu who suggested they do so.

That man has no place in these proceedings. I've given him too generous of a leash for too long. Best to cut him off soon, in case his ideas above his station become too big a problem.

A chill rippled through her.

Perhaps that had already happened? Min still struggled to believe Jedda would frame her like this on her own initiative, but the artificer had been left alone with Abalendu. Min recalled Abalendu's hand on Jedda's shoulder just as they were departing on their rays, and she shuddered again.

The room seemed to darken as Min was left alone with her thoughts. She took up a book from her small shelf – *Nestor's Companion*, a former captain's reading suggestion she had never gotten around to – and opened at where she left off.

Despite her intentions, Min read very little over the next few hours.

Her blank stare at the book was interrupted when Zoya opened the door to her room.

"You've been called outside. We've moved proceedings to the Mudhut," was all the warrior said.

Min almost jumped out of the bed, too excited to question why it was Zoya who had been sent to fetch her.

Min's suspicions did arise, however, after the trek across Stickle's shell to Brightest's home, when she saw who was waiting for her in the small room she was led to. It was Brightest and Abalendu.

"Where's Holtz?" Min asked, her heartbeat slowing, each thud becoming more pronounced. "And Sung?"

"Sit down, First Officer," Abalendu said, indicating a seat at the top of the table.

Staying standing, her collar seeming to tighten, Min looked at Zoya, then back to Abalendu. "Would someone like to explain to me where Holtz and Sung are? It should be the other naval officers who are taking charge of the investigation, not civilian passengers and their bodyguards."

"Do you know," Abalendu said, looking at Min for the first time, clearly not able to help the grin that broke across his face at that moment, "I thought that too. But then we had a deeper look into things, and – what do you know – we were not quite following procedure."

It was at this moment Min glanced at Brightest. The old man's face was free from anger now. In fact, he was looking at her intently. There was no accusation there at all anymore, but the intensity of that gaze suggested he wanted… something from her.

"I'm not following. How could you possibly have priority over my officers—"

"Sit down," Zoya said from behind, a Parasite Glove-covered hand resting on Min's shoulder. Min shuddered at the artefact's touch, knowing what it had done to Zoya.

Min sat.

"Where are my officers?"

"Did you know," Abalendu began, leaning back in his seat, "that Zoya is a colonel in the military? Yes, she's my bodyguard, and yes, she's a wielder of a Parasite Glove, but her official military rank is colonel."

"Fascinating," Min replied, "but I don't see what that's got to do with us. The *Narwhal* is a naval vessel. When she's at sea, I'm in charge, and if not me, command falls to my officers."

"Ah, but the *Narwhal* is not at sea anymore, is she?"

A pause.

Bugger me.

"We realised that fact makes matters more complicated. Isn't that right, Zoya?"

Behind Min, the warrior made a sound in her throat.

"When any New Windward citizens are threatened on foreign soil, that is a military matter."

"There are no citizens here. We're all naval—" Min's eyes fell on Abalendu.

Bugger me.

"Yes, given the situation, and the threat posed to the innocent passengers, all decided it would be best if the military intervened in this situation until the danger had passed."

Min struggled to sit still, every instinct screaming at her to jump out of her seat to find her officers, to do something about this farce.

She had been worried about Sung, wondering if the first mate might act on her prejudices and attack Min's innocence.

With Abalendu, she was certain where she stood. She knew this stuck-up ponce would be more than willing to lock her in her room for the three years it was going to take them to get back home.

Luckily, it was not Abalendu who was in charge.

Min turned her seat around, dragging its legs upon the wooden floor, until she was facing the warrior behind her.

"Okay, Zoya, let's say I agree to this. That you're in charge. How do we proceed?"

Zoya's eyes flicked away from Min. "Don't talk to me. Talk to my assistant."

"Your assistant? You don't have an—"

Behind Min, Abalendu coughed.

No. Bugger me, no.

Min scraped her chair back round to stare incredulously at Abalendu. "Really?"

Abalendu shrugged, again failing to hide his grin. "Well, you know, I do need to stick close to her. She is my bodyguard, after all."

He looked over Min's shoulder, presumably at Zoya, and then straightened himself in his chair. "Now, then, First Officer Choi, tell Colonel Zoya why you ordered the *Narwhal's* artificer to steal this Eshak piece."

"If you're taking a record, I'd like to state – not for the first time – that I gave no such order. In fact, I've not seen any evidence to confirm Jedda did actually—"

"The existence of any such evidence is no longer your concern. So, you are claiming Jedda is lying?"

"That's certainly one explanation for it."

"What other explanation could there be?"

"She's been tricked into thinking I gave the order? She's been forced? Threatened?"

Abalendu glanced back at Zoya again. Gorya's hell, Min wished she could see the Kisiwian behind her.

Abalendu continued, reading from the notes in front of him. "Are you really trying to claim that you did not order this golden Eshak piece to be stolen in order to repower the *Melodious Narwhal's* core? That would be possible with the artefact, would it not, Brightest?"

Min's mouth had already opened to speak when Abalendu diverted the question to Brightest instead.

The old man shrugged, his gaze still fixed on Min.

"But it is powerful, isn't it? The power it contains should be more than enough to make a skyship fly again, correct?"

Brightest stared directly at Min. "I suppose so. If it could be properly harnessed. But it belongs to Stickle. She needs it to survive."

"As you say, yes," Abalendu said, glancing back over Min's shoulder. "But it must be possible to harness the power, since you did so to help your Stickle Bond to it. Perhaps you gave away some of the secret to First Officer Choi, and that was what spurred her towards theft?"

This… this isn't about me, Min realised suddenly, her eyes meeting with those of Brightest.

They haven't come in here to determine my innocence or guilt. They brought Brightest in here to make him sing, to give away the secrets of his Eshak piece.

Brightest looked back at Abalendu, his face softening. "Nothing I can remember, sorry."

And Brightest knows it. Holamo's lonely hell, he knows they're trying to play him.

All at once, Min felt a bubbling from within, her muscles tensing, and she knew her anger was threatening to take control of her actions. Abalendu had the Eshak piece, clearly, and it now seemed likely Zoya was in on the ploy as well, although that possibility shocked Min. Zoya had always been such a stickler for the rules.

It did not matter which regulations Abalendu threw at her, how much he tried to hide behind laws and protocol; Min knew exactly what was happening here.

Theft, and conspiracy to mutiny.

She would have their heads for this, Parasite Glove or no.

Min shifted her weight to stand, to bellow at the top of her lungs so any of her men that might be close enough could assist in her apprehension of these criminals. Then she caught Brightest's eye again.

His movements spoke to her: a singular glare and a slight shake of his head.

No, he was saying.

Not yet.

She forced herself to relax, slowly, unsure why Brightest was delaying her actions. If he knew what was going on, surely he would want to act as quickly as possible to save Stickle.

"What about you, First Officer Choi? Can you recall any information Brightest may have given to you that spurred on your theft? Brightest, rest assured, you can trust us; with the criminal apprehended, any information you can give us about how she might have tried to harness the item's power could help us to find out where it has been secreted."

"There..." Min began, hesitant. "There's nothing. I wasn't told anything. Didn't even know what it did, at the time, just knew that Jedda wanted it."

What is it you want from me, Brightest?

Then Min saw something move in Brightest's hands. It was a tiny white spider, about the size of Min's smallest fingernail.

His eyes darting between Zoya and Abalendu, ensuring they were not looking, Brightest shooed the spider away from him, and the creature began to crawl down his leg. Min saw that a thick, semi-pearlescent web was trailing from the spider's rear.

The moment she realised Brightest was sending the spider to her, she also noticed the other end of the webbing was attached to Brightest's hand, a reddened lump where the substance had somehow been embedded.

"Do I have to repeat myself, First Officer?"

"What, sorry?" she said, snapping out of her shock, looking back at Abalendu. "I guess you have to, yes. You've got to understand this is a lot to take in, being framed and all."

"You think you are being framed?" Abalendu asked. His face was so serious, Min was almost convinced she was sailing up the wrong river with her suspicions, before she remembered who she was talking to.

"Yes, well, you can understand why I might be paranoid."

Min's biggest problem now was that she had lost track of the white spider. Not wanting to rouse Abalendu and Zoya's suspicions – she was certain the warrior would be paying close attention to her activities – Min looked to Brightest instead.

Brightest's eyes were fixed on Min's leg.

Shit. Shit.

Abalendu lowered his head to look at his notes. Willing to risk Zoya catching her movements from behind, Min tipped her head just enough to look at her foot. She was in time to catch sight of the spider disappearing into her boot.

She sat upright, rigid, staring at Brightest in disbelief.

She was going to start shouting. Forget the fact that she was currently up for theft, she was going to—

Brightest opened the palm of his right hand – the hand with the webbing impaled into it– and made a subtle calming gesture.

Min, quite unsubtly, darted her eyes down to her boot, and back to Brightest, giving the best 'what-the-bleeding-bloody-hell?' expression she could muster.

Trying not to draw attention any further, Min shook her head urgently.

Brightest nodded back at her. The bastard gave a small smile. Then the spider bit her.

"First Officer?" Abalendu said.

Min had thrown herself forward in her seat, masking her cry with a groan.

"Uh, don't mind me," Min said, composing herself as best she could. "I just can't believe crap like this keeps happening to me," she said, as much to Brightest as to Abalendu.

"Apologies. I didn't think they'd let us speak freely any other way."

That was Brightest's voice. He was speaking to her, but without moving his lips.

"Brightest?" Min thought, trying to reply to the old man inside her head.

"Yes, it's me. The spider is allowing us to—"

"Did you just send that spider to bite me?"

"Yeah, it's strange, the spider's bite seems to create a link between hosts for its venom—"

"You prick. You bloody prick."

"Well, First Officer, this is a side you've not shown me before. I think I like it."

"I think I hate you."

"That's a start."

"You know it wasn't me who stole the Eshak piece, right?"

"I'm not a complete idiot, yes. That became fairly apparent once the double act here started subtly asking about how exactly they could use Stickle's gift to power your ship. But frankly, I don't care if you are innocent or not. All I care about right now is how to save my friend's life."

"It's going to be tricky if Zoya is on Abalendu's side."

"She's on his side."

Min could not help but shake her head at this.

"I don't think so. You don't know her – she is military through and through. I reckon Abalendu sent her on the trip with us to get her out of the way. She won't break the rules."

"Maybe not, but she's certainly willing to bend them. You'd be surprised what someone is willing to do once you tell them they won't get to see their babies again."

"You need to get me out of here."

"Do I?"

"Yes, of course. Once the crew hear about this, even Zoya won't be able to stop us taking back control. When we have them in captivity, my first job will be to get Stickle her Eshak piece back."

"You think it'll be that easy?"

"You've met Abalendu. Everyone else has been on the ship with him for almost a month. Do you think any of them don't hate his guts?"

Brightest chewed his lip.

"The crew are confined to the *Narwhal*. I can't get to them – there are a few loyal to Abalendu posted as watch. Supposed to be for my safety, but I can't help but feel—"

"That they're keeping you here. Boramu's noisy hell. Who are the turncoats?"

"Ole and Uj."

Ole was not a surprise – one of Sung's lot, he had made his loyalties clear during the fight on the beach – but hearing Uj's name, a fellow Goryeoan, hurt. Min had taken a shine to the young apprentice, and had hoped he looked up to Min the way Min had looked up to the captains she had apprenticed with.

But I'm not a captain, am I? Does it always have to come back to that fact?

"Okay, you're going to have to break me out, then. Got anything to take down Zoya without causing her any harm? Or do you have a way to sneak me out?"

As if she could sense Min saying her name, Zoya walked between Min and Brightest, her leg pulling on the spider's web, severing the connection.

Brightest's voice in her head fell silent.

Looking at the old man, Min saw Brightest motion with his hand.

Wait. Patience.

"Clearly, this isn't going anywhere," he said out loud. "She's not going to talk. What kind of... persuasion tactics are you New Windward lot happy to employ in situations like this?"

Abalendu considered the question, but Zoya spoke first.

"We don't torture."

Abalendu looked at her, disappointed, but nodded in agreement. "No, we don't stand for that sort of thing, I'm sorry to say." Min could believe he genuinely was sorry.

"Well, if that's the case," Brightest said, "there's nothing here for me." The old man stood. "I'll find Stickle's Eshak piece myself."

Zoya moved to Brightest's side.

"Where do you think you're going?" Abalendu asked.

"To relieve myself," Brightest retorted, staring Zoya in the face as he did so. "And then to solve my problems on my own."

He began to storm out of the room, but turned around at the last moment.

"My invitation is revoked, by the way," he said, a parting shot. "You lot are no longer welcome in my home, and as soon as you can, I expect you to leave this island."

The insult hung in the air for a few moments.

"Duly noted," Abalendu finally replied, then returned to his notes.

Brightest left, and Min suddenly felt very alone, despite the two people still left in the room. Alone, and a little bit afraid.

But why should I be the one who's afraid? I've done nothing wrong. It's these two, Abalendu in particular, who've framed me and conspired to mutiny. If Brightest can see it, the Narwhal*'s crew will see it too, if they're not already aware.*

It's Abalendu and Zoya who are in trouble now.

With that thought, Min stood.

"Tell me, what made you think you would get away with it?"

Abalendu, with Zoya now standing behind his shoulder, looked up from his notes. "Oh, you're still here? Whatever are you talking about?"

"Taking over the ship? Stealing the Eshak piece? Framing me? What made you think it would actually work?"

She thought for a moment he would try to deny it. Abalendu looked at Zoya, and the warrior behind him looked unsure, almost guilty.

Then Abalendu turned to Min and grinned. "Well, it's working so far, isn't it?"

Min was not looking at him anymore. She was looking at Zoya, her mouth open, but struggling to find the words.

"You knew?" Min eventually said, the accusation and confusion clear in her voice.

Zoya flinched, lowering her gaze.

"I wasn't that surprised by him." Min nodded sharply in Abalendu's direction. "But... you knew? I was so sure he'd lied to you as well."

The Kisiwian looked away, but clenched the fist encased in her Parasite Glove. "I had no choice. Your way, I'll be dead before we ever get home again. At least Abalendu will give me the time I was promised with my family."

Anger took hold of Min's tongue. "And how will they feel, I wonder, when they learn their mother is a traitor?"

It was probably for the best, all things considered, that this was when the wall exploded.

Min's head rang, and the generous spread of pain reminded her distinctly of when she had first been pulled through the rift.

She heaved herself from the rubble, just in time to see a glass shape shatter as Zoya's fist went through it.

The Flagonknight. Brightest had brought the Flagonknight.

Sure enough, the creature was reforming in front of Zoya, but the warrior was ready for it, smashing the glass form before it had time to fully coalesce.

However, this time the Flagonknight seemed to be faster; the reforming components of it gripped Zoya in place, and the warrior's grunts of exertion told Min she would be kept busy. With no sign of Abalendu – was it too much to hope the asshole had been killed by the explosion? – Min knew this was her chance to run.

Brightest joined her as soon as she left the walls of his home, flinging Min her officer's sabre. The joy at being able to hold her weapon gave Min a fresh burst of hope.

"The crew," Min said, gasping at the effort to keep running. "We've got to get the crew roused and ready, in case Zoya is planning on being aggressive."

"Thank you, Brightest," Brightest grumbled. "I hope you appreciate me tearing my home apart for you," he said, as they ran down towards the beach.

Min ignored him, instead casting her gaze upward. One of the many rifts that orbited the purple Darkstar was hovering above them now, its long orbit taking the rift closer to the water's surface than Min had seen any of the others travel. This gap between worlds was considerably different from the one that led to the pink bubbles; the rift above them now was three times the size as the previous one, and it was crimson, a deep red that crackled with barely-contained energy rippling around its exterior. The nearby rift eclipsed the Darkstar, bathing the entire island in its red light.

The sight of the red rift, and her first glimpse of the *Narwhal's* main mast, spurred Min on.

"To arms!" she shouted as she made her way to the beach. "Grab any weapons you can, quickly!"

Her sabre extended, she jumped atop a nearby barrel, and the *Narwhal*'s crew gravitated towards her.

In the distance, Min fancied she could hear something roaring. The Flagonknight could not roar, could it? The sound made Min shiver.

"What's going on?" came a voice from the assembled crowds. It was Sung, pushing herself to the front. "You're supposed to be locked away. What's going on?"

"We've been betrayed," Min said, frustrated that Sung was the first of her officers to come forward. When was she going to catch a break? "There aren't enough of us here," she said to one of the apprentices, lingering closest to the *Narwhal*'s gangplank. "I don't care if people are off-shift, this is an all-hands moment. It might be us against a Parasite Glove."

"What's going on?" Sung repeated. The first mate, along with many of the assembled – curse Min's luck, it was mainly Sung's shift she found herself speaking to – did not seem to be reacting to Min's urgency in the way she had hoped.

"We've been betrayed," Min said again, and then took a deep breath.

She had only witnessed one inspirational speech: Captain Ajal's, just before breaking through a small pirate blockade. The speech had gone badly, but luckily that crew happened to have more faith in their first officer – one Officer Choi – than their captain, and the blockade had been broken nonetheless. Back at the academy, they had actually told Min such speeches did not exist, or at the very least they should not – such romantic notions had no place in the real world.

Min had agreed with her teachers. Right up until this very

moment, when she realised that a rousing speech was exactly what her crew was waiting for.

"Listen," she shouted, trying to be heard over the growing noise of the assembling sailors.

"Listen!" she shouted, raising her sabre, as if piercing the commotion like a narwhal's tooth through ice.

To her amazement, they did.

"Everyone, I know we have not had things easy. Nobody wants to be in our position – stranded, told that we are years from ever getting to see our loved ones. Bloody hell, some of you thought you had it bad before we got sucked in here." She found Sung, staring at the first mate as she spoke the next words. "Some of you never wanted this job in the first place. Some of you didn't want to get bossed around by someone like me."

She broke eye contact with Sung, sweeping her gaze across the rest of the congregation. "But we will get past this, crewmen, I swear to you. We will see our families again, and we will not lose ourselves to get back to them. We'll return to them, with our souls and our honour intact.

"But it won't be easy. Not only do we have this sodding place pushing against us, some of our own are pushing too.

"You all know Abalendu. You all know Zoya. They are trying to do things their own way. Lies. Theft. Treachery. They feel that is the best way to get back home.

"I don't know about you lot, but I don't want to have to report back to the admiralty and tell them how low I stooped to save myself. Do you think that is how they want us to represent our country?

"I don't want to be ashamed to tell my family what I did. I know I could never look at them properly again if I made others pay the price for my return.

"So we're going to have to fight them. I know going up against a noble and a Parasite Glove is not what anyone wants, but we're going to do it, because we know it's the right thing to do, and because it is our job. Because we're better than that. Because we're loyal to New Windward.

"Now, are you with me?"

One or two of the younger crewmen – Kanika and Shreya, Min noticed – gave her a half-hearted cheer. However, most of the crew before her were silent.

Min made a mental note to listen better to her former teachers. Inspirational talks were a terrible idea.

"Not having much luck, are you First Officer?"

Still on her barrel, Min spun around to face the source of the voice. The first person she saw was Zoya. The warrior was breathing heavily, her shoulders slightly hunched to allow gasping breaths to fill her lungs with more air. An angry gash, although visibly healing through the Parasite Glove's powers, wept blood across her forehead. Min could swear a few new lumps of Parasite Glove had spread up her arm.

However, it was not Zoya who had spoken. Stepping out from behind Zoya came Abalendu, clutching a metal rod that Min recognised straight away; it was the one Brightest had used to subdue the Flagonknight when they had first met him.

Min turned to give the old man a withering glare. "Really? You couldn't have taken it with you?"

Brightest shrugged. "Didn't want to take it out of the house. Might lose it."

Min rolled her eyes, and looked back to the pair. Zoya was tired; good. With the Flagonknight having taken a toll on her, and with the strength of the crew behind Min, perhaps Abalendu and Zoya would just back down, instead of making this bloody.

Because if Zoya was going to use that Glove against them, it would indeed be bloody.

Overhead, red light crackled as the low-flying rift made its lazy way through the sky. For that moment, both sides were silent, staring at each other.

"Step down, Zoya," Min shouted, making sure her voice was heard over the commotion from above. "You've made a few bad choices, but no major harm has been done, yet. Come back to the fold now, and your family's honour will still be upheld."

Zoya sneered at Min's words, but it was Abalendu who spoke. "And why would we back down, First Officer, when it is you who has been making the wrong choices? Your position is not as strong as you think."

Arrogant prick. The way he smiles, like the womb he was spat from immediately made him better than the rest of us. Hope I can get a good punch on him before this is over.

"Surrender into my custody, Abalendu Seekwalla, before the crew are forced to take action," Min said, her eyes now firmly fixed on the ringmaster of this mini-mutiny.

"Um, First Officer?" Brightest said from just behind Min. Min waved her hand at him, urging him backward. This was New Windward business. The crew needed to see her solve this by herself, without relying on a civilian.

"I think you should pay attention to your friend, First Officer," Abalendu said, his knowing grin irking Min more than she cared to admit.

Min turned to speak to Brightest, but stopped with her mouth open.

Brightest had his arms pinned to his side, each one held by a member of her crew. Sung had a dagger drawn, its point an inch from the old man's throat.

"What—" Then she saw. The rest of the *Narwhal*'s crew – about half of the total number seemed to be gathered here now – were all looking at her. Their weapons were drawn, but they were not readying themselves to move against Sung's treachery. They were watching Min, tense, frames rigid, ready to attack her if she gave them reason to. Some looked guilty, some seemed genuinely angry, but it was clear they were all against her.

And Min had been the last to know.

"You chose him over us," Sung spat at her, her dagger pricking Brightest's neck dangerously. "You had the chance to take us home, but you chose him over us."

"What? I never—"

"Oh, you did, First Officer," Abalendu said, stepping forward, the coward growing some balls now that he had people to back him up. "You knew all along that Brightest here held the key to getting us back home – his precious golden Eshak piece – but you didn't want to upset him by taking it away. Really, you left us all no choice."

Min, mind reeling as she tried to figure out when she had lost all these people, looked back to the rest of her crew.

"I am captain—"

"You're not though, are you?" came a voice from the crowd, just as Min realised how badly she had misspoken. "Might think you are, but nobody else does – nobody here, and nobody back home wanted to pin that rank on you either."

Min's throat suddenly ached, feeling twice the size it normally would.

"I have command of the *Melodious Narwhal*," she said, trying again, ignoring the quavering of her voice, "and I order you all to stand down and return to your cabins. This indiscretion will be dealt with in due course."

A stupid order. If there was any chance of them actually obeying, it would have left Min and Brightest alone against Zoya, which would have been suicide.

Luckily – if she could look at it that way – nobody listened to her.

"Sheath your weapon, First Officer," Sung said, drawing blood from Brightest's neck, "or your friend gets it."

Sick with frustration, watching the crimson trickle down the old man's throat, Min did as she was told.

"Don't give up!" Brightest said, his eyes darkening. "They won't dare do it. Doesn't have the guts, this one. Don't do it. Call her bluff."

Min shook her head. "You don't understand. She's already thrown everything away by turning on me. After pulling a stunt like that? I don't know if there are any lines she wouldn't cross to get what she wants."

She thought of her grandfather, at that moment. The man who had not wanted her to join the navy, who had never really allowed himself to believe in the idea of New Windward, who had warned her, and eventually pleaded with her to stay and work at his school, promising that at some point the people – the foreigners, he called them – she had allowed herself to trust would turn on her.

Walking closer, Abalendu clicked his fingers. Ole and Jeet, who apparently had been waiting for this wordless order, stepped forward to restrain Min.

"No need to fear, First Officer," Abalendu said. "None of us are barbarians. None have sunk so low as to be actual pirates. We just want to get home. You will be confined to your cabin until we get back to New Windward, and then we'll let the admiralty decide who was in the wrong."

A likely story, Min thought. *What are the odds that I'm allowed to make it home to tell my side of events?*

"What about me?" Brightest asked. "What about Stickle? You'll give us back the Eshak piece?"

Abalendu laughed. "Oh, we'll leave you alone," he said, "but we're keeping the Eshak piece. We need it to get home."

Brightest exploded, ripping himself from the grip of the crewmen, lunging at Abalendu.

Zoya, however, was faster. She caught Brightest's punch with her Gloved fist, leaping into the attack just in time. Brightest glared at her for a moment, his teeth clenched. It looked for a brief second as if Brightest was holding his own. Then Zoya flexed her fist, and Min heard something crack inside Brightest's hand.

The man did not cry out, but he gave a grunt of pain and pulled back from her, his rage dissipating, allowing the seamen to get a hold of him again.

Instead of working further at Abalendu, Brightest then turned his gaze upon Min. It was not a friendly one.

"You promised," he said, almost spitting as he did so. "You promised to save Stickle. But now she's going to die."

Beside Min, Abalendu was saying something, but roaring inside her head drowned out his words as firm hands grabbed her and led her toward the *Narwhal*'s gangplank.

Brightest was right. She had promised, and she had let him down.

It was as if she were not even trying to keep that promise anymore.

Like she had given up.

"Give up," she heard her grandfather say. "Come back home."

To the others, it must have seemed like Min acted out of the blue. They were walking up the gangplank that suspended Min and her escort over the sand of Stickle's beach. She threw her head back first, knocking her captor in the face. Feeling his grip on her loosen, Min ducked, delivering a wild sweeping kick to Ole's legs. Disarmed by fresh blood in his eyes and a lack of ground under his feet, the Iceman plummeted to the sand below.

Ahead of her, Kanika – who was pushing Brightest forward – turned to see the commotion. Min just grabbed the apprentice and threw her, tossing her over the edge to join Ole beneath the gangplank.

"What—" Brightest began to ask, but Min was already rummaging through his bandoleers until she found what she wanted.

Finding the small flute, Min pulled it out and blew on it. Just like before, no sound came out.

"What're you doing?"

"Keeping a promise," Min said, urging Brightest up the gangplank onto the deck, taking another deep breath and blowing on the flute again. "Come on, keep moving."

The deck, however, was occupied by far too many members of her crew.

"First Officer," apprentice officer Jung said, his blade drawn, face pale as he advanced on her.

"Jung," she said to the young Goryeoan, "I don't care about that piece of metal you hold in your hand. You've heard about what I did to the pirates that boarded the *Colossus*, when I had command of her? Have no doubt I can break you just as easily."

It was all bravado, of course. He would be trained just as well as she was, if not better, if he had been educated since he was a young boy. However, there were stories out there about Min, especially in the academy, and sometimes tales like that could be more powerful than a good blade in one's hand.

Jung stepped backward, unsure, giving Min and Brightest the room they needed to run to the helm, exactly where Min wanted them to be.

She gave another blast on the flute. How long was it going to take them?

The red lightning around the rift above crackled again, as if taunting Min.

Too long. It would take them too long.

Half a dozen crewmen were advancing on her now. All familiar faces, some distraught at having to approach her in this way, others close to relishing the experience.

Suddenly, there was a splash from the water behind. One of the rays they had ridden on earlier burst from the water, soaring over Min's head and landing in front of them. The creature hit the deck with a slap, and then pushed itself off the wood, hovering there, still, waiting for them.

"Only one brave enough to take the leap, eh?" Min said, dragging Brightest with her, throwing him on top of the ray.

"Got no harness," Brightest grunted. "Don't carry everything on me, you know. Without a harness, got no way to control it."

"Let's see how far prayer goes as a navigational tool, then," Min said, kicking at the ray's side.

There was a thump on the *Narwhal*'s deck. With all the commotion going on, the noise should not have stood out, but Min turned, cold fingers squeezing her heart at the sound of it.

It was Zoya.

Despite the situation, despite their familiarity with one another and Zoya's recent betrayal, the warrior's face was all business, as if this were a normal day for her, part of the routine.

Flexing the hand that bore the Parasite Glove, Zoya walked forward.

"Brightest, we need to go," Min said, urging the old man into action.

"I told you," he grunted, "without a harness, there's no way to control them."

"Surely this is a strong enough message," she said, digging into the ray's side with both knees, not just a gentle nudge, but forceful, violent, trying to get her message across using the medium of pain. "Sorry," she said, in a half-hearted whisper.

The ray leapt from the deck as if it had been stabbed, propelling itself and its riders towards the closest body of water.

Unfortunately, Zoya was quicker. Not quick enough to get to Min and Brightest, but her outstretched, gloved hand managed to get a hold of the ray itself. Min felt a sharp tug as the ray's flight was slowed by the additional weight, but it still managed to make it over the side of the *Narwhal*. Holding on for dear life, glancing behind just before they hit the water, Min was treated to the sight of Zoya's gritted teeth just before they submerged.

They breached the surface seconds later, Zoya still holding onto their mount. The ray was careening through the waters now, still illuminated a bloody red by the low-passing rift, but Zoya held on to the tip of the creature's tail and was being pulled along behind them at high speed.

"Kick her off," Brightest shouted to Min.

With only a little guilt, Min agreed, stretching her body downward to be able to deliver the heel of her boot to Zoya's face.

She felt a small crunch with her first impact, but the second almost spelled disaster when Zoya reached out her ungloved hand and grabbed Min's boot. If it had been the Parasite Glove, things might have been over there and then, but fortunately the ray chose that moment to bump upon the water's surface, causing Zoya to lose a grip on Min, but not on the ray itself.

Instead, slowly, Zoya began to work her way up the ray's tail, hand over hand, pulling her body against the force with which she was being dragged through the water.

"She's not going to stop," Min shouted. "We've got to dive!"

"Are you crazy? Without a harness, that's madness. And there's no way to get the ray to—"

Min shoved her elbows into the area where the creature's head should be, and the ray dove under the water.

As they plunged beneath the surface, Min felt the reality of the descent of her own life as well. She had been told she was the brightest of her year at the academy. She was the only one of her cohort to have been given command of a vessel upon graduation. This was supposed to have been a simple mission, a research task in safe waters.

Still, she had failed. The worst thing that could have happened had happened – her crew had turned on her, not trusting her to do right by them.

Despite her belief over the last few years, Min finally realised a simple truth: she was not good enough. Certainly nowhere near as good as she had thought she was.

As the deeper waters threatened to crush her, Min turned to look at Zoya. The warrior was similarly struggling with the increased pressure as the ray continued to dive. Beside her, gripping onto Min's jacket tightly, Brightest lay with his eyes closed, muscles straining.

Feeling the pressure become too much, Min released the ray, pulling her elbows from its head.

The ray reversed direction, as if sensing the distress of its riders, shooting up.

From what Min could tell, they lost Zoya almost straight away, the reversal in direction the final thing that was needed to shake the warrior's grip.

Still, now that Min had released her control of the mount, she was powerless, using all the strength she had left to hold onto the edge of the creature as it shot to the surface.

It was not a gentle arrival as they broke the water. At the speed the creature was travelling, it propelled itself into the sky, just as Brightest had used the rays earlier to climb the floating rocks.

Min lost her grip almost immediately, but found she could not care.

As she sped through the air, the ray falling back to the sky beneath her, Min's gaze found the lone landmass that was Stickle, able to make out the *Narwhal* still beached on her eastern shore, scores of ants scurrying around on the *Narwhal*'s deck and at her side, doing the bidding of their new master.

Dimly, Min realised she should have been falling.

Looking up at the direction she was still travelling in, she saw she was caught in the pull of the passing rift, its red light cackling mockingly as she fell toward it.

This time, as she was pulled apart, Min cared little about the pain.

Nothing the rift did to her could compare with what had already happened..

She had lost the *Narwhal* and its crew.

She had failed.

Sixth year of solitude, day fourteen

We have a chance. Star's shadow, Stickle has a chance now.

As her size has increased — she doesn't seem able to stop growing — I've become more and more desperate. I always knew it was inevitable, that she'd end up eaten by the dragon, but the idea of it has been harder to get to grips with over the years. When it was first her and I alone in this place, losing Stickle would have been like losing a favourite pet; I would have been gutted, but life would have gone on.

Now, though? If Stickle dies…

I think I might die too.

Over the last year, I've been looking for resources for myself through the rifts, but I've been trying to find a solution for Stickle, too.

I had no idea what I was looking for. My best bet had been to find a rift low enough and large enough for Stickle to travel through herself, but that never worked out. The few that actually met that criteria did not open out onto water, and I'm pretty certain Stickle wouldn't survive long with only land around her. Also, in case you haven't noticed, large bodies of water often hide large problems; the last thing I want to do is to take Stickle to another world, just to have her eaten by something else.

We've gotten good at surviving here, in the Darkstar Dimension. Trying our best to figure out the dragon's movements, planning our own accordingly.

But I don't want Stickle to just survive. I want her to live.

However, I think I might have found something that'll help us with that. The last world I visited, I brought something back with me. Something powerful, something that its previous owner… well, I'll try not to think about them too much. One step at a time.

If I can harness the power of this Eshak piece, if we can use it, somehow, against the dragon, then Stickle will never have to fear from that monster again…

TEN

Min landed in the dirt with a thump.

She groaned, as much from the hard landing as from the agony of being torn apart and tossed to another world.

However, the physical pain seemed like a respite when Min's memory returned to her, reminding her of all that had just occurred.

She had lost her crew.

Groaning on the inside, face in the dirt, Min forced her head up. Half-heartedly, chin still resting on the ground, she looked around.

The new world, the one within the low-flying red rift, could not have been more greatly removed from the Darkstar Dimension. Whereas the sea surrounding the Darkstar was composed of dark waters, this land was red, dry and rocky, reminding Min of the stony deserts of the Wastespan back home, where parties of scouts could lose themselves in the endless canyons and caves if they did not stick to known routes.

This dead world seemed a fitting exile for her, then. Dead, like all of Min's prospects. All of her promise.

Close by, Min heard a familiar groan.

She rolled on her side to see Brightest lying in a similar position to her, some twenty feet away. He raised his head and spat some blood onto the dirt.

Brightest looked her way, scowled, and then turned on his back to look at the sky.

Min turned too. Above them, perhaps some thirty feet, was a smaller version of the red rift that had lit the scene of her betrayal.

The old man looked at the rift, frowning. Then, with more

grunts, he pulled himself to his feet.

Groggily, without any particular purpose behind it, Min did so too.

"Well, this is just brilliant," Brightest finally said. "Taken me away from where I need to be, with no real way of getting back."

Min opened her mouth to respond. She should have retorted, reminded him that she had just saved his life. But really, when it came down to it, she did not really care what he thought. Not now, especially after she had already failed. So she closed her mouth again, ignoring the insult.

Unlike the last world Min had visited, this was not a gentle, undulating landscape. The place they had been brought to this time was desert-like, but the flat of the land was punctuated by rocky outcrops, bursting from the earth like pimples on a sailor's arse. In one direction – Min had no idea how compass points worked here – those rocky crags became more exaggerated, growing into large hills. Brightest picked that direction, pursed his lips, and began to walk.

"Wait," Min shouted, hurrying to keep up with him. "Wait!"

Brightest did not stop, and glared when she reached his side.

"Haven't you got somewhere better to be?"

Min shrugged. She really had no idea what to do now. Her life had been the academy, sailing, the dream of someday becoming a captain. Was that a dream she could still follow? Abalendu and Zoya had taken that from her, hadn't they? Taken her ship and crew.

Holamo's lonely hell, it was worse than that. The crew had chosen to get rid of her.

Min had nowhere better to be. She had no idea where she was supposed to head, no idea what she was supposed to care about.

"You know this place?" she said, ignoring Brightest's bitterness.

He nodded, grunting. "A regular world. Used to come here quite a bit. It's where my home came from, actually."

She looked at him, her face a question.

He shrugged. "Made a deal with the locals. Still," he said, turning to look back at the small rift they had fallen through, "something's different from the last time. There's supposed to be a platform there, to make it easy to move back and forth through the rift." He stroked his beard. "Wonder what's going on."

"Anything we should be worried about?"

"I've got enough to worry about already. Can't afford to be distracted by someone else's problems."

That attitude flew in the face of all Min's training. The academy would suggest investigating any disturbances, in case they affected your crew, or New Windward in general. A small part of Min, a part that had not yet come to terms with her colossal failure commanding the *Narwhal*, wanted to push further.

The rest of her decided Brightest must be right. He was the one who had survived for so long on his own. Only a few days in this place and Min's life had fallen apart. She needed to be more like him if she was to go it alone.

"You know the people here, then?" she asked him. "Is there some kind of king or businessman you've been in touch with? Someone who can help us?"

Brightest moved his head from side to side, making a clicking sound in his throat. "It's a bit more complicated than that, but I should be able to work something out."

"Complicated? Isn't it always?" Min attempted a weak smile. Brightest caught it, and turned on her.

"Let's get something straight here," he said, pointing at Min, wielding his finger like a particularly passionate teacher attacking a blackboard with a stick of chalk. "We are not going to be pals. This isn't going to be a nice little adventure where we get to be best buddies at the end. You people have been nothing but trouble since you turned up on my beach. My friend – my actual friend, who I've been with for most of my life – might die. So don't expect me to stick my neck out for you, don't expect me to like you. And do expect me to smack you in the face if you try to smile at me like that again."

Min the first officer would have remained stoic under such an onslaught, not wanting to lose face under pressure. Min the exile, however, struggled to keep her composure, instead turning and walking in the direction they had already been travelling in, in order to hide her crestfallen face.

"So," she said, trying to change the conversation, and to keep her mind off her broiling emotions, "you said things are a bit more complicated in this world. What do you mean? Is it something about the locals?"

As if in answer to Min's question, the locals arrived.

She heard them just before they appeared. There was a

rhythmic stamping, militaristic, and then a dozen loosely humanoid figures moving in a perfect rectangular formation marched around the closest of the rocky outcrops.

The closest these things resembled to anything back in New Windward was a goat, especially in the face. The natives of this world had long, flat faces, with their mouths at the very bottom of their chins, and their emotionless black eyes positioned on either side of their heads. What passed for horns on these beings did not seem to be made of bone, for Min could see whatever it was protruding from these creatures' heads flop around a little as the approaching unit – by their formation she assumed they were some sort of organised fighting force – noticed them, and wheeled around to approach, their spear-like weapons taken off their shoulders and put into a ready position. Still, the effect was goat-like, not least because of the thin white fur that appeared to coat each of their bodies.

The bodies of these creatures, however, were the least human things about them. The least goat-like things about them as well, for that matter. The natives' torso came in two parts, attached by a very thin waist, reminding Min more of an ant or wasp's body than anything else. That, and their thin, spindly arms and legs.

They also had two pairs of arms. That was a particular detail Min was certain would haunt her future nightmares.

"What the actual f—"

Brightest put up a hand to silence her.

"Just let me do the talking," he said. "You've done more than enough. And don't stare at their doka, either. They hate that."

"Their doka?" Min asked, but he had already left, raising his right hand to greet the newcomers.

By the hells, Min thought, jogging alongside him, her eyes bouncing all over the creatures' bodies. *What's a doka? Probably the floppy horn things, but what if that's the name for their bodies? Or their extra arms? Or – Boramu's hell, it could even be the name of their spears. Best just to play it safe, and not look at them at all.*

Brightest started to speak first. He surprised her by making a loud guttural bleating sound, moving his hands in front of him in small circles to accompany the noise. Min stared at the ground just in front of the lead goat-ant, trying to look as passive as possible.

The bleating continued on both sides, and seemed to be getting more forceful, especially from the creatures.

"So," Min said during a lull in the conversation, when the goat-ants were talking amongst themselves, "I guess you know these guys well, if they built you a house? They're going to be able to help us out?"

Brightest grunted, and she noticed then the man was sweating. "Something isn't right here," he said. "Something's up. Also, why are you looking at the ground all the time? You're freaking them out."

Min opened her mouth to protest, but then the lead goat-ant lifted his spear and gestured toward them. Immediately, the other soldiers – Min was now convinced that was what they were – did likewise, spreading out in a circle around Min and Brightest, the leader bleating loudly at them, almost crowing.

"Well, crap," was all Brightest said as a pair of soldiers pulled his arms roughly behind his back and began to bind him.

The leader of the crew continued to bark at Brightest as the man's hands were roped behind his back, and two of the creatures lifted him up, holding him horizontal above their heads.

Another pair of the creatures approached Min.

"Brightest?" she asked, completely unsure of the situation.

"Things aren't working out exactly as I thought they would," Brightest shouted as Min was similarly trussed up and carried on the shoulders of two goat-ants. "Seems there's been a change of rulership since I was last around."

"Brilliant." Min's heart sank.

"Yeah. From what I can gather, these guys work for a distant descendant of the family line I was in touch with. Apparently there was a revolution a dozen generations ago, and these new guys aren't as big a fan of off-worlders."

Nearby, the leader barked back at Brightest.

"Ah, looks like they now view the rift – and everything that comes through it – as one of the greatest blasphemies of their world. Bit of a change from my day."

"Wait, did you say generations ago? Just how old are you?"

He grunted. "These guys have short lives. I mean, really short. A day on this world – about thirty hours or so."

Min looked back at the goat-ants, and noticed the sun was setting in the distance. She also noticed the fur coating the creatures getting considerably greyer.

Brightest gave a little chuckle. "You should be honoured, you know," he said, his voice laced with irony. "Capturing you will probably be the highlight of these guys' lives."

Min looked down with wonder at the two goat-ants carrying her. Already, they were starting to stumble, their bodies growing feebler as old age began to set in. This deterioration continued for the hours they carried her across the rocky wastes of their home world, their missteps becoming more frequent, the creatures noticeably bending lower under her weight the longer the journey went on.

The length of the trip afforded Min some time to think, to figure out how to piece things together after the mutiny had so thoroughly taken them apart. She and Brightest had to get out of this place, of course. Despite the ill that had befallen them, Min was reassured by the old man's presence; she struggled to believe he had survived for most of his life living within the Darkstar's light, only to die a few days after she arrived on the scene. He would think of something to save them, and she would ride in his wake, back to safety.

But what then?

Min would not go back to the *Narwhal*, of course. They had made it very clear they did not want her, and that she had nothing to offer them. If she was being honest, there was a very high chance the ship would no longer be in the Darkstar Dimension if she was able to get back to it; with the golden Eshak piece, Min had no doubt Jedda was up to the challenge of getting the crystals working again, to fly them back home.

Min would be stuck in the Darkstar Dimension for the three years it would take the rift to New Windward to reappear, and then she could skulk off back home by herself.

The navy would not want to hear from her. Well, they would probably be interested in punishing her for her failures, but after that, their door would be closed.

Min was certain her family would accept her back. Her grandfather had made it clear he had always wanted her to teach at his school, and she knew her father would always have a position available for her on one of his fishing boats.

Not a position in command, of course. There would be too many painful memories down that route. Min would be happy with a job that kept her on the waves, and away from having to make any more difficult decisions.

She would never be a commanding officer on a ship again, and she certainly had no interest in being a captain, not even on a fishing boat.

A captain. None of this would have fallen on Min's shoulders if the *Narwhal* had actually been given a proper captain. Why in Frathuda's windowless hell had the navy put her in this position anyway? Even if she had been a promising new recruit, nothing good would ever have come of putting a vessel to sail without proper leadership. Come to think of it, how could they possibly have even gotten permission to...

Min gave out a small cry as she realised a thin line of blood was trickling from each of her nostrils; bound as she was, she was unable to tend to the flow.

She was surprised at how unsettled the goat-ants were by the nosebleed, but Brightest eventually convinced them to untie her for long enough for Min to pinch her nose and stem the blood. As she stood there, hand held to her face, her wary eyes on the goat-ants' readied spears, Min wondered about the nosebleeds that had happened over the past few days; Abalendu not long after they arrived in the Darkstar Dimension, Brightest during their walk to meet Stickle. They must all be under a considerable amount of stress for their bodies to act up so much.

After a few minutes, Min was bound again, although this time it appeared to be a considerably greater challenge for her aging captors to lift her back up. For some time, Min had hoped the creatures would waste away before they got Min and Brightest anywhere, toppling as they marched, leaving the two humans alone and bound out in this rocky desert. However, as they reached the foot of the mountains, Min spied a multitude of cave entrances bored into the rock of those slopes, and surmised this was where the creatures lived.

"Brightest, you can get us out of here, right? Got a plan?"

"I'm working on it, yeah."

"Got something in those bandoleers of yours to catch them off guard?"

At Min's words, the leader stopped the march, spinning around and barking at Brightest, finger outstretched. Min was shocked by the length of the thing's beard now, and by how white it was. She was more shocked, however, when the creatures responded to her question by clawing at Brightest, pulling his bandoleers from him.

The look he shot Min as he endured their probing was purest thunder.

"I guess they can understand us?" Min said sheepishly.

"What gave that away?" Brightest growled.

They were taken into one of the lowest holes bored into the mountainside, which connected to a warren-like maze of tunnels that had been linked inside, illuminated by dimly glowing fungi. The tunnels and rooms they were pulled through were saturated with light depending on whichever fungus colony was growing in the crevices of the nearby tunnel walls.

Finally, they were thrown unceremoniously into a green-lit room. None too soon, Min thought, getting one last look at her captors as they turned their backs on them. The goat-ants were now hunched, their movements painful, the tips of many of their beards brushing against the tunnel floor. Min fancied she caught a glimpse of cataracts covering the eyes of one of those who had borne her through the desert.

Then she was left alone with Brightest.

"That's it? Are they just heading off to die somewhere?"

Brightest shrugged as well as he could with his hands still bound behind his back. "Not without providing a hearty meal for their sons and daughters. I imagine a haul like this will go down in legend."

It took Min a moment to realise what he meant.

"You don't mean us? They're going to eat us?"

He gave another shrug.

"You let cannibals make your house for you?"

"Don't be ridiculous. They're hardly cannibals, eating humans. That would be like saying you're a cannibal for eating a chicken or a goat. Although I suspect you'll never look at a goat the same way after this experience – if you're lucky enough to have an 'after'.

"But, yes, they do indeed eat people, I'm afraid. I'm sure you wouldn't turn your nose up either if your only other options were mushrooms or rocks."

"You don't seem too concerned." Min squinted at the man lying on his back on the floor. "You must have some kind of plan brewing. Maybe something hidden somewhere under that cloak?"

Brightest shook his head. "They took everything. And if I'm honest with you, I'm terrified. But I didn't survive for sixty-odd years in the Darkstar Dimension by panicking every time a near-death experience popped up. I'm thinking. And that's considerably more difficult to do with you chattering away all the time."

"Sorry, bit of a nervous reaction. I get that a lot, actually."

"Do people eventually just tell you to shut up?"

"It has been known to happen, yes."

"Does it work?"

Min glared at Brightest, and did her best to retreat into her own thoughts, leaving the grumpy old man to his.

She had lost the *Narwhal*.

It had chosen to get rid of her.

Holamo's lonely hell, how could she have been so stupid?

There was a reason it took so long for captains to work their way up the ranks; she was a fool to think she deserved to be promoted earlier.

It was not just a matter of experience – she had plenty of that. The academy had made sure, with their endless drills, voyages, and gruelling apprenticeships. She had seen more action in her short years on the waves than many of the *Narwhal*'s crew who had spent their lives there.

It was also a matter of perception. Nobody could expect old sea dogs like Sung and Holtz to willingly take orders from an officer whose face had yet to be scarred by the biting salt of the sea.

They were not ready for her.

Min sat in the cell for a long while, working over that thought in her mind, like a child obsessing over a much-loved marble they had just wagered away.

No, that was wrong. That was not the problem. It was not that the crew were not ready for Min. The fault was not with them.

The fault was with Min.

She was not ready to lead.

She had been so certain of her brilliance, so sure her teachers were right, that she was a shining star of her generation, and was already years ahead of everyone else.

She should have recognised that praise for what it was – flattery, encouragement to push herself harder. Not cold, hard facts.

But Min had allowed herself to believe she was better. She had spoken to the crew as if she were better.

And then they turned on her.

This was a less favourable marble to play with, but Min did so anyway, scoring her fingers on the jagged edges of the newly fractured glass, worrying at it, allowing it to prick her.

She had gone through life thinking she was great. One of the best.

She had always been wrong.

Min cast her mind back to Sung and her crew mates, the withering glances Min would often receive from them. She saw those glances echoed in the memories of other crews throughout her apprenticeship. She saw her grandparents, watching her with disappointment and sadness as she packed up her belongings and made off for her first day at the academy.

They all knew it, Min thought. *They all knew I had far too high an opinion of myself.*

They all knew, but I was blind.

"Looks like it's up to you, then," Brightest said, pulling Min out of her dark thoughts.

She realised she had been crying, and hoped the dim light of the fungal luminescence was not enough to show Brightest the truth.

"What?" was all she could manage without her voice threatening to break.

"You've got to understand this galls me a little to say, but I'm too old to do what needs to be done, especially with all my tricks gone. It's up to you."

The look of the *Narwhal's* crew when they had all stood against her fresh in her mind, Min shook her head. "I don't believe that for a second, Brightest. You've lived your life like this for so long, always having an answer for every situation."

He nodded. "I do have an answer. It's you."

She shook her head again, more vigorously this time. "You've got the wrong person for the job. What you wanted was a proper leader – a proper ship's captain – to have come through that rift, to lead her people courageously, to have her ideas followed to the letter. Instead, you got me. Who am I? I'm someone fresh out of education, who isn't as good as she thought she was. You need anyone but me, Brightest. Just like my crew don't need me any longer."

Brightest barked a laugh in response, so loud that one of the passing goat-ants peeked its head in to check nothing was amiss.

After it had gone, Brightest continued.

"You don't think your crew needs you?" he asked, a mocking edge to his voice.

Min glared at him, then turned away, her face crimson, the tears threatening to return.

"Then you're almost as big an idiot as they think you are."

"It doesn't matter what you think," she spat back, still not daring to look him in the eyes. "They've made their choice. They reckon they're better off without me."

"Oh," Brightest said in mock realisation, leaning back against the wall, "I've got this wrong. I thought you were concerned about the safety of your people and the survival of your mission. But it turns out this is all about you instead."

"Bollocks," she said, giving a half-hearted kick in his direction.

"Yeah?" he replied. "Bollocks? So you think they are better off with who they have now? Captain Scholar Know-it-all and his tamed attack pet? Well, I'll tell you something, First Officer Choi – they don't have what I have. I've survived in this place by using my gut, by making split-second decisions, by being able to see the risks that others couldn't. That's what you need to survive the Darkstar. And those two? They don't have it. They don't have what your crew needs."

"And you think I do?"

He nodded.

"My first clue was how well Stickle took to you, but I really saw it when you took control of that ray jumping across the rocks. Took me years to build up that amount of guts when riding those things. And that's what your crew needs, if they're going to survive that place. Someone who'll wrestle a ray. Someone who can crash-land a skyship with style. Someone willing to duel a goat-ant man in mortal combat to make their way back to them."

"I've never duelled a goat-ant man before."

"Yeah," he said, scratching the back of his head and grinning, "I was getting to that."

The new leader readily accepted Min's challenge. Freshly hatched overnight, the creature's skin still beige and hairless, the strongest of today's generation was more than willing to prove himself in front of his kin.

"Now, here's some good news," Brightest told her. They stood in their cage on the edge of the arena, the stands above them beginning to fill with a horde of excited goat-ants. "Apparently this is just a fight to first blood. You draw first blood, you win."

"It sounds like there's some bad news coming."

The old man tutted. "From what I gather, these guys are pretty sparse on the whole 'blood' front. Most of their insides are bone dry. You'll need to knife him through the heart to get any wetness from him."

"Brilliant. Whereas he'll win from the smallest cut to me?"

Brightest nodded. "Yup. At least he won't have to kill you, though."

"Oh good. So I can still be nice and alive when he claims his prize and eats me."

Brightest gave a mirthless chuckle. "So negative. How have you survived for so long with that kind of attitude?"

The stands above them appeared to be full to capacity, with the spectators now braying in unison, some kind of chant to let the organiser know they had to get on with it.

"I don't know," Min said to Brightest, swinging her sabre, which had been returned to her for the fight. "It kind of feels like I'm picking on this guy. I mean, he wasn't even born when I got here, and now I'm meant to kill him? Feels a bit unfair."

Across the arena – a tall dome that appeared to have been carved out of the mountains for just this purpose – the goat-ant Min had challenged put his hands on the head of a much weaker one of his kind that was bowing before him.

Brightest scrunched up his eyes as he observed the creature. "I don't think you have to worry about it being unfair," he said, as Min's opponent crushed the other goat-ant's head like a watermelon.

"So, they're strong," Min said as an already-greying pair of guards opened the cell and pulled her from it.

"It can kill you, if that's what you mean," Brightest said.

"Yep. That's what I meant. Any tips?"

"Try not to die?"

"You are a true gentleman. Thanks."

With that, Min walked into the gladiatorial ring.

She looked at the crowds gathered on the tiered platforms around her: a multitude of aging goat-ants, bleating hungrily as their champion stepped forward. The sound seemed to dry up any moisture in her mouth.

Min felt the familiar weapon in her hands, wondering how in Frathuda's windowless hell she was going to walk away from this alive.

Combat had never been her strongest skill. She could hold her own in most regular fights, that was true, but against anyone properly skilled she was slower and weaker. Her strength – or so she had thought, until recently – was the management of her people, and her planning.

The goat-ant leader thundered toward her, a wooden club in each of its four arms, braying like a thing possessed.

The only goat Min had ever known was the one her grandmother had kept to tend the lawn outside their school. That little bastard had hated Min, and had taken every opportunity to butt her with its horns when she got too close.

Not much has changed, she thought as she dived to the dirt to avoid her attacker.

The crowd roared around her with approval as she tumbled in the sand.

First blood, she thought, as she felt the grit beneath scratch her skin. *By the hells, I'd better be careful here, or I'll hand the match to him myself.*

She almost lost a second time as the leader charged again, and Min fancied she could see Sung's port watch jeering at her from the stands to her right. She dived at the last second, but felt the brush of one of the creature's clubs as it passed a hair's breadth from the side of her head. Min knew she could not keep this up much longer.

A bit like commanding the Narwhal, she thought as she picked herself up from the ground again, the goat-ant leader already turning for a final pass, taking a moment to bray for the crowd, who echoed his cry in appreciation of their leader's superiority.

Her face reddened as she thought back on the other crews she had worked alongside, at the dark faces that had always lurked on the edges of those gatherings, glowering at her every time she spoke.

I was convinced my training made me better than them, had let myself believe the lies my teachers told me.

How many of them had hated her as well, for her arrogance? How many others had been a small step away from mutiny?

How could she have been so blind?

Then, as the goat-ant lowered its head for a final charge, her graduation surfaced on the broiling sea that was her memory, fighting to be reflected upon one last time before death.

"They would have died without you," the admiral said, handing her sabre to her, a line of praise that would later be echoed when she was to learn of her first command, a command that would also involve escorting the admiral's own son.

A moment later, the scene was echoed again, but this time not with Abalendu's father.

"We would have died without you," the crew of the *Stalwart Colossus* told her on the morning after the pirate assault that took their captain's life, the assault that Min had eventually routed with her quick – if unconventional – thinking.

"Bet they didn't teach you that at the academy," the first mate had whispered to her as she had taken the helm. He was right, of course – there had been no classes on how to use harpoon cannon to propel yourself into the air to reach saboteurs on the main mast, or how to use your own body to douse a flame intended for oil-soaked sails. If anything, those skills had come from Min's earlier life, from her many escape attempts from her grandfather's school as she tried to return to the world the old man had been so determined to hide her from.

The goat-ant charged closer, and Min's memories raced.

She remembered earlier that day – was it really the same day? – when she rode upon the back of the ray, flying among the rocks in the sky. The look of amazement on Brightest's face when she took control over her mount.

"It's you," Brightest had told her, only minutes ago. "Your crew needs someone like you to keep them alive, someone able to think on their feet, someone able to improvise. Someone able to see the solutions that others can't."

Another thud. Death took one step closer.

Min raised her arm, and slashed a cut down it with her own sabre.

The coliseum gasped. Even the charging goat-ant faltered, looking at the crowds above to see what had happened.

"First blood," Min shouted, showing the red of her arm to the onlookers, blood dripping from the shallow cut to decorate the dust of the arena floor. "I claim first blood!"

The collected spectators were a mess of confusion. Some of

them cheered when Min raised her arm, but there was just as much – if not more – grumbling from the stalls.

The leader was yelling at the crowds, pointing at Min and then shaking his head. By the way he was stamping his feet, she could tell her ploy was getting to him.

Min smiled, gave a yell of victory, and then raised her cut arm again. The crowd responded with a few more cheers.

Still smiling, Min sought out Brightest in his cell on the arena's edge. She showed him her wound where she had drawn first blood, nodding, indicating that everything was all right now.

Brightest, eyes wide, incredulous, stared back at her, and shook his head slowly.

No. No, things were certainly not all right.

The few cheers that Min had elicited died away quickly, especially as Min's opponent brayed loudly, flailing at the audience, making it very clear to everyone there – including Min, who had no clue how his language worked – that he was the only winner in the arena tonight.

Ah, Min thought. *Not going to win with a bit of biological trickery. Hope these guys have hamstrings, then.*

The goat-ant leader – still focussed on turning the crowd to his favour – roared once more, but the roar turned into a high-pitched squeal as Min walked up behind him and slashed her blade across the backs of both his knees.

For the second time during the battle, the crowd went silent, the only noise in the arena now the squealing of the leader, scrambling around in the dirt as he struggled to grab any of his clubs that lay close by.

Min was not much of a fighter, but even she had no problem with odds like this.

She looked back to Brightest, who remained rigid with shock, but gave her a small smile as she raised her blade into the air.

"Shall I finish him?" she shouted to the crowd.

Min had no idea if they understood her words at all, but her intent was clear enough, and after a second's pause they roared in approval.

"Sorry, old chap," Min said to the crippled goat-ant as he struggled to pull himself away from her. "You know, I would feel a lot worse about this, but you did just squeeze some innocent guy's head between your hands, so—"

Her blade swung down, removing the leader's head from his neck, and ending his torment.

Brightest was the first to walk up to her, hands clapping.

"I knew it! Knew you could do it!"

"Yeah," Min replied, unable to stop herself beaming. "Yeah, looks like I'm not spent yet."

"So, all you have to do now is pick one of them to marry, spawn a few hundred eggs tonight, and we can leave in the morning."

"I'm not falling for it."

"Ah. You learn far too quickly. Well, as the new leader of the Mortocorian, are you happy for me to make negotiations on your behalf?"

The great task that Brightest set for this generation of Mortocorian was to rebuild the structure back to the rift. Half of the goat-ants set forth to complete the task overnight. The rest of them prepared a feast to celebrate their new ruler.

"I don't think I'm particularly happy with this leadership thing, Brightest," Min said, looking uncomfortable under the iron circlet they had placed on her head. "After all, if we're leaving tomorrow, what will that do to their society?"

"Not to worry, I've already planned ahead," Brightest said, clearly enjoying himself at the banquet table, piling up a plate of what Min assumed was food, despite its apparent similarity to the contents of Cook's waste buckets. Still, Brightest was comfortable enough, especially wearing his bandoleers again, having had them returned after Min's victory. "We're leaving tonight, to take off on a great spiritual journey into the desert. If you don't return by the morning, they are to choose a new leader. And, you know, worship you as a god."

Min eyed him. "Give up the jokes, Brightest. You aren't going to trick me anymore."

Then she caught a flicker of something on the edge of his lips.

"Frathuda's windowless hell," she exclaimed. "You aren't joking, are you?"

He shrugged, palms outstretched innocently. "Well, look, it makes sense, doesn't it? Builders like these guys are rare, and they're a resource we almost lost because of how volatile their culture is. We can't just keep jumping in every day to make nice with that particular generation, can we? Godhood just seems more enduring. You'll thank me if we need to come back here again."

Min felt distinctly uncomfortable now. "It just seems wrong, that's all. Impersonating a god."

"What are gods, really? I've met a few to claim that title, and they aren't all that."

"You've met gods?"

"Pfft, so they say. But what makes a god? Throw a bolt of lightning, make the earth shake? I've seen magicians who can manage that. Should they just claim they're gods too? We will live tens of thousands of these creatures' lifetimes. How much more godlike do you need to get before it seems appropriate to you?"

Min mulled over Brightest's thoughts while enjoying the majority of what was served to her, avoiding the roasted reshu at Brightest's suggestion.

In the quiet of the night, when yesterday's generation were slinking off to die, and tomorrow's were testing the thin membrane of their egg sacs, Min and Brightest left.

The structure that had been built beneath their rift was a simple enough affair, and Min could see Brightest's Mudhut in the architecture, although this work appeared to be more sophisticated, more ornate. Still, not a lot of progress seemed to have been made by the goat-ant builders in the last few thousand generations.

Min and Brightest climbed the solid stairway to the rift, waiting at the edge of the red umbra that crackled before them.

"This is it," Min said, summing up her courage to throw herself into the rift again. She could not say what put her off more; the pain of the voyage, or fear of the conflict that waited on the other side.

Brightest nodded, the mirth he had shown at the feast having faded from his face during the walk back.

"What's the plan?" he said. "Where will they be keeping the Eshak piece?"

"We need to find Jedda," Min said. "If she was the one who grabbed it, she won't want to let it out of her sight. Also, she's probably the only one on board who could make sense of it in the way they want her to. She's the one I'm hoping to turn back to our cause."

Min neglected to mention she could hardly believe Jedda had turned on her in the first place.

"Fine," Brightest said, and with no more words he stepped into the portal, evaporating into a red mist before Min's eyes. Taking a deep breath, Min followed.

Ninth year of solitude, day thirty-seven

It's time to make my mark here. Years ago, I decided to make the Darkstar Dimension my home. Now, it's time to make a home in the Darkstar Dimension.

The tent I've been using on Stickle's back has expanded over the years into a proper campsite; extensions to the first tent to provide different rooms, plenty more just for storing the different artefacts I've found during my travels. At least two of the constructions I put up just through boredom.

Stickle doesn't mind. In fact, she encourages it. She's grown bolder ever since she harnessed the power of the Eshak piece to take on the dragon, and I reckon she half thinks of herself as an island now. Seems to get a kick out of me living on her back.

But my 'home' was getting a bit embarrassing. The final straw was when a pair of humans, newly pulled here by the Darkstar, washed up on Stickle's shore, wondering where the other people were. It took them a while to believe it was just me that had created all the mess.

They moved on, eventually, but by then it was clear I needed to make some changes, have something a bit more permanent to live in.

Thankfully, I already had the people in mind for the job. Most of the worlds I visit don't have any intelligent life, and those that do are often unaware of the rift that connects them to the Darkstar.

Some, however, have visited the Darkstar Dimension already, and the rift to this place is a constant presence in their lives. Such is the case with the Mortocorians.

Now, I'll be the first to admit that these guys are a bit weird, but I'll be damned if they aren't great workers. It was simple enough to strike up a deal with their ruler – an emperor, I think? – trading metalwork for labour; theirs is a world with not much in the way of any kind of ore, so they were more than willing to sell their own children's and grandchildren's lives (literally, based on how long the construction took) to piece my new place together.

They seemed to have an issue making sense of any kind of drawings or diagrams, so I eventually just told them what I needed the building for, and let them do their own thing.

Two days. Two days was all it took for them to carry the brickwork through the rift and piece it together for me.

I'll admit, it looks a bit odd with all its mis-matched cubes, and the brown is a bit drab, but...

It's home. For the first time in a very long while indeed, I have somewhere I can call home.

ELEVEN

Pain.

As expected, Min experienced immense pain.

Pain, and the rushing of air.

With the agony of her body reconstituting itself, it took some moments for Min to become aware of what was happening.

When they had first entered it, this rift had been high in the air above Stickle, and the only way they had reached it was by being catapulted upward by the ray Min had hijacked.

There was no ray to catch Min this time.

Luckily, there was only water underneath them now. The fall was far enough to be dangerous, but thankfully not far enough to guarantee a shattering of bones upon impact. Min managed to angle herself to do a proper dive into the black, but lost her composure almost immediately under the water. Last time she was down in the blackness, she had found it immensely difficult to orientate herself, and now she was intensely conscious of the moving thing in the deep darkness she had spotted when the ray had last pulled her under.

Thankfully, she had a clear landmark showing her the way to the surface – the purple glare of the Darkstar shone like a beacon, its distorted light in the rippling water Min's only clue as to where the surface lay. She spotted Brightest frog-kicking his way to the top, and followed.

The first thing she noticed was that the *Narwhal* was not there. Neither was Stickle.

Min paddled in circles for a moment, panicked, until she burned off that nervous energy and allowed her brain to engage.

"The rift kept moving," she said to Brightest, more to show that she had figured it out than to inform him, as the old man did not appear to be surprised by the turn of events. "We've been on that world for a day, and the rift has continued to orbit the Darkstar." Brightest nodded, chewing his lip. "That's about it. Hope they haven't done anything stupid in the meantime."

Min scanned the distance where the sea folded up into the sky, and tried to make out which of the distant lumps of rock might actually be a turtlemoth with a skyship beached upon it, but struggled to see anything that gave away Stickle's location.

She tried not to think about the fact that if the dragon had attacked in the time they were away, there would be nothing left to spot.

Giving up looking for Stickle, Min's eyes drew upward, towards the many objects orbiting the Darkstar. After a few moments of searching, she found what she was looking for, and pointed at the blue-green rift. "There's New Windward," Min said, "and no sign of the *Narwhal* up there. They've not figured out how to make her take off yet, anyway."

Brightest looked at her, his brow creasing. "What do you mean, 'they're not up there'? It's already too late, I told you before. It'll be three years until the rift appears on the surface again."

Min looked from the old man to the rift high above. Although it was moving too slowly for Min to make out its path, she knew from Brightest's orrery that New Windward's rift was turning closer and closer to the Darkstar itself, and would soon be consumed. "But the rift's still there. Surely if they can get the *Narwhal* to fly now, it won't be too late to get home?"

Brightest's eyes widened, as if just realising something for the first time. "When I said it was too late, I meant it."

"But," Min's eyes rose to the New Windward rift again, "it's right there. If we were able to get the *Narwhal* airborne again, couldn't we just fly up to it?"

Brightest shook his head, watching Min carefully. "The distance was never the problem, Min. It's the dragon."

Min looked at the Darkstar, so close to the New Windward rift now. There was no sign of the dragon, but she knew the beast was there, somewhere, clinging tight to the Darkstar's surface.

"The dragon is incredibly territorial. I've seen people and creatures making that mistake, flying too close to its lair. If your *Narwhal* even made it halfway to the rift, the dragon would take umbrage, and make an example of them."

Min's mouth dried. Boramu's noisy hell, if only they had this information at the very beginning, it might have put Abalendu off his plan to begin with.

No, she thought, after a moment. *Abalendu would never have believed it. He'd never have believed it, unless it had been his idea.*

Either that, or in his arrogance he would try to come up with a way of dealing with the dragon.

Slowly, she looked back at Brightest, who was studying her.

"I was right, you see," he said.

"What?"

"About your crew. That they need you. The idiots who have taken charge are going to get them all killed. They need someone like you to keep them alive."

She realised he was right. Perhaps she was the best person for the job after all, whether they liked it or not. She could not help but smile at the thought.

"How're we getting back to them?"

"Well, normally we'd go by ray, but I assume you didn't manage to keep hold of my whistle in all the commotion earlier?"

Red-faced, Min checked her coat, just in case she had subconsciously pocketed the instrument. But no, Brightest was right – she had dropped it, or it had been dislodged from her hand in the flight from Zoya.

"We have other ways," he said, "don't stress. Got to be careful, though."

"I don't like the sound of that."

"See," he said, flashing her a quick grin, "I knew you were a smart one."

Brightest fished around inside his bandoleers and brought out a smooth metal cylinder, which he held above the water's surface.

"Right, this is going to be tricky. I need to get inside."

"Okay? Isn't there a lid? Can't you just unscrew it?"

"I can, yes," he said, "but that's not the issue. You're going to unscrew the lid in a moment, but you can't – let me repeat that: you cannot – allow the contents to get wet."

Min, her legs starting to ache as she constantly treaded water to keep herself afloat, looked at the rippling black liquid that surrounded them for miles in every direction.

"What happens if it gets wet?"

"Do you have tsunamis where you come from?"

Min paused. Yes. Yes, she certainly did.

Suddenly, opening this cylinder did not seem to be the best idea.

"Is there another option?"

"We could swim?"

Another pause.

"All right, hand me the case."

As slowly as she could, taking strong, even kicks with her legs to stop herself from bobbing up and down too much in the water, Min found the lid of the cylinder with her left hand and unscrewed it. As soon as she did so, the air seemed to tremble around her, as if the container held movement itself, trying to leak out now its cell was open.

"Fine," Brightest said, "hold it there." He swam over to her, trying as carefully as possible to not cause any commotion in the water, and slowly raised a hand up to reach inside the cylinder. "Just need a pinch."

He withdrew his fingers, pulling out something Min had never seen in her life before.

They were petals. Pink petals, in a shape like two feet bonded together at their heels. The petals were hard to look at, almost as if they were quickly vibrating in Brightest's hand. She could hear them humming.

"Close it," he told her, his eyes locked on the open container. Min closed the container, straining with all her might when pulling the lid shut, to ensure a proper seal. Only then did Brightest visibly relax.

"Reckon you can keep ahold of this one without losing it?" he said as she stowed the cylinder away. She did not give him the satisfaction of rising to the jibe.

Danger now gone, Brightest crushed the three petals in his hand, and sprinkled the pieces onto the water before him. The water around them rippled where the flakes touched, causing small waves that rose just as high as Min's head, and pushed out from them in perfect circles.

"What is it?" Min said. "Are you calling the rays? Something else?"

Still treading water, Brightest nodded toward what passed for the horizon in this place. Min squinted, seeing that something was coming toward them.

It was a boat.

She was so shocked to see it, her coordination failed her, and her head ducked under the water for a moment.

"Holamo's lonely hell, a boat? Are there people on it?"

"You often find people on boats, don't you?"

"There are other people here?"

"What, living close to the Darkstar? Oh, yeah, sure. Of course there are. You reckon with all the rifts that float above us, and all the random crap that gets pulled here, that I'm the only one who decided to stick around? There are a few natives, and more who regularly pass through. Most of them you wouldn't really call 'people', though, but this guy fits the bill, I guess."

"Who is it?"

Brightest smiled. "Why don't you wait and see?" His features suddenly became serious. "Let me do the talking, though. That's very important."

As the vessel approached, Min got a better look at it.

Her first impression was that it was small, considerably smaller than the *Narwhal*. In fact, as the boat got closer, Min was convinced it could very well be a single-man vessel, and would comfortably contain no more than three people at the most, especially if they were spending long stretches of time on it.

The boat was also primitive. As it approached, Min could see it was a twin-hulled boat – the hulls seemingly each carved out of a single tree – strung together with a wooden platform that Min could swear was attached to the hulls with twine or rope. What was most prominent about the boat was the structure that had been built on top of the connecting platform, which was effectively a small house, reminding Min of the buildings she had come across on the more remote islands back in her own world – wooden walls made from vertical planks, topped off with a roof of straw or some kind of fern leaves.

To Min, it felt as if she were watching something from a history book sail toward her.

"Does this guy live here, then?" Min asked Brightest, eying the straw hut on the boat's deck.

He shrugged. "You know, I'm not actually sure. He's never let me down when I've called him, though. Remember, let me do the talking."

The longboat came up alongside the pair, and Brightest pulled himself onto the deck using a rope ladder on the side, which seemed to be made out of some kind of woven vine.

Min had never been more thankful to step onto the deck of a ship. If she had been in more comfortable surroundings, she would have fallen onto her rump and given her legs the time to allow the burning sensation caused by the constant treading to subside. However, Brightest immediately approached a bead curtain which barred the entrance into the central hut, and beckoned Min to follow.

Inside, Min was reminded more than anything else of Brightest's treasure trove. The interior of the hut was an eclectic assortment of cages, boxes and desks. Unlike Brightest's hoard, where most items were covered and hidden, here everything was on full display. There was a large assortment of weapons, mostly swords, propped up in various containers that reminded Min of how her grandmother had stored umbrellas. One large glass jar seemed to be empty, but every time Min turned away from it she was certain she caught movement inside it from the corner of her eye. There were various paintings hung randomly from the walls, often not sitting straight, and most of them were instantly forgettable, except for one of a young woman, painted from behind, watching others play together in a lake. Min was wistful for the unadulterated blue of the sky in that image, and wondered when she would next get to relax as that unnamed woman was.

"You two should get together more often, you and the guy who owns this stuff," Min told Brightest. "Seems like you've got a lot in common, all that hoarding. You should compare collections."

"Mine's better." Brightest sniffed. "And he's a terrible man to swap with. Drives the hardest bargains. Look, there he is now. Remember—"

"Yes, yes, I'll shut up."

Turning a corner in the jumble, they came across what Min could only describe as a counter, the kind one would find in any shop down New Windward's main street. Behind this counter sat the oddest clerk Min had ever seen.

Most shop clerks back in New Windward had no qualms with some face-to-face action with their customers. This man, however, sat cross-legged on his counter, naked. Naked, except for his mask.

Wanting to look anywhere except at the man's unmentionables, Min stared with horrid fascination at the false face he wore. Unlike traditional Goryeoan masks, which were shaped to match the contours of a human face, this man's face was a flat rectangle of wood, the length of which went almost as far down as his belly button. There was a face painted on it in some kind of green paint, but it seemed stretched somehow, almost childlike, as if it had been put on by someone who had forgotten exactly what a human face looked like, or by someone who had only ever heard one described, but had never seen one themselves.

As the owner of the boat began to speak to Brightest – in a series of pops and whistles that were accompanied by fits of dramatic arm gestures, the man's limbs flailing about like a drowning swimmer – Min walked away from the shopkeeper, trying to get a peek behind the mask. Disturbingly, despite the fact that Min was certain the man's attention was entirely held by Brightest, the mask appeared to be looking at Min the entire time, turning to her even when she stood at a right angle to him, although the rest of the man's body was pointed firmly toward Brightest.

"I only want some fish," Brightest said to the man, indicating one of the tanks that sat to the right of the counter top. Looking inside, Min saw something that resembled a trout, if the creature had been allowed to gorge on lumps of lard for the last few years.

The masked salesman spoke again, the strange clicking language rattling around inside Min's head. It sounded aggressive, and Brightest seemed to be acting as if the man was throwing a multitude of death threats at him, but Min got the impression from the salesman's high-pitched clicks and pumping hand gestures that he was enjoying the exchange.

"For some fish?" Brightest said, the words exploding from his mouth. "You want all that for some fish?"

"Is there something special about them?" Min asked, wondering how exactly this fat trout was going to get them back to the *Narwhal*.

"No," Brightest said, rounding on her, seemingly forgetting all about the fact he had asked her not to speak. "See, even she gets it. There's nothing special about it; it's just a fish, but you're asking me to chop my arm off for it."

The masked man clicked and whirred again, leaning back in his seat, hands behind his head, relaxing.

Brightest swore under his breath, and slung his bandoleers over his head.

"What's up?" Min asked him as he rooted through his belongings.

"He says the price is for the rescue, as well as for the fish."

"Rescue?"

"He found us floating in the middle of the sea, with no boat or island close by. Reckons he saved our lives."

"He doesn't know us that well then, does he?"

Brightest looked up at her with a twinkle in his eye.

"Damn," he said, still smiling, "I should have let you do the bartering, shouldn't I?"

He pocketed a few items from his bandoleers, but passed the rest over to the salesman. "Here you go," he said, "that's everything I can afford to give you."

The salesman clicked again.

Brightest's hand flew to the pocket he had just put his items into.

"I need these, you parasite. I need them to survive. There's no point in me getting what I want from you if it basically leaves me dead afterward. Not great for you, either, if you're looking for repeat business."

The masked man's response was unintelligible to Min, but the way he reclined on his desk suggested he would pass the rest of his days quite happily if he did not get any custom from Brightest in the future.

Then the salesman turned to Min, and clicked in her direction.

"Her?" Brightest said dismissively. "That one? Oh, she's worthless. Got nothing of value, do you?"

Min tried not to smart at his response, seeing it for the deflection that it was.

The salesman, however, was not fooled. He pointed at Min again, more urgently this time.

Brightest frowned, then looked at her. "Got anything on you to shut this guy up?"

Min immediately reached into the side of her jacket she had stored Brightest's cylinder in, the one with the humming petals, but she noticed her companion's eyes widen straight away. Sensing his distress, she withdrew her hand, as if finding nothing there.

Min patted herself down a few times, and then looked at the salesman with open palms.

"Nothing, I'm afraid. It's like he says – completely worthless, me."

The salesman clicked, pointing at Min's belt.

Her heart dropped.

He was pointing at her sabre, the one given to her upon graduation at the academy.

Brightest must have seen her stricken look, as he was the first to speak.

"Oh, that thing? You don't want that. Most useless weapon I've seen in my life. Not even sharp. Couldn't cut a loaf of bread. The only time she tried drawing it on someone, the enemy almost died laughing at the sight of it. Not worth your time."

The shopkeeper did not relent.

"It's okay, Brightest," Min said after a moment, unclipping the blade from her belt and passing it to the thief masquerading as an honest salesman. "If it'll get us back to Stickle and my people, it's okay."

Brightest hesitated for a moment, then took the sabre from Min and presented it to the masked man. "And I hope you choke on it, you bloodsucker," Brightest said, as he fished into the tank and pulled up the overweight trout. "We'll be taking ten minutes or so outside, unless you need some of our toenails to pay for that time?"

The salesman waved at Brightest dismissively, already focussing on the sword now, cooing as he pulled it from its sheath.

"Bloody parasite," Brightest muttered as they left, the purple rays of the Darkstar blinding Min as she walked back into its light.

"I don't get it," Min said, looking at Brightest's purchase as it gasped for breath in his arms. "What do we need that for? It's not going to carry us to where we need to go. Right?" She was doubtful about her last statement, only because this place had surprised her so much already.

"This thing? Nah," Brightest said, and he picked up the trout and threw it overboard.

Min could not help but cry out, almost as if he had taken her sabre itself and thrown it into the sea.

She gripped onto the wooden railing of the narrow boat, tense as she watched the trout's luminescence flicker to life. She was certain Brightest knew what he was doing, but she had no clue what that might be.

The trout did not seem to do anything unusual. Like the rest of the sea life in this strange place, it had begun to glow as soon as it hit the water. She could not spot anything out of the ordinary about it, except for the fact that the trout was a bit larger than most of the specks floating by underneath them, and that its colours changed, bright yellows slowly melting into hot pinks, then on to fiery orange.

When it first hit the water, the fish seemed stunned, as if it had forgotten how to act when not enclosed within a glass tank.

Then, with a few flicks of the fish's tail, it was gone.

Min, nervous, turned to look at Brightest. He seemed bored more than anything else, and still irritated by the shopkeeper.

She could not figure out what he was doing.

"Has this got anything to do with the rays?"

"Nope. Only way I know to get in touch with those guys was my flute. This is for something else. You'll like this."

Min first became aware of something happening below the water when the narrow boat rocked slightly, and a dark object – the only life Min had ever clearly seen under the water that did not glow – moved under them, its bulk blocking out the light from the smaller fish that swam further below the surface.

Min was aware of other dark shapes circling the boat, at least four in total. From what she could gather, each was about the size of a large cow, possibly a bit bigger.

Brightest still did not seem concerned.

"What are they?" she asked him, convinced this was their new ride he had summoned.

"Don't recognise them yet?" he asked, just as the creature's head broke through the water.

This thing's face reminded Min of the beak of a snapping turtle – rigid, cliff-like lines that spoke of an unforgiving bite. Between the thing's jaws, Min caught sight of a rainbow tail disappearing down the creature's gullet.

The other circling shapes did not raise their heads above the water, but instead broke the surface with the shells on their backs, which moved around the salesman's vessel like rafts caught in a current.

All of the creatures had twin purple growths sprouting from their heads, like antennae on an ant.

Min gave a gasp of realisation.

"Stickle! It's Stickle! Or, you know, others of her kind. Turtlemoths."

Brightest nodded. "That's right. Getting in touch with their kind is easy enough; Stickle could never ignore a big fat fish. Problem is, we've no method of actually controlling them."

He hunched down, lowering himself as close as possible to the chewing turtlemoths. "But," he said, as much to the creatures in the water as to Min, "I'm willing to bet that once these guys learn of the trouble Stickle is in right now, they'll be more than willing to lend a hand. Isn't that right?"

In response to Brightest's question, the remaining turtlemoths reared their heads, all responding at once with the hooting that Min had come to recognise during her time on Stickle, coming at a considerably higher pitch from these smaller creatures.

"Better get started, then," Brightest said, casting a final glare back to the shopkeeper's hut. "These guys are loyal, but they aren't half as fast as the rays."

Min winced again at the thought of the flute. Conscious of the time she had lost them, she glanced up at the Darkstar again.

"What do you think? Will we make it?" she asked, as she and Brightest lowered themselves on to the backs of separate turtlemoths. "If it hasn't woken while we were away, how long do you think it'll be before the d—"

Brightest interrupted her with a clicking of his tongue. She looked at him, surprised.

Brightest indicated their mounts with a nod.

"We're lucky this lot surfaced for us. They're large, for turtlemoths. And therefore nervous. Without protection, this is about as large as turtlemoths get here in the Darkstar."

He looked at her knowingly, and Min understood. Turtlemoths did not stop growing. Stickle was proof enough of that fact. They did, however, grow large enough to be worthy of the dragon's attention.

And these creatures were about as large as a normal turtlemoth got.

Min patted her mount on its back, and glanced nervously up at the Darkstar again, harbouring its dormant host.

"Let's go, then," she whispered to her steed. "We've got a ship to catch."

Twelfth year of solitude, day two hundred and fifty-three

I had a few purposes behind getting this building put upon Stickle's back. Sure, I wanted to send a message, to myself more than anything: this is where I live. This is me.

There were other reasons, too. I've got some plans I want to set in motion, stuff I want to do, and I needed a place to make them happen in.

Well, I've got a place, now. Time to get started.

My first job was to do something a bit more meaningful with all the information put in these books. I've got volumes of information about the rifts, now. Descriptions of what they look like here, floating around the Darkstar, and what to expect on the other side. Measurements of movements, speed of deterioration of orbits, stuff like that.

I tried drawing a map of all these facts. It's impossible. There's just too much going on, too many different objects – rifts, rocks, buildings, ships – floating up there, all behaving differently.

One of the rifts I visited a while ago – yellow swirl #4 – opened up into some kind of building of learning, where the inhabitants seemed to be dedicated to a lifetime of study. They showed me around the place, and the sight in there that I just couldn't shake from my mind was a giant moving model they had made of the stars and planets.

I spent a few days there, getting the engineers to show me how it all functioned. Reckoned something like that would work beautifully for the Darkstar. Mine will have to be more complicated than theirs, obviously. It'll take ages to get it working properly, and I'll have to tend to it constantly to keep it up to date, with all the rifts appearing, disappearing, and reappearing.

But I've got time, haven't I?

There seems to be a pattern to a lot of these rifts reappearing. I just feel that seeing this all happen in front of me, instead of numbers and facts in a book... that'll help me make more sense of it.

Take the rift the others went into, for example, the ones who got pulled here with me, back at the very beginning. I've seen the rift to their new home reappear four times since they all left the Darkstar Dimension. If I track things better, I reckon I can predict when something like that might happen again.

I'm not interested in going into that place, mind. I've no interest in reopening old wounds. Also, by not sending anyone my way when the rift opened on their side, I guess they aren't interested either.

That's fine. I've got plenty to do over here now.

Wouldn't want that kind of distraction.

TWELVE

The turtlemoths carried the pair over the dark sea, in the direction the red rift had travelled from. There were only four of the creatures in the beginning, but as they continued to travel, more of the beasts joined their procession. A few hours later, Min had lost count of the shadows that followed in their wake, but the extra company lifted her spirits. She was not certain if the turtlemoths could help at all, but it was enough to feel that she and Brightest were no longer two against the rest of the crew.

Min was convinced she could see a distant object that might well be Stickle, bent around the interior sea of the Darkstar Dimension, still far enough away to seem part of the sky instead of the horizon that her mind tricked her into believing still existed in this place.

Brightest perched on the turtlemoth that travelled beside her. He was alert, tense, his eyes fixed forward, intent on getting back to his friend before the dragon awoke.

Min was not certain she could ever call a creature like Stickle a friend. Certainly, she was fond enough of the turtlemoth, which was surprising given the short time she had spent with it, but she was fond of cats as well. That did not mean she called them her friends.

Min looked again at Brightest. When he was enjoying himself, when he was riding rays or bartering with masked salesmen, he seemed vibrant, almost youthful.

Now, with nothing to distract him other than the worry of what might happen to Stickle, Brightest looked old.

He had lived a long time here, he had told her. Perhaps, over years without any human contact, Min could indeed learn to call an animal a friend.

"Why did you stay?" Min shouted across to him.

Brightest, distracted by his fruitless scouring of the distance, frowned as he looked at her.

"This place," she said, "the Darkstar Dimension; there are countless worlds attached to it, including the one you came from. In all the time you've been here, you've never found one you would prefer to call home? You've never found a safer place to live?"

"Oh, there are safer places all right," Brightest said, resuming his sentry-like position. "Plenty of worlds out there where someone could settle down, maybe even start a family, die old and fat. Just not for me. None of those worlds are for me."

"Tell me about it," Min asked, chancing her luck. He had refused to elaborate on his past when she had first asked him, but a lot had happened since then.

There was a long silence. Just as Min felt that Brightest was ignoring her, he spoke.

"I was young when I was taken here. Much younger than any of your crew, but still old enough to remember a bit of my life before the Darkstar. I remember where I came from most of all, the Spire that was my home. Where I came from... it was different from most places I've been to since..."

He drifted off for a bit, apparently deciding how to continue.

"There was a bunch of us at the time. Almost thirty, I think. Thank goodness, because I was useless back then. Wouldn't have survived a day."

Min was surprised at the number of people once with Brightest, finding it difficult to ever imagine him as part of such a large group, but did not let her amazement show.

"We did what we could to survive. People died, of course. People always die. Dragon, drowning. Just people generally unsuited to surviving outside of the perfect bubble they had created for themselves back on the Spire.

"But eventually, there was a small group of us. A group of survivors. There were ten at one point, I think? That lasted for a while, but those numbers began to dwindle.

"Our leader, he was the one who decided to start exploring the other worlds. We had given up trying to get back home. Star's shadow, even then most of us weren't interested in getting back to the Spire, but they were unhappy with the Darkstar." He turned to smile at her. "In case you haven't noticed, it can be a tad perilous out here."

She smiled back. "You didn't want to go though, did you?"

Sorrow crossed Brightest's face, and he turned from her again. "No. No, I wanted to stay here when they eventually found somewhere, a world of their own. They didn't… they didn't really understand why I wanted to stay. Especially not…" More silence, as Brightest took a deep breath. "They didn't understand."

"Why did you want to stay?"

Another deep breath. "Well, you know, by that point I had met Stickle. She wasn't half the size of these fellas yet, but I knew even then she would need help surviving here, and we couldn't take her with us.

"Also," he said, turning back to Min, "I can't understand why anyone would want to leave this place. I mean, just look at it."

He gesticulated back to the starlit sea they were sailing upon. In the waters beneath, shoals of fish twinkled in the clear, dark depths that never seemed to end, instead folding up into the sky, a phenomenon that still caused Min's head to hurt when she tried to make sense of it. Above them, the Darkstar loomed in all its glory, painting the entire scene – Brightest and Min included – a vibrant purple. And up there, in the endless twilight of the sky above, was mystery, wheeling around the Darkstar in the form of colourful doors to countless worlds.

"How could anyone," Brightest continued, "live a full life in one world, when they've tasted so many, and know there are endless wonders out there to sample? Even me, even at my age, I know I have a wealth of new experiences to discover before I'm done."

As he spoke, Min soaked in the sights around her, the multitude of worlds that circled above the twilight sea. She never would have expected to see anything like this place, never in all her life. Not even when the professors at the academy were relating stories of the lands they had travelled to, far from New Windward. Certainly not as a child, when the arrival of her grandparents seemed to close so many of the doors Min had loved to walk through. In that moment, Min understood Brightest perfectly.

This place was wonderful.

"So," he said, turning back to Min, his face an equal mix of excitement and regret, "why didn't I go with them? My countrymen, my friends, my... I couldn't. I just couldn't. I'm as much a slave to the wonder and glory of this place as they are to the notion of a happy farmstead to grow old and weary in. I just don't understand why I was the only one to feel that way."

You aren't the only one, part of Min wanted to say, but she kept quiet. She could not be like Brightest, even if that choice was available to her. She had made a promise to her people, and to their families. She would get them home, even if that meant abandoning the life of adventure that Brightest had chosen.

A life that certainly appealed to Min as well.

"Any highlights?" she asked, trying to pull him out of the dark thoughts he was threatening to wallow in. "What's been the best experience you've had here? The most amazing?"

He looked wistful, smiling. "In the early days," he said, "when the others were still here, there was... Stickle was about the size of a large dog. I had built myself a canoe, and we were on the water together, scavenging. I was taking a break, daydreaming, looking up at the sky, and I saw something I've never seen since. A new rift opened, high up, close to the Darkstar. That's not completely shocking, there are new rifts opening all the time, but this one was purest white light, and I could almost swear there was music floating down from it, reaching me on the water, even though I must have been miles from it.

"And then they started to come out of the rift."

"Who?"

Brightest shook his head, smiling. "I have no idea. They never bothered to come down, didn't even look in my direction, even when I told the others later and we tried to light a beacon for them.

"They were whales, Min. Giant whales, impossibly massive creatures floating through the sky. Not flying like the dragon, but properly floating, as if they were swimming, but up there." Brightest pointed up to the Darkstar. He was getting excited now, and Min saw the memory still captivated him. "The whales, there were countless numbers of them, and they were decorated – or, I don't know, maybe they grew out of them – in countless warm glowing lights. And then, as if that was not enough, I saw the people."

Min listened to him, transfixed by the image in her mind.

"From what I could tell, there were people swarming all over those whales, each of the travellers seeming to be composed entirely of light. It took me a while to realise what was happening but it finally occurred to me – these light-people were riding upon the whales, like you or I would ride on a ship on the waves. This was their fleet, and who knows where they were travelling to?"

"What happened to them?"

"They passed on. No sooner had they started to appear than another of those white rifts opened, and the Whalefleet continued through that. It kept up all week. There must have been hundreds of them, Min, each as beautiful and as haunting as the last. I would do my chores, same as everyone else, but any spare time I got I would sit by the shore, close to Stickle, and watch the Whalefleet pass by. Eventually the last one must have gone through, because at one point I looked up and the sky was empty."

"You've never seen them again?" Min said, her voice flat, distant; she already knew the answer.

Brightest shook his head, but did not share her sadness. "No, but I've seen countless other sights that have been almost – almost – as spectacular. And that's why I have to stay here, Min. That's why the Darkstar Dimension has been my home for most of my life. How will I ever have the chance to see them again if I leave? What if the Whalefleet comes back just as soon as I decide to go away? How many other Whalefleets – or sights like it – does the Darkstar have ready to show me before my time here is done?"

Seeing the look of adoration on his face, a look that seemed oddly out of place on one so old, Min would have agreed with Brightest there and then. If not for the danger they constantly faced, if not for the crisis Min was facing with the crew of the *Narwhal* right now, she would absolutely agree with him. In fact, perhaps the constant danger was what appealed to her, was what was making this experience so intoxicating. Travelling on this world that seemed so in flux, with rifts popping in and out, with strange creatures inside ready to eat intruders.

With dragons the size of planets eclipsing the sky.

Underneath Min, the turtlemoth jerked. She looked around to see that Brightest's was doing the same, still travelling toward Stickle, but trembling under the water, the constant vibrations making life extremely uncomfortable for its rider.

"What is it?" Min asked Brightest.

His face was dark, and one glance at it made Min's heart sink.

"What do you think? Look."

Min followed Brightest's gaze upward.

She had not noticed the dragon unfurling itself from the Darkstar, presumably during Brightest's story. The country-sized beast was now wheeling in the air behind the Darkstar, stretching its wings after its rest.

"Gorya's frigid hell," Min muttered, her hands suddenly cold. "Stickle."

Brightest nodded, his own face drawn. "Or, you know, us."

Min looked at the small school of turtlemoths that had gathered around them during their trip. "Would it come for us when there's larger prey available?"

"Not sure. It doesn't always make for Stickle, even though she's an obvious target. Guess the dragon has enough sense to realise Stickle blasts at it every time. And these turtlemoths are about the right size to get the dragon's attention."

"They're tiny," Min said. "Wouldn't even be a mouthful for something like that."

Brightest shrugged. "Agreed, but it doesn't seem to stop the dragon. Anything larger than these guys, with the exception of Stickle, gets eaten eventually."

Min looked at the dragon again. "Brightest," she said, her voice low, "it's pointed at us. I think it's coming this way."

It was indeed heading in their direction. After completing a circuit of the Darkstar, the dragon had given one flap of its great wings, and, although still distant, was now gliding toward them.

The turtlemoths noticed too. Their movements had become more frenzied, panicking in the water, not bucking their riders, still making toward their goal, but with the staccato jerks of creatures on the verge of breaking.

"Might just be a coincidence," Brightest said. "Darkstar Dimension is a large place. Could have spotted anything out in this stretch of water."

Min watched the dragon getting closer, the span of its wings eclipsing the Darkstar, showing a black, bat-like silhouette framed by the purple rays of the uncanny light source behind it.

"Do you think it's a coincidence, Brightest?"

The old man swallowed.

"No," he said eventually, as the dragon continued its flight. "No, I think it's coming for us."

Min lost all sensation in her hands. She had to look down at them, to convince herself she was still gripping tight to her mount's shell.

"Could they dive? Couldn't the turtlemoths just leave us here, and dive down deep, come back for us when it's safe?"

Brightest shook his head. "Look at the size of it, Min. There isn't anywhere deep enough in the Dimension for them to hide, no caves down there to shelter in. The water isn't a deterrent for this thing, I've seen it go under countless times for its prey. If the dragon has spotted these guys, their best bet is to find some land to shelter under, or to hope something else catches the dragon's eye before it gets here."

The looming creature was now halfway between the Darkstar and the turtlemoths. Looking at the size of it, Min could not imagine a landmass large enough for her mount to hide under, or one thick enough that the Darkstar Dragon could not break it apart in order to claim its prey.

"We need to split up," Brightest said after a short while. The dragon had continued to approach, the turtlemoths were becoming more frenzied in their movements, and it was becoming increasingly apparent the dragon was heading, if not for them, for something in their general direction.

"Get away from each other. A few miles away. At least then, if it comes for one of us, the other might escape. Sticking together now pretty much guarantees death in one bite."

Min did not like the sound of splitting up, but struggled to give a good argument against the suggestion, so instead gave a resigned nod.

Brightest whispered to his turtlemoth, gave a "Yah!" of encouragement, and then his mount veered off to port, with a good number of the turtlemoth pod following. Min's mount stayed its course, with her own collection of creatures following behind.

"You know," Min said to her turtlemoth after a while, "if you all want to survive this, it might be a good idea for the whole pod here to split up. Might be only a couple get taken, instead of everyone, if the dragon does attack." Min looked behind and counted about a dozen of the turtlemoths still following her, ranging from a similar size to her current mount to those the size of a regular sea otter. Children, Min realised.

Her turtlemoth gave a hoot of understanding – clearly Stickle's intelligence was not linked to her enormous size – but the pod did not disperse. It took Min a moment to figure out why.

"They're your family, aren't they?" she asked it. Another hoot of approval.

Min understood. Without guaranteeing who would be chased if they split, the pod was choosing to stand together, instead of fragmenting and hoping only a few survived.

All, or nothing.

A bit like Min with the *Narwhal*. Min could bail out now, let the turtlemoths go on without her, wait out the next three years on her own, and eventually return to New Windward herself, assuming she could survive the Darkstar Dimension for that long. The thought, however, had never seriously crossed her mind until now, and she still did not regard it as a viable option.

If she were a turtlemoth, she would never be able to live with herself if her children were eaten while the parents survived.

Min looked at the dragon again, and felt a rush of relief. It was no longer aiming for her, instead wheeling off to port, no longer focussed on her pod.

However, its true target was just as obvious.

The Darkstar Dragon was aiming for Brightest.

Min watched in horror as the beast's maw opened. She caught a glimpse of teeth like ivory daggers, each ten times the size of the largest tower in New Windward, glinting in the purple light of the Darkstar.

She saw Brightest, then, before the dragon made impact. He was just a speck in the distance, so far away it was a struggle to properly make him out. What she first thought was a grey cloak waving in the wind was actually his mad hair and beard, billowing behind him because of the speed his turtlemoth was travelling at. Brightest was standing on his mount, his arm pointing forward. Min got the impression, from his choppy movements, that Brightest was shouting something, but she had no opportunity to catch his words, because the turbulence the dragon's descent was causing – still close enough to disturb the water and air around Min – made it sound and feel like a hurricane raging.

The dragon hit the water behind the turtlemoth pod, its jaw wide open, its belly rupturing the black depths like a cannon ball ripping through wooden hulls.

Min got the briefest glimpse of Brightest being thrown from his mount as the dragon's explosive impact shook the water like jelly.

He looked like a broken puppet, thrown through the air, arms and legs moving helplessly.

Then the dragon lunged forward in the water, jaws still open.

A few seconds later, it was airborne again, its belly a little fuller.

Min braced for the impact of the massive waves rippling out from the scene of the carnage, taking a few seconds to reach her pod.

However, as the first wave took her, throwing her from her mount and pulling her under the surface, far from the relative safety of the turtlemoth pod, Min's mind could focus on only one thing.

Brightest was gone.

She was alone.

Twenty-first year of solitude, day eighty-eight

I can't figure out the point of that damned dragon.

The rest of this place, in its weird way, makes sense to me.

The Darkstar exists, right? It's hungry, it pulls stuff to it through the rifts, to sort of feed it, I guess. Certainly seems to guzzle magic like nobody's business. And people like me end up here, as a result of the Darkstar punching holes in different worlds.

Most of the other stuff in here, it looks like it's been pulled in at some point or other.

But the dragon?

I can't figure it out.

I mean, it seems to be linked to the Darkstar somehow, right? I've never been that high up, but I'm pretty confident I'd be burned to a crisp before getting anywhere near touching distance of the star, so something must be going on with the dragon to let it survive the experience.

Maybe that's just a dragon thing? Even back on the Spire, we had stories of dragons.

Wouldn't be a total shock to me if dragons were real somewhere, and one got pulled through a rift and managed to survive in here.

I mean, that's what I've done, right?

But that doesn't ring true to me. If the dragon was living on a rock or an island here, then yeah, that would work. But something almost the same size as the Darkstar, something that lives wrapped around it?

And that doesn't even explain what the creature feeds on. There just aren't enough living things on the Darkstar Sea to sustain a monster that size. Even if the dragon got to snack on half a dozen turtlemoths the size of Stickle every day, there's no way that would be enough to fill its belly. Since it doesn't have that source of food anyway, how does the dragon stay alive?

Again, that must have something to do with the Darkstar. It feeds from it, somehow? Maybe all the magic-draining going on has something to do with keeping the dragon fed?

There must be more going on here, but I'll be damned if I'm ever going to be able to figure this out.

Clara joked once that the Darkstar was just a massive egg, and someday it was going to hatch.

That doesn't work for me either, but…

I'll figure it out. Eventually.

THIRTEEN

Pulled under the water, distracted by the loss of her only companion, a lesser person would have given in to despair. Min certainly felt its familiar fingers, clutching at her chest, threatening to rise to her throat, regaining the grip they so recently had after the mutiny.

Min, however, would not give in to those emotions again. She was the best of the academy's graduates. She had saved the lives of at least two of the crews she had apprenticed with, and had gained the respect of many of her mentors. She had survived everything the Darkstar Dimension had thrown at her in her short time here, and she would be damned if one dragon would be any different.

Aware that she was becoming familiar with the experience of being pulled under the waters of this place, Min found the purple light of the Darkstar and began to kick up, the light from above vibrating wildly as the commotion caused by the dragon still raged, the disturbance also affecting the currents under the waters, buffeting Min every which way as she strained to reach the surface, and fresh air.

Fortunately, the turtlemoths found it much easier to control themselves in these difficult conditions, and they proved to be considerably more loyal than Min's crew members. The turtlemoth that Min had been riding on for the last hour drew up alongside her, inviting her to grab onto its shell. Then the creature surged up, allowing Min to gasp in some much-needed breaths.

Her first instinct was to look for the dragon. It was moving away from them, but Min could see the creature was wheeling in the air, not flying in a direct line away.

It could very well be planning on returning. Very unlikely a small pod of turtlemoths could provide a satisfying mouthful for a creature like that, and certainly nowhere near a meal.

Still, if the dragon was going to come back for them, there was nothing Min nor the other turtlemoths could do. But she could at least do some good, in the hope that the dragon was finished with them, for now.

"Head over there," Min said to her turtlemoth, pointing at the area the dragon had descended upon, speaking to her mount with the authority she would normally use for giving instructions to one of her seamen. "There may be survivors. They'll need our help."

She could not see how anything might have survived that descent, but she had also known Brightest long enough to not put anything past him.

Min had experience sailing into waters just after battle. During her time on the *Stalwart Colossus*, before they had broken the blockade Pirate Lord Moran had established along the Goryeoan Strait, twice they had arrived less than twenty minutes after an attack upon New Windward vessels. Arriving too late, the waters had been filled with barrels and planks, the last remnants of scuttled ships, and also people; often dead, but sometimes survivors.

Here, the dragon had left nothing. There was no sign of any of the turtlemoths, not even any evidence of underwater scavengers drawn toward where blood mingled with water. The dragon had descended upon this place, and appeared to have left nothing.

Not twenty feet away, something broke above the water's surface, gasping.

It was Brightest.

"How?" Min asked the spluttering man as she pulled him onto her mount's shell, both in awe and overjoyed at the man's survival. "How could you possibly…?"

"It bucked me," he said, continuing to fight for air, showing his age now more than he ever had before. "My turtlemoth, at the last moment, when we were in the dragon's mouth, it flipped over and threw me out."

Min's own mount, as if in response to Brightest's tale, gave a few small hoots, considerably higher pitched than those Min had grown accustomed to hearing from Stickle.

She patted the creature's shell in response, hoping her touch would console it.

"The dragon," Brightest said, still sprawled out flat on the turtlemoth's back, "it isn't coming for us anymore."

Min looked up to the sky, elated. The creature – which had been moving back in their direction – was wheeling away, having spotted something else of interest close by.

Min's heart fell, however, when she saw the dragon's new target. Brightest clearly spotted it too, as he gave out a low moan from beside her.

"Stickle," he said. "It's seen Stickle."

Sure enough, the island that was Stickle was now in view, perhaps another twenty minutes' travel from where they were, but considerably less time for the dragon.

They had managed to travel all the way over the sea, just in time to see their friends and crew eaten.

"Go!" Min shouted, falling onto her knees on the turtlemoth's back, the rocking sensation of that action seeming to jolt the creature to life, spurring it forward. Min knew the fight would be over in seconds, but she had to do something. She had saved Brightest's life by not giving up. Perhaps she could do something similar for some of her crew as well.

However, it seemed the *Melodious Narwhal* was not as helpless as she had thought.

They saw the dragon lurch in the air before they heard the crack of thunder that had dealt the blow to it.

"What was that?" Brightest said, just as Min spotted a flash of green fire coming from the side of the *Narwhal*.

The dragon flinched again, interrupting its descent, just as the sound of the explosion reached Min's ears.

"The cannons," Min said, awestruck. "They've got the cannons working again."

A third volley sounded, and this time brought further success – the dragon wheeled away, losing interest in its difficult target.

Brightest gave a whoop of victory. Then he noticed the shock on Min's face. "Why should I not be as happy about this? What am I not seeing?"

"The cannons," Min said, "they shouldn't be working. If they've gotten the guns working, that means they've found a way to power the core."

Brightest's smile disappeared. "The Eshak piece."

Min nodded, at the same time noticing the Darkstar Dragon

was not making a line back for its home. Instead, the creature was circling high above Stickle, as if considering this creature that so consistently thwarted it.

"They've figured out how to harness the Eshak," Min confirmed. "If the repairs are finished – and they weren't far off from getting that sorted under my command – then there's nothing to stop them from taking off."

"They're all as good as dead, then," Brightest said.

Min shook her head. "No, they're not," she said, "not now that we're here."

She patted the turtlemoth's shell as the creature bore them on, toward their goal.

∞

When they got close enough that Min was concerned lookouts might spot them, she and Brightest submerged, hanging on to the back of their mount's shell, only popping their heads up now and again to get a breath of air. Unlike most of the other denizens of the Darkstar Sea, the turtlemoths did not give off any light of their own, so Min reckoned they would not attract much attention. Even if they did, the lookouts would just report the unusual creatures, and not much should be made of it.

They were borne to the *Narwhal* with no events. Min was impressed to see that the ship had been pushed back into the water, and seemed to be coping with the experience well enough, although it still listed slightly on the starboard side.

Ballast probably shifted during all that time on the beach, she thought. *Surely someone's thought to check that by now?*

It would not make much of a difference when the *Narwhal* was airborne, but her officers should know better than to overlook a detail like that, especially Holtz.

"We head for the belly," Min said. "Get Stickle's Eshak piece before anyone knows we're here."

Brightest nodded. "Should be easy enough, if Zoya and Abalendu are elsewhere – don't think you have anyone else too tricky on your crew? I can get the piece back for Stickle to Bond to it quick enough, but that won't do us any good if they just decide to take it again. I can probably come up with some tricks to deal with Zoya if I get enough time in my trove, but I don't have anything that can sort the entire crew. What are we going to do about the fact that everyone else has turned on you?"

This was the question that had been worrying Min ever since they came back from the goat-ant world.

"We need to find Jedda first," she said. "I'll bet my arse she's in the belly, mostly because the Eshak piece is there too. I want to know what Abalendu's got on her, what exactly he said to get her – and all the others – to turn." She chewed her lip, thinking. "Got to look for Holtz, too. Didn't notice him, or a lot of his watch, when everyone turned against us. Life will be considerably easier if there are some more people on our side. Then I'll tell the crew the truth: if they listen to Abalendu, they're going to end up as dragon food. Can't really afford to avoid a warning like that, can you?"

Reaching up to the *Narwhal's* hull, Min put her hand onto the polished wood, and let a warm sense of comfort flow over her

"You sure you're up for this?" she said to Brightest, eying the closest porthole above them, a good thirty feet up. It would be tough enough for her – a sheer climb, with few decent hand and footholds – but Brightest was about three times her age.

He grinned, reaching into his pocket and pulling out a twine container of gelatinous sludge that he spread over his palms. As he did so, the substance hardened, forming finger-length spikes on each palm.

"Want some?" he asked, throwing the container to Min. "The people who gave it to me used it as a weapon, threw it at their enemies." He raised an eyebrow, looking at the spikes on his fingers. "I prefer my use."

"What are you planning on doing to my ship?" Min asked, her voice cold, eying Brightest's hands with suspicion.

"Not your ship anymore," he said, pressing his palms to the *Narwhal's* side, where the spikes embedded into the wood with a crunch that set Min's teeth on edge.

She pocketed the container, preferring to take her chances with falling to the water than damage the *Narwhal* any further.

"Time we went about changing that."

They made it up to the porthole with no interruptions, although Brightest's every movement with those dreadful spikes made Min fret about the carpentry that was going to be required to repair the damage he was doing.

The porthole led to a small storage room not far from the belly. Min wriggled through the hole with little effort, her diminutive size playing in her favour for once.

It quickly became apparent that Brightest was not going to have the same level of success.

"I could make it a bit bigger," he said, considering the porthole while hanging by his left arm. Despite the climb, he did not seem to be finding the strain particularly difficult to cope with. "Got a jar of ceramic termites somewhere. If they're still alive, I reckon they could make short work of the wood—"

"You are not eating my ship," Min said, her voice flat.

"It wouldn't be me. It would be the termites."

Min continued to stare at him, deadpan.

"I'd rebuild it later, obviously. I'm sure I know a world with wood that would match this perfectly."

"No," Min said, the finality in her voice confirming that this conversation would not continue. "We'll have to change plan. Do you reckon you could reach the deck from here?"

Brightest looked up and sighed.

"You're asking a lot, you know. I'm an old man."

"I'd noticed. Can you make it?"

"I can," he said, adding under his breath, "but I don't see the problem with the termites. Didn't have an issue with making a Flagonknight rip a hole in the wall of my home for you, did I?"

"I'll meet you on top with the Eshak piece. Just keep out of sight."

Brightest nodded, and was about to recommence his climbing when Min thought of something else.

"Erm, it's okay to touch it, right? The Eshak piece? It's not going to burn me, or turn me into a squirrel or something?"

"Probably not," Brightest said, as his face disappeared from the porthole, "but there's always a first time."

Only partially reassured, Min crept out of the room and along the corridors she knew would bring her to the belly. Above, noises betrayed movement on the main deck, but Min was thankful there was no activity down on her level.

Upon entering the belly, the first thing Min noticed was the core crystal itself. It was lying on its side in the corner of the room, freed from all supports that had bound it to the *Narwhal's* systems, drained, disused and unwanted.

Back in Min's homeland – not New Windward, but Goryeoa, where her mother and father had travelled from – in her great-grandfather's time, island states went to war over items like the *Narwhal's* core. Funny how quickly it had been discarded in this new world.

Instead, in the middle of the room, floating above the pipes that had originally been attached to the core, was the golden Eshak piece.

Min was instantly wary. There was no way something of that importance would be left unguarded, and certainly not for very long. She probably only had a small window of opportunity to grab it and get out of here before she was discovered.

She listened for noises that would give away the inevitable guards. The corridor back up through the decks was noisy, but that was movement from the crew outside, presumably getting ready to set sail now the *Narwhal* was powered again.

Min heard nothing nearby, until the sniffing began, a sound that punctuated the silence of the belly, prompting Min to hold her breath.

Not certain where the noise was coming from, Min crept into the room.

It was Jedda. The artificer was sitting on the floor behind the core mount, her knees pulled up to her chest, her eyes red, goggles on the floor beside her.

Jedda's head whipped around as Min came into view, and the artificer stared at her for a moment, mouth wide, apparently not comprehending what she was seeing. Jedda lurched forward, and it looked as if she was about to reach out for Min, a look of relief on her face. Then, rethinking her actions a split second later, Jedda recoiled, throwing herself back to the floor, scrambling away from the first officer, covering her eyes with her arm and giving out a low moan.

Deeply uncomfortable with Jedda's reaction, and even more mindful of the noise her former friend was making, Min dived forward to put her hand over Jedda's mouth.

Jedda struggled, giving out a wail before Min could clasp her hand properly onto the girl's face, and the artificer seemed to still be trying to avoid looking at Min. Then, presumably when she realised she was not going to win the struggle, Jedda's head snapped into position, her eyes wide and fearful, rooted on Min, the artificer's nostrils flaring with each breath she took through them. She fixed Min with the same gaze Min fancied a condemned man would look upon an executioner with.

"Jedda," Min said, speaking quickly and softly, trying to communicate equal parts haste and compassion, "I can't let you make any noise. Don't want them to hear." She stopped for a second, to give Jedda time to register what she was saying. "I'm not going to hurt you, Jedda." Another pause, and Jedda still did not respond. "I'm not going to hurt you, okay?"

Her eyes not changing, Jedda nodded once, and Min could feel the panic in the girl's movement.

"I'm going to take my hand away, but you can't make any noise. Understand?"

Jedda nodded, eyes still locked on Min's.

Sending a rare prayer to Frathuda, god of enemies – and to Jedda's ancestor gods for good measure – Min removed her hand.

Jedda started to cry.

"Oh, Min," Jedda said, through tortured gasps, "I'm sorry. I'm so sorry."

Then Jedda reached out for Min, her face red and contorted, mouth pulled back in a grieving grimace, nose running, hands clutching Min's jacket in desperation. Jedda pulled her face into Min's shoulder and started to bawl, reminding Min every bit of her six-year-old cousin breaking her arm when falling from the New Windward rooftops.

"By the hells, Jedda, it's all right," Min said, at first unsure of what to do with her hands, completely thrown by this grown woman acting like a small child. She held Jedda tightly, feeling the artificer shake in her grasp. "It's okay, Jedda," she said, softer this time, allowing her sincerity to bleed into her voice, almost causing it to break.

Despite the need for haste, Min held Jedda, allowing the artificer to cry, both so that Jedda could calm down, but also to stop herself from joining in. That would be far too unprofessional. She was, however, glad Brightest was not here. Min found herself overwhelmingly embarrassed at Jedda's reaction, and at how it made her feel.

She was the one who had been framed. She was the one who had been chucked into another dimension. How was it fair that Min ended up being the one who felt guilty?

After a while, Jedda pulled herself back from Min, sniffing, rubbing her face, looking away from the first officer.

"Jedda, I'm not angry at you," Min said, returning to the task at hand, "but I need to know: what happened? What did they say to get you to lie about me?"

Jedda, still not looking, began to speak haltingly, as if she did not trust herself to talk properly. "Abalendu," she began, kicking off her admittance with the exact name Min had expected.

Min missed the next few words Jedda spoke. A wave of anger rushed over her at the mention of the scholar, its roaring filling her ears and her eyes. Min saw the mess fragile Jedda was now in, and knew exactly whose feet to lay that shame at.

I'll kill that bastard.

Min must have let some of her thoughts show on her face, because Jedda recoiled from Min when she glanced at her.

"It's not you," Min said, reaching out a hand to grab the artificer before she lost her again. "It's him. I just got mad when I thought about him, sorry. Try again – what did he say?"

"He told us all you were working against us, that you didn't care about us anymore. I didn't believe him, of course, but some of the others did, and when you shouted at them at the end of the first day, a bunch of them decided that was proof Abalendu was telling the truth. That you weren't looking out for their best interests anymore. That you were more interested in hanging out with Brightest, and in mucking around in this new place.

"I should have stuck with my first thoughts, but the others kept badgering me about the core, and about this Eshak piece, and you know how much I like my games, and nobody ever really wants to talk to me about that stuff, and how often does gaming and artificing come together like this? I mean, I couldn't not chat with them, and they got me thinking..."

Jedda took a deep breath, shuddering as she did so.

"When you went away on those rays, that's when Abalendu came to me, along with a big bunch of the others. You know I'm not good at stuff like this, Min. I hadn't thought there was a big problem, but I reckoned if so many other people had spotted the problem, maybe I had just missed it. Maybe it was important that I got my hands on the gold Eshak. And, you know, Min, I did want to touch it, just to see what it felt like..."

"I know, Jedda, I know. But Jedda, I've not chosen Brightest over the crew. I've not chosen him over you. That's not what it's about. What Abalendu wants to do, what he's made everyone do... it's everything we stand against, Jedda. Everything New Windward shouldn't be. We were formed to stop the pirates, to work together against those who want to take from others for their own gain.

"We're supposed to be better than that. We have to be, to show the world – our world – that people can be better."

Jedda nodded, detached herself from Min, and stood. "Can we still fix this?"

"Yes, Jedda, but we need to be quick. The dragon is abroad, and Stickle doesn't have long."

Jedda rubbed at her eyes, stooped to pick up her goggles, and fitted them back onto her head, nestled among her black curls. Then she looked at Min, her eyes still red, but determined.

"What can I do?"

Forty-third year of solitude, day three hundred

Another world of water.

Damn, but I'm sick of water worlds.

Tend to have decent food in them, I guess, but fish take effort to catch, and I already have to put a good bit of work into getting to the rifts in the first place.

Once, I walked through a rift straight onto farmland ready to be harvested. Why can't there be more farming worlds out there?

After realising I was in yet another world of endless ocean, I was about to turn around and head back through the rift when some of the locals approached me. They actually looked pretty similar to my people, but they'd never heard of the Spire before.

Said the place was called 'Jigu'; turns out there are plenty of islands for people to live on in this world, the rift just didn't take me near to any of them.

I wonder how many other worlds out there I've written off, just because the rift happened to open up on a particularly boring part of it?

These locals, they claim the place really is mainly water, and everyone lives on the islands dotted around it. Doesn't sound too dissimilar to life on the Darkstar, really. Except, you know, without the variety and adventure my life has to offer. Yes, and without most of the constant death I have to deal with as well (although apparently there are some major pirate issues these folk have to put up with).

After a quick chat, I jumped back through the rift as fast as I could, leaving those poor saps sail off to whichever shore they were headed toward.

I don't know how anyone could stand a life like that; bland and predictable.

FOURTEEN

Minutes later, the two of them made it to the *Narwhal*'s deck. There was only a light sentry between the belly and the deck, two ordinary seamen, and Jedda got rid of them by requesting some more parts from Brightest's Mudhut. After betraying Min, she had everyone's trust, and with Min and Brightest gone the greatest threat to Abalendu's plan was Stickle, and the gargantuan turtlemoth could do little to affect the small creatures that ran about her shell.

They found Brightest close to the deckhouse, comforting one of the Darkstar rays that had been captured and bound to the deck, presumably for some of Abalendu's experiments later.

"You have it?" Brightest said, seeing the two approach. His urgency had grown again, especially with the dragon's increased activity above. It had remained circling Stickle, but had not attempted to attack her, yet.

Guilt plain on her face, Jedda reached into her pocket and pulled out the golden Eshak. "I'm sorry," she whispered softly.

The barrels Brightest was sheltering behind exploded as a figure leapt into them, throwing Jedda – and the Eshak piece – to the side.

"I'm not," Zoya said, glaring at Min.

Min went cold; this was the last person she wanted to tangle with.

"Zoya," she said, not wanting to give the warrior a chance to grab the Eshak piece on the deck nearby. "Zoya, this is madness, you've got to stop. You of all people should be better than this. You can see what's waiting for Stickle," she said, indicating the dragon above. "Surely your honour won't stand for letting something like that happen?"

Zoya spat. "The life of an animal, in place of seeing my children again? I do not think so."

"Stickle is more than that, and you know it," Min said, wishing for all her life that she had not traded her sabre away to the floating shop, for all the good the weapon would do her against the Parasite Glove. "And what about Brightest? Is it worth it to steal from him, just to get back home?"

"For my husband and my family?" Zoya said, raising her fist. "Yes. A thousand times, yes."

Zoya's fist hit the deck. The planks Min was standing on shattered, throwing her and Jedda to the now-fractured ground. Jedda gave a cry as she slipped through the gaps in the once-proud *Narwhal*'s deck. Min was fortunate enough to be thrown clear, but did not avoid all harm – her face was peppered with cuts from where splintered wood had torn into it, and one particularly nasty shard was now protruding from her right thigh.

Looking around, Min first sought the Eshak piece, worried it might have been thrown overboard in the commotion. It would do nobody any good if that disappeared – Stickle needed it just as much as Abalendu thought he did.

She saw the gaming piece rolling along the deck, stopping at a pair of barrels strapped to the portside railing. However, in that moment, Min noticed two more things that made her heart stick in her throat.

First, she saw the dragon – as if sensing the commotion below it – wheeling around once more, directing itself toward Stickle, giving out an almighty roar as it plunged back at them.

Foremost of concern, however, was Zoya.

She had Brightest, was holding him upright, her Parasite Glove wrapped around his neck.

She had murder in her eyes.

"Brightest," Min shouted, hoping Jedda was okay, wherever she had fallen to below. Min tried to move toward the old man, but the shard of wood sent a bolt of pain up her leg, causing her to collapse to the ground.

Brightest grunted, his jaw clenched, eyes locked on Zoya's. "You aren't so tough," he said, his voice distorted under the strain of the warrior's grip.

Min pulled herself across the broken deck, reaching for Brightest.

Above her, from the quarterdeck, a familiar voice sounded, and Min felt the hairs on the back of her neck stiffen in revulsion.

"Coming in at three o'clock," Abalendu's voice echoed across the *Narwhal*. "Give her another taste of it."

The *Narwhal*'s cannons groaned, but did not fire. Abalendu's head peeked over the quarterdeck railings.

"Zoya," he barked, paying little attention to the rest of the combatants below.

Min, fighting against the pain in her leg, managed to make it all the way to the Kisiwian's foot. Instead of trying anything against Zoya – Min knew she had no chance of making the slightest bit of difference to the warrior – Min reached out a hand and grabbed Brightest's.

"Zoya," Abalendu barked again. Behind him, the dragon loomed, making straight for them, getting larger as it approached. "Get the Eshak piece down into the belly now, or we're all about to become dragon food."

"No," Min gasped as Zoya raised Brightest high, pulling him out of Min's reach.

"You were brave," Zoya said to Brightest, before tossing him over the side.

The old man's limbs tumbled like those of a rag doll before he hit the water's surface.

Zoya ignored Min; instead, she picked up the golden Eshak piece and went below, making her way to the belly. A number of seamen moved forward, grabbing Min's arms and hauling her to her feet, ignoring her cries as the wooden shard cut further into her thigh.

As Min was half-led, half-pulled up the quarterdeck steps, Zoya must have remounted the Eshak piece, as the ship's cannons fired, forcing the dragon to once again roar and wheel away, unsure of this new threat.

How long would it be, Min wondered, before the dragon realised that nothing worse was coming? That the *Narwhal* was just sitting around, waiting to be eaten?

Abalendu must have been thinking along the same lines.

"If we're all back on board," he said, issuing orders to those around him, "I can't see any reason not to just take off. Let the dragon have her food, and we can get a head start on things."

"You can't do that!" Min shouted. Abalendu looked at her properly for the first time since her return.

"Oh, hello, First Officer," he said, self-satisfaction oozing from his grin. "Welcome aboard the *Melodious Narwhal*."

"You bastard," she said. She noticed that her disapproval was echoed in the faces of some of the seamen around her.

"Abalendu, you've got to stop this. You're putting the lives of everyone on the *Narwhal* in danger. Brightest says the dragon won't let you up to the rift now; it's too close to its home. As soon as you sail the *Narwhal* anywhere near to the Darkstar, the dragon will attack. Everyone will die, Abalendu."

The scholar did not appear to hear Min, but she could see a few more of the crew paying attention.

"How convenient, First Officer," Abalendu said, inspecting his fingernails. "A key piece of information has just happened to come to light that supports your point of view? Odd that nobody mentioned this before, isn't it? One might even claim it is suspicious, that maybe you're just making up facts to try to regain command of this ship."

"Just like you made up facts to take command in the first place?" Min spat back, unable to help herself, lunging forward against the grip of the crew holding her. "You told everyone I didn't care about getting home, that I have other priorities. That just isn't true."

"Yeah it is," Sung said, walking forward. "Yeah it is. We heard you. We all heard you. When Master Seekwalla here first brought up the idea of using the game piece. You said it didn't belong to us, that it wasn't an option. Well, clearly you were wrong, right? It is an option, and it's working. We've just fired on the dragon using that magic, and we're going to fly home now too."

Abalendu clapped Sung on the shoulder. "Well said, First Mate, well said. Remind me to talk to my father about a promotion for you when we get back to dry land."

Min barked out a mocking laugh. "You're joking, aren't you? Promotion? Your father will be ashamed of you, Abalendu, ashamed of everyone here. Mutinying against your commander? Stealing from the natives, forever sullying the name of New Windward in this place? Basically, acting like the pirates we were formed to put a stop to? You won't get a promotion, Sung. Once the admiralty hears about what you've all done here, you're going to be locked away for life. You'll certainly never sail under a New Windward flag again."

"Careful, First Officer," Abalendu said, now looking directly at her, a sly grin crossing his face. "Careful. Keep talking like that, you might make some of us think it would be better if you didn't make it back."

Beside Abalendu, Sung grinned at the suggestion, but Min caught Ole and apprentice officer Nalla – who had already been paling during the conversation – start, their eyes wide, looking at Abalendu in shock.

You smug bastard, you just did it. You just made the mistake that's going to lose you the Narwhal.

"I'd say your father would be ashamed if he saw you now, Abalendu Seekwalla," Min said, standing tall, facing off against her opponent with dignity, "but I think we both know he already is."

That last remark seemed to hit a nerve. Abalendu's face fell, the smug facade revealing someone bitter and cruel underneath.

"Yes, well," he said, reaching up to pet the dragontoad that was slumbering on his shoulder, "that wouldn't be hard, would it? He's been disappointed with me all his life." Coming out of his internal reverie, Abalendu looked around at the assembled seamen, and at the dragon circling above.

"Time to cast off, men," he said, turning his back on Min. "Let the dragon have her fare – we've got a rift back home to catch."

To Min's dismay, the crew jumped to follow Abalendu's orders.

"And," Abalendu said, turning to look at Min one last time, "will someone do me the favour of dealing with our former commander? We wouldn't want her telling tales to Daddy when we get back, would we?"

Sung pulled out the knife at her belt. However, behind Sung, Ole and Nalla stepped forward; not coordinated, but both fuelled by the same instinct.

It was Ole who spoke first. "You're not serious? We can't do that. We can do a lot of things to get home, but we're not going to murder anyone, especially not the first officer."

Abalendu tutted. "You're not going to murder the first officer, no. Sung is. Be a good sailor; go find a bell to polish or something. Sung, deal with her quickly, yes? We don't want any queasy stomachs upsetting this expedition."

Sung stepped up to Min, but the first mate seemed uneasy now, as if mindful of the unrest in the men behind her.

"Sung?" Nalla said, prompting the first mate to turn around to look at her apprentice. "You're not serious, are you?"

"Don't be an idiot. It'll be over for us if she talks when we get home. You want to get back now, or do you want to wait three more years? This is part of the price, and I'm happy to pay it for all of us."

Ole and Nalla looked at each other.

"Is there still a choice?" Ole asked.

"What?"

"Go home now, or in three years – is that still a choice?"

"Yeah," Nalla added, "because if this is part of the price, then we aren't willing to pay it. Reckon a lot of the lads will agree."

It was Abalendu who spoke before Sung had the chance to.

"What did you say?" His voice was low and threatening, reminding Min of a cat's soft growl before pouncing.

Ole looked nervous, and stepped back a bit. Nearby, other seamen – Chun-Hwa and Jeet – cocked their heads, becoming aware of the exchange.

Oh, it's all falling apart now, Abalendu.

"Look, maybe this was a mistake," Jeet said, stepping forward.

That's right, Min thought. *A bit late, but you've got guts. I like you.*

"I don't like you, Jeet," Abalendu said, raising his chin at his countryman. "I've not really known you for long, but I've just decided I don't like you. Isn't that sad?" While speaking, Abalendu reached a hand up to his dragontoad. This time, instead of stroking the Bonded creature, Abalendu flicked the dragontoad's face with his index finger. The beast awoke at once, hiccupping, letting a small, dense green bubble out of its mouth as it did so. The way the sphere floated to the *Narwhal*'s deck and sizzled when it touched the wood reminded Min of the pink bubbles she had seen in the first rift Brightest had taken her through.

Jeet looked nervous. Nearby, more crew stopped what they were doing, straining their necks to see what was going on.

"Time to get back to work," Abalendu said, "before some of us have to say or do something that others might regret."

"Are you threatening her?" Min asked, deciding it was time for the first officer to step out of the shadows. "It's just, it feels an awful lot like you're threatening her."

There was a murmur of agreement from the gathering deckhands. Min felt powerful, now.

"I mean, she was just objecting to you ordering my murder.

That seems like something she should be able to speak out against, right? But nobody's ever been threatened like that on board the *Narwhal*, have they?"

"Certainly never when you were in charge, First Officer," Sefu said, breaking protocol by coming halfway up the quarterdeck steps to get a better look at what was going on.

Sefu, I could kiss you, Min thought. *I'll arrest you for mutiny straight afterward, of course, but I'll not forget what you just said.*

"I want to make something clear," Abalendu said, turning to look straight at Sefu, his dragontoad now alert. "I am threatening you."

Tension hung in the air between the two of them like a storm cloud approaching a coastline. Just when Min thought Sefu was going to back down, Trude – who had previously been holding on to Min's right arm – jumped forward, the wooden mallet that hung from her belt finding its way into her hand as she brandished it like Min would handle her sabre.

"You don't get to do that," the Icewoman said to Abalendu. "You don't get to threaten one of the crew like that. That's not how you run a ship, right guys?"

Abalendu said nothing, but instead pointed at Trude and clicked his fingers. Bile rose in Min's throat as the dragontoad shuddered, and a green mist spewed from the palm of Abalendu's hand.

No longer fully restrained, Min shrugged her other arm free and dove for Trude's legs. The Icewoman hit the deck with her face, but the acrid cloud – who knew exactly what it would do on contact? – dissipated after passing through the space the seaman had occupied.

"Sneaky bitch," Abalendu hissed, stepping forward to kick Min. "You are so certain you want to send these brave people to their deaths?"

The kick had no real power behind it. What Min was worried about were those Bonded powers, and how far Abalendu was willing to go with them. She assumed that green cloud was poisonous, but she had also seen the dragontoad do much worse than incapacitate, remembering how the Flagonknight had melted away at the touch of those green bubbles.

"Father always said I wasn't much of a fighter," Abalendu said, squaring up to Min, who was pulling herself to her feet. Around them, especially below on the main deck, her crew gathered, weapons at the ready but standing back, waiting to see what would happen next.

Waiting to see who would win, Min knew. They were on the knife edge now, the crew, so close to tipping back to her. Victory here would seal that.

Above, the dragon screamed, and dove again for Stickle.

"No!" Min shouted, and Abalendu used that lapse in her concentration.

This time the attack came from the dragontoad itself, not from Abalendu; the creature spat at her, its spit made from the same viscous green liquid as the bubbles it created.

The projectile, however, was intercepted by Sefu, throwing himself in the path of the spit, taking the green liquid in his face and neck.

Sefu screamed, rolling on the ground, clutching his wound. Min was sickened by the smell of burning flesh, and the hissing steam that arose from the wounded Kisiwian, now being tended to by his crew mates.

Resolute, Min faced Abalendu again, not for the first time missing her sabre. Abalendu, for his part, had gone paler, was withdrawn, somehow.

"There you go," he said, eyes darting around. "Look what you've done. If you had just stayed where I wanted you, that man would still have a face. Stand down now, and nobody else will get hurt."

"Somebody else will get hurt, Abalendu," Min said, standing tall, feeling the eyes of the crew on her, their attention bolstering her resolve. "I guarantee it."

Even though she was aware of how Abalendu had taken advantage of her distraction last time, Min still could not help but look when the Darkstar Dragon finally reached Stickle. Luckily for Min, Abalendu was captivated by the sight too.

The Darkstar Dragon approached the massive turtlemoth tentatively, having just been fired upon by the strange craft berthed on her, and having endured decades of rebuffs during previous attempts on this ever-growing morsel. However, Stickle did not respond to the dragon's approach, other than lifting her head and giving a forlorn hoot.

The dragon reached out one of its great claws – it needed only one, despite Stickle's massive bulk – and latched onto Stickle's shell.

"There you go," Abalendu said. Stickle's hoots became more frantic as the dragon began to beat its wings harder, getting ready to lift this island-creature back to its lair, to feast. "Time to say goodbye to your new friends. I guess that Brightest fellow decided not to stick around for the final showdown."

"No," Min said, reaching into her jacket and pulling forth what looked like a small sphere of twine, "he didn't stick around. Didn't think he'd be able to, to be honest. Lucky for me, he did lend me some of his tricks."

Abalendu frowned, pointed at Min, and clicked his fingers. At the moment the dragontoad opened its mouth to gob at Min, she threw Brightest's climbing goo at the Bondmate's mouth.

The glue bomb did not quite make contact with the dragontoad before the creature let forth its projectile, but Min's aim was true. Instead of hitting Min's face, the dragontoad's spit impacted the glue bomb directly in front of the pathetic creature, causing the glue to explode in a mess of sticky greenness.

The dragontoad pitched from Abalendu's shoulder, its entire head coated with an unholy combination of its own spit and the contents of the glue bomb.

The creature did not scream; it could not, as its entire face was coated with the sticky, burning substance. Instead, it writhed on the deck, strange muffled noises coming from within it. It was easily the most energetic Min had ever seen the dragontoad.

Panicked, Abalendu reached down to his Bondmate to pull the substance off its face, but withdrew his hand with a hiss when the acid started to burn his fingers.

Min looked on guiltily as the dragontoad struggled. It was a relief when Abalendu clutched his temples, screaming with pain as the dragontoad died, severing his Bond with it.

Min stood over him amid a smattering of cheers from the many spectators, agonisingly aware of Stickle's frantic hoots and the fact that the *Narwhal* was still moving away from the turtlemoth. The dragon's wings were beating hard now, each movement making the *Narwhal* rock precariously, the gargantuan creature roaring in triumph. If it normally snacked on turtlemoths the size of the ones Min and Brightest had ridden, what a feast it must think it now held in its grip.

"Okay, men," Min said to the crew on the deck below her, looking expectantly up. She realised Sung was one of those faces, lost in a sea of hope. "Time to turn our ship around and—"

Zoya leapt over the edge of the quarterdeck railing and punched Min in the gut.

It was a blow with her non-gloved hand, and Min was certain the warrior had not hit her with full force, but the pain Min experienced from the attack rivalled the agony of travelling through the Darkstar rifts. It was such that Min lost some time – possibly only seconds – but when the darkness broke, Min found herself lying in a heap among some cracked barrels; barrels broken, Min dully realised, by her own impact with them. Her insides were red and sharp, and Min was convinced something was very wrong in there.

Zoya stood a short distance away, helping Abalendu to his feet. It looked to Min like Abalendu had been crying, and despite her hatred for the man, she did not feel good about that.

Beneath them, out of sight, she could hear Stickle's panicked shouts.

"Break her," Abalendu said to Zoya, glaring at Min with all the hatred of a four-year-old told it was already past his bedtime. "She killed my Bondmate. Break her."

And with a stamp of her heel, Zoya did.

Despite herself, Min screamed when her leg snapped. Another first for her, breaking a bone, which was unusual with all the action she had seen in her young life.

Seemingly satisfied with Min's punishment for now, Abalendu turned to address the crew, many of whom now looked at him with an impotent mix of contempt and fear.

"You good-for-nothing lot," Abalendu began, employing all of his charm. "Not only are you filthy traitors, you're traitors who turned too late. You can't go back now, can you?" he said, indicating the *Narwhal's* port side.

There, to her horror, Min realised she could see Stickle. In the scale of things, Stickle was reduced to a goldfish caught in an albatross' claws, such was the girth of the dragon in comparison, and Stickle had now been lifted high into the twinkling twilight of the Darkstar sky. Underneath, three pairs of flippers flapped impotently as Stickle's head flopped left and right, hooting all the while for some sort of miracle.

"You've nowhere else to go now but home, which is good, as that's exactly where you – where we – all belong," Abalendu said, addressing the men again. "So stop your lollygagging, fire up the belly, and get us aloft."

After a brief hesitation, the crew did indeed get to work. In short order the crystal array that decorated the ship's hull hummed, and for the first time in over a week the *Narwhal* took to the sky.

Min's leg ached. She tried to move it, to turn her ankle, wiggle her toes, and found she could not. Abalendu glanced at her briefly, then looked away, directing more of the men to work the rigging. Some of the crew looked broken, ashamed. Min remembered reclaiming a vessel under control of a pirate lord, upon which New Windward men and women had been forced into piracy, given the choice of working for their captors or death. The looks on their faces, of those resigned to debase themselves, was mirrored on the crew of the *Narwhal* now.

With Sung at the helm, the *Narwhal* angled itself toward the Darkstar, quickly overtaking the dragon, which was moving considerably slower with the turtlemoth in its grip. Squinting, Min could just make out the blue-green New Windward rift, dancing so close to the Darkstar now. Was Brightest right? Would the dragon still attack them, even though it was about to begin feasting on Stickle? She could not tell.

Aching, her defeat assured, Min pulled herself to the side railing, looking at the waters below. The dragon was beneath them now, Stickle's weight slowing its progress. Its purple wingspan obscured its prize, although Min could still hear Stickle hooting as the turtlemoth's fear reached fever pitch.

Then everything changed.

Below, there was a roar. This, however, was not the roar of the Darkstar Dragon.

It was exactly the type of roar that Stickle had used to fend off the dragon when they first arrived.

At the sound of the noise, Min broke into a cutthroat grin. Abalendu's head whipped around.

"What in Master Bartholtocrat's name was that?"

"Oh," Min said, drawing Abalendu's attention to her, "you don't recognise it? Sounds like someone is winning her freedom."

Half the crew rushed to the starboard railing, and for a brief moment of madness Min fancied the whole vessel would upend, tipping them all out into the black.

Stickle – for it was Stickle, roaring as she had done before – let out a blast of sound so mighty that they felt the vibrations through the deck, even though the *Narwhal*'s core was working overtime to accelerate toward New Windward, away from the dragon and its not-so-helpless victim.

The dragon gave a cry of pain and frustration, and Min could see its head move frantically from side to side. A second later, there was a massive splash, the water under the dragon rippling out in concentric circles that would have drowned any lesser islands nearby.

The dragon had dropped Stickle, plunging her back to the Darkstar waters.

Min's favourite moment, however, came when the *Narwhal*'s crew – with the exception of Abalendu and Zoya – cheered. Even Sung clenched her fist in front of her chest in a sign of success.

Abalendu wheeled on Min, who was struggling against her broken leg to prop herself up.

"How?" he asked, his flabbergasted expression almost making the pain of her leg worth it. "Without the golden Eshak, how?"

Min gave her best grin of feigned innocence. "What do you mean, 'without'? Looks like Stickle has her Bondmate back, doesn't it?"

Abalendu shook his head, still shocked. "No, we have it," he said, the hint of a stammer bleeding through his words. "We're flying."

The *Narwhal* began to shudder. Something was wrong in the belly.

Min's grin widened.

"What have you done?" Abalendu said, the curling of his lip bringing joy to Min's heart.

"Me?" Min asked. "How could you think I – a mere graduate of the academy, churned out in a factory of puppets – would be capable of something like this?"

"Take her to the core, now!" Abalendu shouted. "We need to see what she's done."

Min was relieved to see Jedda in the belly. The artificer had blood on her forehead, but other than a crack in one of the lenses of her goggles, she appeared to be fine.

Well, other than the fact that she was staring at the core mount, crying her eyes out, tears streaming down her cheeks.

Min could see why. There in the core mount, replacing the golden Eshak that Min had taken and slipped into Brightest's hand just before Zoya knocked him overboard, was one of Jedda's ascended Eshak pieces.

The piece was on fire; clearly the strain of powering the *Narwhal* for a few minutes had been enough to drain the minor amount of magic from it, destroying the gaming piece.

At first Min thought the process had stripped off the thin layer of gold paint the two of them had applied to the piece before going in search of Brightest earlier, but then Min noticed the hunk of charcoal Jedda was holding, stroking as she bawled while watching the other Eshak piece burn. The first had already burnt out, and Jedda must have exchanged the two so the deception could last longer.

A lifetime of gaming, turned to ash in minutes. No wonder Jedda was beside herself.

So was Abalendu.

He lunged across the room, grabbing Min by the lapels.

"Put another one on," Abalendu shouted, "quick! We're almost there. We can't give up now."

Jedda looked up at him, teary eyed. "Can't. That was the last one. My last one." Seemingly oblivious to what was going on around her, to the shuddering of the ship, and the groaning of the crystal array reverberating through the hull, Jedda only had eyes for the final embers of her gaming career.

"You idiot," Abalendu screamed, spittle speckling Min's face. "Don't you know what you've done? You're going to crash the ship."

Aware she had pushed Abalendu past breaking, aware that even though his dragontoad was gone, this man could still hurt her, Min chose to focus on the glory of the fact that she had beaten him.

"She's crashed before," Min said, looking at him seriously. "She got better."

Abalendu hit Min, then. He slapped the side of her face with the back of his hand, splitting her lip and batting her head to the left.

Min looked back at him, feeling blood trickle down her chin. "Did you enjoy that?" she asked.

"I'm going to enjoy beating you to a pulp before we hit the water, that's what I'm going to enjoy."

Eyes still locked on Abalendu, Min simply said, "You're not going to get a second chance. Colonel Zoya, under mandate three twenty-two of the New Windward military, I'm asking you to apprehend and confine Abalendu Seekwalla for striking a naval officer whilst being under her protection."

The room inhaled.

There were almost a dozen of them in there, packed into the belly that was designed for four people at best. Jedda, Min, Abalendu and Zoya were the key players, but the silence from the remaining seamen and apprentices was probably the loudest, as they held their breath, waiting to see how Zoya would respond.

Abalendu pushed Min back, letting go of her jacket and withdrawing to Zoya's protective shadow, sneering at Min. "You're an idiot, thinking to use my bodyguard against me. An arrogant idiot. Zoya, kill this upstart. All we have to do is grab the Eshak from the turtlemoth again, and we can still get back home. Nothing has changed so long as the rift is still here."

Zoya did not move. She was staring at Min. Damn, why was that woman's face so hard to read?

"Colonel?" Min said, summoning that elusive mix of command and empathy that Captain Marya had impressed her with so much. "Mistakes have been made, Colonel, but you've been given an order to follow a very clear directive from the organisation you swore to dedicate – to sacrifice – your life to."

"You are not military," Zoya said. Despite the warrior's rigid stance, Min was shocked to see a tear running down the Kisiwian's cheek.

"No," Min said, "but you are."

"Ridiculous," Abalendu said. "Even in the end, you are ridiculous. Zoya, finish her, and let's get home."

Zoya did nothing. Min had the pleasure of seeing uncertainty cross Abalendu's face.

He turned to look at his bodyguard, who remained unmoving behind him.

"Zoya, you can't seriously be considering this madness, can you?"

"Abalendu Seekwalla, I hereby order you to your own quarters, for your safety, and the safety of others."

"Preposterous!" Abalendu blurted out. "You are my bodyguard. Father ordered you to protect me."

"Yes. This is for your own protection. If you don't do what I am requesting, I will make you comply through force, and none of us want that."

Despite a great urge to do otherwise, Min kept her mouth shut.

"Enough," Abalendu said, drawing a dagger from his belt, wielding it as a young schoolboy would a pencil on his first day at school; inexpertly. "I'll deal with this my—"

Zoya hit him in the back of the head. He crumpled, but she caught him before he met the ground.

Min nodded at her. "Get him to his quarters," she said, stepping forward. The deckhands that had followed them below – Nalla, Trude and Jeet had stepped to the fore – regarded her as they had before. They were waiting for her command. She was back in control.

"But I need you up on deck as soon as you're able," Min shouted after Zoya, even as the *Narwhal* began to shudder, the now-familiar sign of her crystals running out of power as the lesser Eshak piece crumbled to ash. "You've got to help me crash this girl again."

"First Captain, First Captain," came a voice; Kanika, leaping down the stairs three at a time.

Not quite accurate, but close enough, Min thought. *Better than what they were calling me.*

"Yes, Kanika, report. Are we, perhaps, falling?" she said, a small grin beginning on one side of her mouth.

"What?" the woman said, confused, only now noticing the shuddering of the *Narwhal*, increasing in intensity as the crystal array gave all it could. "No, First Captain, it's the dragon."

All the warmth Min had gathered from her victory evaporated with those words.

"What is it?" she said, even as she limped past the seaman to get above deck again.

"I think," Kanika stammered back at her, "I think it's coming for us."

Already breathless, her broken leg throbbing, the *Narwhal's* crystals beginning to strain and fail, Min hobbled back to the deck to take a look.

Below, exactly in the direction the *Narwhal* was about to plummet, the Darkstar Dragon had turned from Stickle and was facing directly upward.

It was looking right at them.

Sixtieth year of solitude, day one hundred and nine

Visitors have come to Stickle.

This isn't the first time we've had company, but this time feels... different. Their first officer in particular, she seems...

She seems like good people.

I must admit, despite my hesitance when they first arrived, I'm warming to most of them.

Going by the path of their world's rift, it looks as though they'll be stuck with me for a handful of years.

Perhaps...

Perhaps this will be good for me.

FIFTEEN

Time seemed to slow.

Below, like a purple demon unleashed upon the world, the Darkstar Dragon gave a roar that caused the water beneath it to convulse. The beast gave a single beat of its colossal wings and began to push through the air toward them.

The *Narwhal's* crystal array gave an agonised gasp, and Min felt the ship begin to list. She gripped the handrail, preparing herself for the plummet she knew was moments away.

"Oh, ancestors," Jedda said from the railing beside Min, her voice low and quiet.

Min glanced behind to see a number of the crew preparing themselves by gripping onto anything that was bolted to the deck. From the looks on their faces – Nalla fixed upon Trude with helpless eyes, the Icelander giving a lost shrug – Min knew that inside, they were doing the same as she was.

They were preparing themselves to die.

It was like the goat-ant leader charging at her again, her end in the arena inevitable.

Except it had not been inevitable then. Perhaps it was not now.

Her mind whirring, racing through the possibilities available to her, Min's eyes rested upon the ray Abalendu had strapped to the deck, twitching frantically as it sensed something was wrong with the vessel it was confined to.

Forgetting about her broken leg – and for a brief second almost collapsing to the deck with her first step – Min hobbled over to the ray, pulling her knife from her belt.

"Min?" Jedda said. "Min? What's going on?"

"Going to take a small trip, Jedda."

Jedda was aghast. "No, Min, you can't! The dragon—"

"We're dead anyway, Jedda, you know that. Can't hurt to try something."

"But—"

"Now, grab hold of something, and when you see her, get Zoya to pull the wings out, like last time. That's an order," Min said, jumping onto the ray's back just as she cut the last of its bonds.

The beast bucked and slid down the deck as the *Narwhal* began to tilt. Min had hoped this was one of the rays they had ridden on earlier – so it might already know her – but she did not recognise it.

A harness would make this easier, she thought. *And a fleet of warships would be nice too.*

Aware of the increasingly approaching roar of the ascending dragon, Min put her hand on the ray's side, close to where the beast's head should be, like she had with the other one, and with the turtlemoth.

"You can hear me, right? I know you can hear me. And kind of understand me. You know we're all going to die, right?"

The creature did not make any noise, but Min felt from its rhythmic trembling that the ray understood the inevitability of its fate, if not the exact meaning of her words.

"I'm sorry – so sorry – you've been caught up in all of this. I can't promise I can help you make it out alive, can't promise anyone is going to survive this, but I can promise you something. If you trust me, I promise you won't flop about on the deck, waiting for the inevitable to come. I promise that if we work together, we can try to make a difference. If not for us, then at least for some of the sorry bastards on this boat."

Clutching onto her mount's sides, Min and the ray continued to tumble down, running out of deck. As the *Narwhal* began to tip more – listing horribly, the crystals using the last of their magic to hold it in place for a few more seconds – all that awaited Min below was the Darkstar Dragon.

And then the ray underneath Min reacted, as if it had taken the time to contemplate her words and decided that its answer was 'Yes.'

The ray stopped floundering around, and pointed itself in the direction Min was looking. Down, toward the purple death that was gathering speed below.

Then, with a flick of its wings, the ray jumped off the *Melodious*

Narwhal, aiming itself for the Darkstar Dragon.

Without the failing whine of the *Narwhal's* crystals to keep them aloft, Min and her mount soon reached maximum speed, with Min doing all she could to keep a grip on the creature as it fell through the sky toward their target.

Min was awestruck once again by the size of the dragon below. Falling toward it, her mind played tricks on her, all the time convincing Min she was close, almost close enough to touch it, until she realised she had once again misjudged the size of the thing.

It can't even see me, she thought. *I'm so small, it's like me noticing a mote of dust in the air. So insignificant, it can't see me.*

She wished the *Narwhal* was as lucky.

Her sense of up and down became distorted. Even though she was falling, with the blanket of stars spread evenly in all directions, Min's mind adjusted the world, making it seem as if the ray was flying through the air as it normally soared just above the waves. She and the dragon were about to pass each other in space, like one ship leaving a harbour as another arrived, the sailors waving a weary greeting to each other as they sidled by.

She squeezed her eyes shut to shake off the phenomenon, and when she opened them, she saw they were in danger of missing the dragon altogether, as it started to pass underneath.

"Get down," she hissed to her ray, well aware that where she was pointing was not actually 'down' in any fashion, except inside her head.

Luckily, the ray seemed to be having similar thoughts, or at least it was somehow able to sense what Min intended. Angling itself against the rushing air, the ray pointed itself downward, toward the dragon.

Boramu's noisy hell, we're going to miss it, Min thought as the creature's gargantuan head passed beneath. *We're going to miss it and hit the water instead. At this speed, that'll definitely kill us, no matter what tricks this ray has up its sleeve.*

Min had not, however, taken into account the sheer size of the Darkstar Dragon. Yes, she had missed the creature's head, but it seemed to take an age for the rest of the dragon to move past, more than enough time for the ray to reach the dragon's back.

As they came in closer to the dragon, the rolling violet planes of its spine moving at incredible speed, Min felt the tell-tale pull that she had gotten from the floating rocks the last time she had trusted her life to a ray high above the Darkstar Sea. The dragon seemed to have its own pull, just like with those rocks, and as before, the ray adjusted for the new situation, angling itself again so it could soar level with the dragon. Within seconds, Min found herself travelling at speed along the dragon's back, a wasteland of horny outcrops and monstrous spines, instead of falling to her doom.

Seeing they were travelling in the wrong direction, Min used her knees to ease the ray into turning, eventually pointing toward the dragon's head, which now seemed miles away.

Boramu's hell, it is *miles away!*

The dragon was so large, if it was not for the fact the land was moving with each beat of the beast's wings, Min would have sworn she had just walked through a rift into another world, one with raging winds and a rippled, violet landscape.

Now they had turned, the dragon's head – Min's goal – loomed in the distance, a lonely mountain overlooking a wide valley.

Beyond that, Min gasped as she recognised a speck in the darkness between the dragon and the Darkstar: the *Narwhal*.

From what Min could tell, struggling as she still was to make sense of direction, The *Narwhal* was now in full plummet, its crystals having used up the last of the energy that had been drained from Jedda's final Eshak piece.

We're too late, Min thought. *We overshot the head, and by the time I reach it, The* Narwhal *will already have been eaten.*

The dragon seemed to sense its imminent meal. Min saw the creature's head – still a good mile away – tilt back as the dragon opened its jaws.

The *Narwhal* disappeared.

Min slumped forward, her head shaking from side to side as she searched for any reason to hope the ship had survived. She was so close now, so close...

Then Min gave a whoop as a familiar shape shot out from behind the dragon's head, having clearly turned through the air at a tight angle, just missing the beast's gullet.

The *Narwhal* – gliding with the use of its now-extended guidance wings – turned again, speeding along the length of the dragon's body just as Min and her ray had minutes before.

For a brief second, the ship passed close enough for Min to make out a statuesque figure standing on the side of the *Narwhal's* hull, teeth gritted as she pulled on the metal structure of the guidance wings with all her might; Zoya, using her Parasite Glove to force the wings to open. The Kisiwian happened to glance her way, and Min was treated to the warrior's eyes widening as Zoya spotted her first officer speeding along the dragon's spine.

The *Narwhal* quickly fell past, taking Zoya's shocked gaze with it.

You saved them, again, Min thought, just as the Darkstar Dragon roared, twisting itself around to pursue the small ship.

Now it's my turn.

The land before her writhed as the dragon pulled itself around, diving back toward the water's surface, moving with a speed that would easily catch the *Narwhal* before the ship could glide to safety.

However, the *Narwhal's* manoeuvre had given Min enough time to reach where she needed to be – the dragon's head. Specifically, the dragon's eye.

She struggled to recognise the creature's facial features, just as she struggled to recognise the blur of the world around her as anything other than the normal sky. To Min, despite her knowledge of the reality of the situation, this purple wasteland was a world she travelled in. Her friends, her ship, the entire Darkstar Dimension did not exist.

Instead of an eye, Min found herself looking at a shallow, violet lake. The waters of the lake rippled in the strong winds around her, and underneath the surface of the water, the lake bed seemed to be constantly tremoring, twitching. For a moment, Min was mesmerised, captivated by the unworldly sight, completely forgetting where she was and why she had come here.

Then the lake blinked.

Shaken out of her stupor, Min looked in the direction the dragon was flying in. Despite her disorientation, Min was certain she could make out a speck that must be the *Narwhal*, which the dragon was rapidly gaining on. In mere seconds, the ship would be consumed, and all this would have been for nothing.

Time for me to play my part, then, Min thought, her gaze returning to the lake before her.

Bet they don't have any classes on this at the academy; not many first officers – nor captains, I'd wager – that have taken on a dragon by themselves.

Reaching into her officer's jacket, now flowing in ribbons behind her, shredded after everything she had been through, Min withdrew the cylindrical container Brightest had entrusted to her. Carefully, she unscrewed the lid. Inside, the pink petals seemed to hum, as if they knew what was coming.

A tsunami, Brightest?

Exactly what I need right now.

Min tipped the entire container of vibrating petals into the lake beneath her.

The dragon's eye exploded.

Min lost consciousness.

When she first came to, she thought she was awakening in one of the great spirits' hells that her grandmother had delighted in lecturing her about; she thought she was dead.

A few seconds after that, she wished she was. Her body, although it seemed to be floating, ached all over. As well as her broken leg, Min's right shoulder in particular was not in great shape. Dislocated, probably. Also, she realised, trying to make sense of the world around her, she could not see properly. No, it was not a simple case of her vision blurring. Min realised something thick was running down the right side of her face, something warm that did not feel like blood.

My eye. I think I've lost my eye.

Then the rest of the world around Min came into focus. She found she was staring at the dragon, and then realised that the constant roaring around her was the dragon's screams.

It was distant from her, now, the dragon. The explosion – the one she had caused, with Brightest's petals – must have propelled her from it, far enough away for its pull to no longer affect her.

The dragon was convulsing in pain; only one of its eyes lit up the sky above Min, the other a craterous ruin.

Quite a pair we make, she thought, as the dragon, still screaming, retreated to the safety of the Darkstar above.

So, Min thought, using her remaining good eye to look about her, *I'm falling.*

She was indeed. Below, Min could make out Stickle, and the *Narwhal*, still falling, but far from her, getting ready to glide onto the water close to the island-sized turtlemoth.

There was no sign of Min's ray.

This is it, then, she thought, rushing towards the watery surface, still far below. *Not a bad way to go – fighting a dragon, saving all those people – but I didn't think I'd end up smashing myself so hard against the water's surface that my body breaks open.*

Despite her imminent death, a kind of contentment passed over Min. Brightest had been right; she was exactly the kind of leader the *Narwhal*'s crew had needed to survive this place. Hopefully without her, they could still make it through the next few years and return home to spread word of her story, to tell her family of her accomplishments.

Then a rage of amber light flooded from the network of crystals that decorated the *Narwhal*'s hull.

Stupefied, finding it difficult to focus at the speed she was falling, Min rubbed her remaining eye, trying to get a better look.

That can't be, she thought, even though evidence to the contrary was before her; not only had the *Narwhal*'s crystal array fired up, but the ship was changing course, making its way up, flying through the sky toward her.

How? was all Min could think, moving her eyes between the *Narwhal* and Stickle, who had now Bonded again with the only source of magic Min knew could exist in this place. The *Narwhal* had never even made contact with the water's surface, let alone gotten close enough to Stickle for Brightest to give them the golden Eshak piece, an act she knew he would never do anyway, even to save her life.

How, then, was the *Narwhal* flying?

As the ship came close, Min saw Holtz at the helm, bellowing orders at the crew, who were scuttling about the ship's deck in response, finding their rhythm again after so long not working together.

Wheeling around to match the speed of her fall, it was Jedda who shouted at the seamen to catch Min, casting out one of the nets they used to gather herring off the New Windward coast when the conditions were just right.

Min almost laughed at the thought of being fished onto her own ship, but she was too overcome with the mystery of the rescue.

"What was it like?" was the first thing Jedda said to her, seemingly oblivious of Min's wounds. "What was it like, fighting a dragon?"

"Jedda," Min said, collapsing into her artificer's arms, exhausted, "how are we flying? Take me below, now."

Jedda threw one of Min's arms over her shoulder and called on one of the nearby seamen to help her hobble below, even as Holtz took the *Narwhal* down, ready to get her back onto Darkstar waters. A sickening feeling began to grow in Min's gut as to what devilry Jedda had conjured up to power the core again.

"You can stop now," Jedda shouted, even before they had entered the belly. "We've got her, we're almost back. Stop, quick."

The last thing Min had expected to see was Zoya standing in the middle of the belly, her Parasite Glove firmly embedded in the core mount, blue lightning crackling all over her as the mount sucked at the magic held within the Glove. Zoya's eyes were clenched tight, her head tipped back, mouth open in a noiseless scream.

Min's own mouth dropped open, horrified at what she was looking at, clear as to what the ramifications would be.

Despite her wounds, Min pulled away from Jedda and threw herself at Zoya, desperate to detach the warrior from the mount. Zoya, for once, offered no resistance, and together they barrelled across the floor, the *Narwhal*'s crystal array beginning to protest as soon as its power source was detached.

Underneath her, Zoya groaned, and Min looked at the Kisiwian, horrified.

"Zoya, what have you done?"

The Parasite Glove was a source of magic, yes. But Brightest had hinted at the price Zoya paid when she used it. It was clear to Min – and all within the room – that this time, Zoya's price had been high. Half an hour ago, the Parasite Glove had only extended up to Zoya's elbow. In the short time she had held it in the mount, the Glove had grown the entire length of her arm, and now its rocky bumps licked their way across Zoya's chest, and also covered the entirety of the left side of her neck. A thin swirl of growths formed a lazy curl around Zoya's cheek, almost mistakable for some kind of tribal tattoo, if one did not know the awful truth of what the warrior had inflicted upon herself.

"Zoya," Min whispered, "you did not have to do that."

Zoya coughed, and finally looked at Min. "You were right. I had brought shame to my family with my actions. When they hear of me, when you finally get the *Narwhal* home, perhaps this moment will redeem me in their eyes."

"Perhaps."

A few weeks after Min blinded the dragon, the *Narwhal* was preparing to set sail.

The ship's first officer hobbled across the deck, the bones in her broken leg still needing more time to properly knit together. Some wounds healed easier than others. Her shoulder, after a not-so-gentle shove from Holtz, had popped back into place well enough, though Min had been warned it could be prone to coming loose again if she kept abusing it. Min suspected she would find out if that was the case sooner rather than later.

Min's authority over the crew seemed almost as easily repaired. To her delight, she discovered that a large chunk of the crew – almost half, most of whom were from Holtz's watch – had not defected at all. When the mutiny was being planned, Holtz and his people had protested, been overpowered, and had been locked in the deckhouse. That had made Min's job to restore order after mutiny – a commanding officer's worst nightmare, other than losing her ship and crew – considerably simpler. Those who had remained faithful to Min were now the ship's crew, spread thinly across two watches. The mutineers, with a few exceptions, were landlocked, confined to quarters within the Mudhut. They were ostensibly imprisoned until they could be brought to trial before the New Windward naval authorities, although Min was hoping she could find some way to circumvent that. Most of them had supported her against Abalendu in the end, and it would be a long three years for all of them if they were spent on prison guard duty.

What worked in Min's favour was the respect she had gained from the crew, even the mutineers – hells, even Sung, although Min was not going to forget that her former first mate almost murdered her – for her actions against the dragon. The creature had reared its head from the Darkstar only once since Min wounded it, and had flown off in the opposite direction to Stickle. A few of the crew could swear the dragon's right eye remained shut. It seemed that mutilating a country-sized killing machine was a considerably effective shortcut to respect.

Min's own eye, however, was not as easily healed. Aditya had tutted a lot when he had finally convinced Min to lie down on his surgeon's bed. Her wound had stung like the frost of Gorya's hell as he had applied his various poultices to it, tutting some more, but the final assessment really hit home when he had ordered for Hertha to put together an eyepatch for Min from scraps of leather.

The eye was gone. It was as simple as that.

She found the loss did not gall her as much as she would have expected, as she was just so bloody busy getting everything back to order, although it soon became apparent that her skills with a blade had been markedly hampered by its loss, as she repeatedly misjudged the distance between her opponent's weapon and her new sabre; another repair easily managed, though she would always feel the loss of the ceremonial sword.

Walking from the quarterdeck, Min ran her hand over the *Narwhal*'s railing.

You'll have to be my weapon, now. Others can do the cutting. Leave the sailing to me.

Finding the *Narwhal*'s repairs well enough in order, Min knew it was time to begin the trickier restorations.

Her first step was the belly. Jedda was down there, under watch with Shreya, one of the loyal apprentices. Min knew rightly Jedda did not need a guard, but appearances had to be kept up – she had to show the other mutineers there were repercussions to actions, no matter who you were.

Min nodded at the young Zadzerjian as she entered, and Shreya stepped outside.

Jedda raised her head at Min's entrance, then lowered it back to her work, not taking the time to acknowledge the first officer's presence.

"Hello, Jedda," Min said after a moment, when it was clear the artificer was not going to speak first.

"Hey, Min," Jedda said, not looking up.

It was unclear exactly what Jedda was up to. She had requested to work on the core mount – to repair it, she said – a week or so ago. She had been going crazy in confinement, more so than the other mutineers. Min allowed her to get to work for Jedda's own sake rather than the hope it would achieve anything.

"Making much progress?" Min asked, trying to sound casual. Since the artificer's outburst when Min had come back from the goat-ant world, Jedda had been quiet, not engaging in any meaningful conversations. Min thought now was a good time to end that.

Letting out an exasperated breath, Jedda sat up, taking off her goggles to get a good look at Min.

"Some. It's difficult without the Parasite Glove actually here."

"What? Why would you want the Glove?"

Min was somewhat relieved to see that familiar look on Jedda's face: an expression of shock at Min's idiocy.

"Because it can fly the ship? When nothing else worked, the Glove made the *Narwhal* fly again. Sure, the rift is almost gone, now, but—"

"Jedda, we can't make Zoya fly the *Narwhal*. Last time nearly killed her. It wouldn't be worth it to ask her to do it again."

"Oh, I know that. I'm not an idiot. But, you know, Zoya's got months left at best now, right? And after that we'll just be left with a walking weapon. A walking weapon, brimming with magic. At that point, surely it wouldn't hurt to get what remains of her to power the *Narwhal* for us?"

Min stopped, equal parts horrified and intrigued by Jedda's idea.

"Jedda," Min said eventually, slowly. "Jedda, you haven't told anyone else about this, have you?"

"Not yet, no."

Min nodded. "Good. Keep it that way. Keep working on the mount, sure, but just… just don't tell anyone, okay? I'm not sure how they'd take it."

Jedda nodded, not seeming to really understand.

"I'll let you get back to it, then," Min said, rising to leave.

Jedda pulled her goggles over her face, ready to get back to work.

Min hesitated.

"Jedda, you know we're okay, right? Everything that happened with the Eshak piece and Abalendu, you know I don't hold that against you?"

More confusion from Jedda. "I know, Min. You told me, so I know."

"It's just… I know you've been upset, Jedda. Chun said she could hear you crying in confinement. That's one of the reasons I let you back in here to work. I was worried you might think I was still upset with you."

Jedda shook her head. "No, you told me you weren't," Jedda

said again, dismissing her own betrayal as if it were nothing.

"Then what's up?"

Jedda sighed. "My Eshak pieces, Min. I lost my Eshak pieces."

Min understood. In comparison with the golden Eshak, Jedda's two low-level pieces were insignificant, but to Jedda they had represented the entirety of that huge part of her life, now ashes.

"Don't get me wrong, I'd do it all again," Jedda continued. "I'd burn them again, to save the ship, to undo what I did. But Min, I had worked so hard for them, to get any kind of power in them. You wouldn't understand…"

Min remembered her time at the academy, the hardcore Eshak crew gaming in the dorm rooms when she went to bed, and finding them still playing when she woke. Most of the gamers she knew had never managed to accrue any magic at all to their game pieces, although they talked about it constantly. The fact that Jedda had two ascended pieces must have really made her stand out in that community.

And now they were gone.

Jedda seemed to be finished, and turned back to working on the core mount. Min knelt beside her, wincing as her wounded leg protested.

"Three years, Jedda."

Jedda turned to look at her, magnified eyes blinking in curiosity.

"Three years, and untold worlds."

"I don't understand."

"We're trapped in the Darkstar Dimension for the next three years. We've been looking at this as some sort of prison sentence. We need to stop. It's time we looked at this as an opportunity.

"Take your Eshak game, for example. So, you've lost all your meaningful pieces. Basically, you're back to being as far progressed in the game as I am."

Jedda looked almost sick at Min's words, so she hurried to continue.

"But think about what you have now, what none of the other players back home have. Already, you know more about the game than any of them — that it's played across countless worlds, that those worlds have their own pieces and rules. Golden pieces do exist, you've held one, and they apparently get used by pan-dimensional god creatures to play against one another.

"Jedda, you have three years to get out there, using the Darkstar to travel to other worlds, to collect their Eshak pieces, to earn more magic, and to bring them back home to New Windward.

"Jedda, when you get home…"

"Yes, Min?" Jedda's eyes were wide. Her smile had snapped into place.

"You'll be a legend, Jedda. An Eshak legend."

Min left Jedda like that, her mind open to the possibilities their exile afforded them. Never mind the fact that Jedda was currently confined for high treason. Min would figure out a way to sort that, once people's tempers had calmed down. If they were stuck here for three years, she did not want any of the crew to suffer for too long in captivity.

Well, she did not want most of them to suffer, anyway.

Reaching the deck, she nodded at Holtz, who was over at the galley, continuing the debate with Runako the cook about why their sole surviving chicken could not have its own run on top of the deckhouse. Deciding Holtz could handle that one himself, Min left the *Narwhal* via the gangplank. She allowed herself a small burst of pleasure at how the deckhands stood to attention as she passed by.

The walk to the Mudhut was draining, with her injury taking its time to right itself. Still, Min had made certain to be a frequent visitor, not wanting her confined crew to think they had been forgotten.

As she walked, Min allowed her gaze to drift to the rifts that floated above her, a whimsical collection of colours that made her mind spin when she considered how many worlds, how many possibilities, hung over her head.

"And all I have to do is say the word, and we can visit them all," she whispered.

As if in answer, Stickle hooted in the distance, the massive turtlemoth's head turned to the side. Min fancied she could glimpse Brightest's companion's eye.

After a moment's hesitation, Min knelt to rub her hand over the shell of Stickle's back, then continued on.

Making her way into the Mudhut, Min's first stop was Zoya's room.

Jedda was an easy bond to repair in comparison with this one, Min thought. *Problem is, I'm not capable of mending what is broken here.*

Min knocked, and a grunt from within told her she could enter.

Inside, Zoya was sitting in what Min supposed was some kind

of meditative pose, her legs and arms crossed. However, instead of the harmony that some of the Holamian monks back home exuded during meditation, Min could see Zoya's face fluctuate between resting and grimacing.

She's tensing her muscles, Min thought. *Must be some kind of Kisiwian exercise routine, thought up for confinement like this.*

"You can go outside, you know," Min said, wary of breaking Zoya's concentration. "If you need to exercise, we can sort something out."

"This is fine," was the only response given.

Min stood in the doorway, unsure of how to continue.

"Thank you," she said, finally. "I wish you hadn't done it, hadn't stimulated the Parasite Glove so much, but I still need to thank you. You gave your life up for mine."

Zoya's face scrunched up as she tensed her muscles again. After relaxing, the warrior said, "You were right. About me shaming myself, and my family. What I did when I betrayed you, it should not have happened. When you return home, you will tell my family how I won my honour back. Perhaps they will find it in themselves to forgive me when you tell them about my sacrifice."

Min pursed her lips, eyes on the swirl of growth on Zoya's cheek. The warrior had months left, now, not years.

But this place, the Darkstar Dimension, it held many wonders. There were no stories of anyone surviving a Parasite Glove back home, but perhaps in their time here, they could find a way.

Knowing better than to suggest this hope to Zoya, knowing better than to give the warrior any hope at all, Min simply said, "As you were, then," and left.

She had one more prisoner to visit.

The room they had given to Abalendu for his incarceration was considerably larger than his cabin aboard the *Narwhal*. Still, upon entering, it was clear to Min that the scholar was not taking his confinement well.

The place was a mess. Furniture was overturned, food lay uneaten on the desk Brightest had dragged up from his treasure trove. Abalendu's own effects, which Min had ordered brought from his cabin, had been rudely mistreated, with manuscripts thrown haphazardly about the place, the contents of a spilled ink pot running down the chair. Min even fancied a few of the books had pages ripped out of them.

Abalendu himself was not faring much better. It was only now, after letting himself go, that Min realised the daily routine Abalendu must have put himself through to achieve his prim and proper look. His hair was normally treated with an assortment of poultices, smoothed perfectly into his desired style. Weeks of mistreatment had taken their toll, and Abalendu's black locks were wild now, curling from his head like tendrils of smoke from a burning building. The red bitterness of his eyes as he watched her from the corner he was slumped in completed the picture.

"Come to gloat again, have you?" he asked.

Min had never gloated, not outside the confines of her own head.

"How are you doing, Seekwalla?"

"Oh, absolutely brilliant, thank you for asking. Other than the fact that I have been incarcerated by an assortment of lunatics who are going through some kind of mass hallucination, convincing each other that a decrepit wild man and a one-eyed, inexperienced junior officer are somehow going to keep us alive in this knowledge-forsaken hell hole."

The insults were not a surprise. Berating any visitors to his room appeared to be the only pastime that lit the fires behind Abalendu's eyes anymore.

"You do know you've just bought a little bit of time, don't you? Nothing more. If by some miracle we do survive our three years here, my father will have you executed when we get home."

Min suspected that particular conversation was going to go quite differently to how Abalendu was imagining, but decided to hold her tongue; a skill she had been gaining a lot of experience with over the past few weeks.

Instead, Min pulled up a small stool and dragged it over to where Abalendu was.

"Seekwalla," she said, sitting down, accompanying his name with a long sigh. "Three years is a very long time. I think we could spend that time in much better ways than bickering whenever we meet."

The scholar said nothing, but shot Min a look of such derision that she nearly left there and then.

Instead, she continued. "I don't want our mission to fail."

Abalendu barked a laugh. "We're long past that, aren't we? You've destroyed the ship's core, stranded almost thirty of us in an unknown place. It is a miracle nobody has died yet. By the time our three years is over, Colonel Zoya will be as good as dead."

Min shook her head to dismiss the hurt that truth carried with it.

"I think we can still find Glimmerwrought."

This time, Abalendu stared at her for a good few seconds before bursting into more laughter. "Glimmerwrought? What kind of fool do you take me for? What kind of fool are you? That mission failed when you got us lost in this place. I know most of you didn't believe in it in the first place, so the fact you're bringing it up now is proof of your delusion."

"I didn't believe in it," Min said, leaning closer, "but that was before I saw the Darkstar, and what it can do. A stopover between worlds? A place of infinite possibilities? If anyone was going to find Glimmerwrought, it would be us, in this place, with time on our hands."

"Infinite possibilities?" Abalendu said, scoffing. "I'd hardly call an empty sky and a sea full of colourful fish 'infinite possibilities.'"

"When I travelled through that rift, I met a race of creatures with the bodies of ants and the heads of goats. They lived only one day long. The creatures that waved goodbye to me as I left were the grandchildren of the ones who captured me in the first place. They now worship me as a god."

Abalendu stared at her, opening and closing his mouth for a few times before uttering a meek, "I don't believe it. Preposterous."

Min stood up. "I agree. And that's why we need you. The people of New Windward won't trust the word of simple sailors. They'll just assume we made up stories to explain away phenomena we don't really understand. They won't trust us, but they might trust the words of a scholar. They might trust you.

"We need you studying these things, making them un-preposterous, so the people of New Windward believe us when we return to them with tales of the worlds we've explored in our time here. Finding Glimmerwrought would be a drop in the ocean compared with the treasure trove waiting just outside for us."

She turned to leave.

"You," Abalendu began, just as she reached the door, "you're letting me go? You're really thinking of freeing me?"

Min just looked at him. Abalendu was in proper shock now, his face incredulous.

"No, Seekwalla, I am not thinking of freeing you. You convinced almost half my crew to turn against me, and your dragontoad's attack left poor Sefu's face a ruin."

Abalendu curled his lip at the mention of Sefu's name, looking away from her in disgust.

Min continued, "I plan on taking you back to New Windward in captivity, to stand before a court of your peers and to answer for your crimes, as I will do with the rest of the mutineers. But I do not plan on just letting their able bodies and your able mind rot over the next three years. We could do so much for New Windward in that time, if we could just agree to work together."

"Why? After all... why would you possibly want to work with me?"

She turned away from him, making for the door, wanting the shocked loss on Abalendu's face to stay with her for a while. However, she stopped in the doorway before closing it, turning her head to the side so Abalendu could see her face.

"When I was a child, my grandmother had a porcelain kitten. It was odd, maybe even a bit ugly, but she prized it above anything else she had brought to New Windward from her home. I smashed that kitten, Abalendu. I was stupid, I didn't listen to her, and I ended up smashing something that meant the world to her."

Abalendu scoffed. "Not an unusual story. Children are always destroying their parents' belongings. I couldn't sit properly for a week after cracking the glass in my father's telescope."

Min looked back at Abalendu, then, and despite everything the man had done to her, she could not help but feel pity for him in that moment.

"My grandmother did not beat me, Abalendu, although I expected her to. Do you know what she did to me when she found me crying over the remains of her prized statue?"

Abalendu looked at Min in confusion, clearly struggling to understand why she was telling him this.

"She hugged me. She walked across the room to me, tears already flowing down her cheeks, and she took me in her arms and hugged me."

Abalendu, forehead creased, just shook his head.

"If I was following the rules, Abalendu, if I did exactly what the navy told me to do, I'd lock all of you mutineers up and misplace the key for the next three years. That's how I've been told to treat people under my command who make terrible choices, who make unforgivable mistakes. But I think, if we are to be stuck here together for so long, perhaps we need to become more to each other than just people in a chain of command."

The scholar's mouth opened and closed, as if searching for words. Finally, still very unsure of the situation, Abalendu spoke. "You're not... you're not planning on hugging me, are you?"

Min looked at him in disappointment. "Get smarter, Abalendu Seekwalla. I need that mind of yours to stop making such stupid mistakes."

With that, Min closed the door and turned the key in the lock, taking small satisfaction in sealing the scholar in behind wood and brass.

As she walked away from the cell, she could not help but think of her grandparents. Despite their disapproval of so many of her decisions in her adult life, she could not help but feel they would be happy with this one.

Brightest was not in the Mudhut. After the sessions with Zoya and Abalendu, Min wanted cheering up, and over the last few weeks, Brightest had been the most reliable source of levity. Seaman Chun, charged with keeping watch on Abalendu's room, informed her Brightest had made his way over to the *Narwhal* a short while ago. Chuckling at how they had just missed each other, Min made her way back to the ship.

She finally found Brightest in the captain's cabin, just off the officers' saloon.

"There you are," she said upon entering. "Whyever are you in here?" She would never have thought to look inside the unoccupied room if he had not left the door open behind him.

Brightest, toying with a telescope that had been hooked to the wall in a sad attempt to decorate the cabin, turned to look at Min. She was surprised at how serious he was, how quizzical, with a face she would expect a high-level Eshak player to be wearing when faced with a challenging opponent.

"Minjun," he said slowly, his eyes flicking from the telescope to her face. "What happened to the *Narwhal's* captain?"

Min's forehead creased. "There is no captain. You know that. I'm in charge, but they only promoted me to first officer."

Brightest looked back to the telescope, slowly shaking his head. "That doesn't seem right. That doesn't seem right, does it?" As if it were a struggle to do so, he looked back at her. "What aren't you telling me?"

She shook her head, confused now. "Not telling you? You know everything. What do you think is – oh!"

Min raised her hand to her own nose just as she saw a trickle of blood begin from Brightest's right nostril. Her hand came away red, a flow of blood beginning to drip from her face as well.

She laughed, reaching into her jacket for some handkerchiefs, one of which she passed to Brightest, who thanked her awkwardly.

"So strange," she said, smiling at Brightest after they had both gotten their noses under control. "To happen at the same time – that ever happened to you before? So strange. What were we talking about again?"

Brightest, puzzled, looked back at the telescope he had left on the captain's table. Then, a grin parting his confusion, he picked up the telescope and offered it to his companion.

"Thought it was time we made some plans, figured out where we were going next." He indicated the large window that looked out the *Narwhal's* stern. "Figured it would only be fitting if you had the first pick."

Realising what Brightest was saying, Min took the telescope from him with relish, scanning the heavens above them and the plethora of rifts that wheeled about the Darkstar, inviting exploration.

"What about that one?" she asked, telescope to eye, pointing at a circular rift whose colour undulated from pink to orange.

Brightest tutted. "Pretty sure that one is too close to the dragon now. Should be back in a few months, though, and we should look out for it; no food in there, but their beaches are to die for."

"Okay," Min mused, scanning the sky again. "How about the green one over there?"

Brightest chuckled. "Ah, the old green boot world. You'll like it; lots of stairs, locals willing to trade. Should be well positioned for us to fly up to it tomorrow, if you'd like?"

Something else had caught Min's attention, however.

"Brightest," she said, removing her eye from the spyglass, pointing at a bright pinprick of light that had just sparked into life above them. "Brightest, what's that?"

He took the telescope from her – almost grabbed it – and raised it to his eye. Then, hand trembling, Brightest passed the implement back to Min.

"What's wrong?" she asked.

Brightest said nothing, just shook his head, his mouth open, and indicated for Min to look into the sky again.

She raised the telescope to her eye, focussing in on the dimming light. It took Min a moment to realise what she was looking at.

It was a person. The humanoid figure was glowing silvery-white, its light continuing to dim, making it easier for Min to make out the newcomer's details. More shocking than anything was the fact that this figure, up there high above the black sea, appeared to be standing on top of a similar-sized creature that reminded Min of a dolphin, travelling through the sky atop this celestial mount.

Then, with another flash, the lone rider disappeared.

"What was it?" Min asked, lowering the telescope to look at Brightest in wonder.

Brightest's expression was not very different from her own; Min was surprised to see a fat tear running down the old man's face. He was grinning from ear to ear.

"It's one of them, one of the people I told you about. They're coming. After all this time… I never thought I'd see it happen."

"The Whalefleet. Minjun, the Whalefleet is returning."

Min looked back up at the sky, sharing Brightest's smile, gripping the lowered telescope with barely contained excitement, contemplating all the Darkstar Dimension was offering her.

Three years.

Three years of exploration.

Three years of discovery.

Three years of adventure.

A WORD FROM THE AUTHOR

This is not my first book.

For those who have not come across my books before, my first novels have been written in the Yarnsworld – a land ruled by stories, where folktales are a way of life, and knowledge of them is requirement for survival.

Much has been said about the adventures of the Magpie King, taniwha, and Bravadori met in those books, but one comment from an early review stood out for me: they called *They Mostly Come Out At Night* one of the weirdest books they had ever read.

'Weird' had not been my intention with that novel, but it felt like a good challenge to rise to.

With *The Flight of the Darkstar Dragon*, 'weird' was very much on the table.

I think I'll always return to the Yarnsworld, in some form or another, but I realised there were other types of stories I wanted to tell that weren't quite suitable for that setting. Something a bit lighter in tone, something more adventurous, heroic, and fun.

That was what spurred on the creation of the Darkstar Dimension, and the characters that now populate it – I wanted to tell stories about larger than life people, set in a place where it felt like anything can happen. I've gone on record before to say that some of the closest inspirations have been Stan Lee and Jack Kirby's original run on *The Fantastic Four*, or that feeling I got when I turned on *DuckTales* on a Saturday morning – they had such a variety of adventures – rewriting history, solving mysteries etc. – but it all still felt consistent, and thrilling.

Hopefully that childlike discovery and excitement is what I managed to recapture for you.

I'm returning to the Yarnsworld next, and am already well into *To Dream and Die as a Taniwha Girl*, but will be back to the Darkstar Dimension soon with *The Return of the Whalefleet*. Until then, please take the time to head online and review this book – I cannot over-emphasise what a difference that makes when helping me reach new readers.

Also, don't be a stranger! You can reach out and chat to me over on Facebook or Twitter, and also keep up-to-date with my writing by joining my Readers Group over at www.benedictpatrick.com.

If you have yet to discover the Yarnsworld, new subscribers to the Readers Group will also receive a free copy of *And They Were Never Heard From Again*, one of my favourite Yarnsworld tales so far:

Thank you again for reading, and I'll talk to you soon,

Benedict
September 2019

The standalone fantasy book that readers are calling a delightfully weird, dark fairytale.

The villagers of the forest seal themselves in their cellars at night, whispering folktales to each other about the monsters that prey on them in the dark. Only the Magpie King, their shadowy, unseen protector, can keep them safe.

However, when an outcast called Lonan begins to dream of the Magpie King's defeat at the hands of inhuman invaders, this young man must do what he can to protect his village. He is the only person who can keep his loved ones from being stolen away after dark, and to do so he will have to convince them to trust him again.

They Mostly Come Out At Night is the first novel from Benedict Patrick's Yarnsworld series. Straddling the line between fantasy and folklore, this book is perfect for fans of the darker Brothers Grimm stories.

Start reading today to discover this epic tale of dreams, fables and monsters!

Manufactured by Amazon.ca
Bolton, ON